Time Snatchers

Time Snatchers

By
Lenard F. Hines

E-BookTime, LLC
Montgomery, Alabama

Time Snatchers

Library of Congress Control Number: 2006931542

ISBN: 1-59824-300-4

First Edition
Published August 2006
E-BookTime, LLC
6598 Pumpkin Road
Montgomery, AL 36108
www.e-booktime.com

PART ONE

The Abductions

Chapter One

The clock on the wall showed the time to be five-thirty pm on this Tuesday afternoon. The man hunched over the computer was showing no sign of being aware of the time. He was too engrossed in what he considered to be a break at last in the numerous reports of missing young girls. His Interpol Liaison office in New York had been the focus of a deluge of reports featuring missing young women cases ever since the Department of Homeland Security had been reorganized to encompass all regional offices across the nation in their quest to uncover a pattern. Therefore, at least a clue to why so many missing persons had simply vanished from the face of the Earth was what Lank had been looking for. It had been very difficult and no easy task, with the limited resources at hand to make much progress toward this end, but with the persistence of a hungry dog any morsel of food tossed at him, he had finally uncovered what he thought to be a very viable clue. Lankford F. Miller, at least that was what the name label on his desk purported him to be, finally, with a heavy sigh, backed away from the computer screen only to glance up at the wall clock and wonder how time had slipped away so fast. As he settled back in his chair the phone rang and with a practice hand he deftly picked up the receiver. The voice at the other end immediately began to speak. "Lank, this is Jeff, I need to see you here right away. There has been another kidnapping right here in our town. I just got the report in. It's so weird," Jeff told him. Jeff and Lank went back to the gulf war days when they conducted secret missions in Baghdad, along with two other outstanding friends, Lewis Praddle, and Raymond Beatey.

Jeff was the director of a sub-regional bio-terrorist office located in St. Louis, Missouri. One of each states tie in with the Interpol Liaison office in New York. Interpol Liaison office worked hand in hand with Department of Homeland Security in Washington. Lank felt his skin go cold at the thought of another kidnapping. This was the nineteenth time a report had been made in Missouri in just the past three weeks and this one right in the city of St. Louis.

"Ok Jeff, I'm on my way. I'll call you from the plane and let you know when I'll arrive," Lank retorted into the phone. He had not meant to be quite so tart in his response but it had been a long day. He was anxiously awaiting the opportunity to mull over the information he had viewed as he brought the file up on the screen with the hope he could connect a few dots and get an inkling as to why so many young women had been abducted. Only women, not a single case of a young teenage male or older for that matter had been reported in the last month.

Sure there had been a couple of instances of young boys, but they had been abducted by sex offenders who had quickly been caught. Lank knew their habits and haunts down to the letter "T" thereby enabling him and his agents under him to quickly round them up. Only one other case involved a domestic issue where the biological dad had taken his eight-year old son who was residing with his mother in another town, from school. This had taken a month to get everything worked out but finally the case came to court and the judge after reviewing the mother's divorce decree had agreed that the father only had visitation rights.

When the abduction from the school had taken place the mother had dialed 911 and that was why Lank was knowledgably of the case at all.

The flight was not so bad. His secretary had been very thorough in finding him the quickest flight to St. Louis. He had contacted Jeff by phone informing him the time he would arrive in St. Louis and not to meet him as he had a rented car waiting at the airport and would drive to his office.

When Lank arrived at Jeff's office he walked briskly down the hall and went in without knocking. Jeff had leaned back in his chair talking on the phone. With an "I see", and "You don't say," thrown in occasionally, a person would not have known anything was going on. Finally with a shove back from his desk and while rising up slowly from his chair, Jeff muttered a goodbye and replaced the receiver. Turning to Lank, he began to convey his knowledge of the latest missing young girl.

"Lank, I know this is going to sound weird and unbelievable, but it is according to a reputable eyewitness," Jeff said with all seriousness on his face. "A state trooper witnessed the abduction right here in St. Louis."

Lank listened intently until Jeff had told him all he knew about the recent case. Lank, finally, after looking out the office window for a moment or two, said in a quiet and controlled voice.

"If this is true, we need to interview the trouper and judge for ourselves if he is telling the truth. Your right Jeff, this is weird. We need to find out just what the trouper saw and why he said the young girl just simply vanished. We also need to know why the trouper waited until a missing report was issued. Did he know the girl and if he did not know her, how can he be sure this is the same girl he saw vanish?"

Jeff quickly agreed and with a look of relief on his face told Lank an interview was set up for eight am tomorrow morning at the HQTRS of the trouper. After a few additional thoughts were voiced by the two, Lank made his departure from Jeff's office.

Lank spent three days in St Louis at the Interpol sub-regional office pouring over Jeff's interview reports of the nineteen young women who had disappeared. Finally satisfying his curiosity he called the airport to confirm his return flight and saying goodbye to Jeff and his secretary. He departed and after turning in his rented car he made his way down to the gate for his departure.

On his way to his home after spending all day catching up on reports in his office, Lank was tired and told his secretary he was going home.

Lank went over the information he had acquired from the computer and what Jeff had told him, trying to fit just one piece of the puzzle in place. Having no luck at this he quickly turned his attention to the driver of a car that was in the process of passing him. Lank noticed the driver was a pretty girl probably in her late teens. She looked over at him as she passed by and smiled. Lank smiled back and thought no more as the car eventually disappeared in the distance.

Approximately ten minutes later as Lank was continuing down the road he suddenly noticed a car in the medium lying upside down, obviously it had flipped several times. The accident had just happened, as no other cars had stopped to render assistance. Lank quickly pulled his car off onto the medium clicking his emergency lights on, noticing there were no sign of anyone trying to emerge from the car. This was not a good sign he thought to himself.

Upon further observation he noticed it was the same car that had passed him a few miles back with the teenager driving. He had remembered the smile she had given him. Even at his age it gave him a warm feeling. Lank approached the driver side of the car and stooped down long enough to peer into the car. When he stood up there was a look of amazement on his face. He muttered something unintelligent and proceeded to peer into the back seat of the car. This only confirmed what he had suspected. There was no one in the car. This could not be. There was no shrubbery or any place to conceal anyone. As he thought on this he heard a car pull up and as he turned toward the car a policeman from New York's finest emerged from the car and upon recognizing him said with a hint of a smile, "Hi Lank, what you got here?"

Lank responded with a greeting that was meant to be jovial but was filled with tension. Lank recognized the officer from his many encounters at High school functions. Their daughters were in the same grade and friends with each other. "I don't know what is going on Joe, but something is just not right". Joe quickly raised his eyes to meet Lank's stare.

"What do you mean Lank?" Joe asked with a quizzical frown on his face.

"This accident just happened a few minutes before I arrived on the scene and when I looked inside the vehicle there was no occupant."

"Where could the occupant have gone? There's no place within a hundred yards for a person to hide in," Joe stated, as he peered inside the car just to make sure for himself. Joe was thinking to himself, probably someone had stopped and picked up the person and had left prior to Lank's arriving on the scene. He knew Lank had already entertained this idea. Anyway agent Lank

Miller was a very through man with a lot of experience of investigating unusual occurrences.

"What do you think might have happened here?" Joe asked nonchalantly, not realizing Lank already knew the occupant was a girl.

"I don't rightly know at this point, but I can tell you the driver was a teenage girl, probably in her late teens."

"How do you know that?"

"Well she passed me back a few miles," He said. "She smiled at me as she passed."

"You'd recognize her again?"

"I sure would," Lank responded. "I think we had better get a tow truck out here and run a license check."

"Yep I guess that would be our best bet," Joe said. "No use looking for her as she obviously is not here".

"OK Joe, good to see you again," Lank told him. "I'll be off then."

"Right on, I'll fax over to you the identity of the owner as soon as I get it."

"Yeah, this might turn into another of those missing women cases," Lank replied. "See you."

"Take care, see you around."

Chapter Two

Lank returned home after his brief conversation with Joe at the accident. He still was at a loss as to where the young girl had gone. Maybe Joe would have the answer by morning. He had to go into the office early anyway to be able to call Jeff and question him about any further developments as to what his questioning of the young officer that had witness a vanishing woman had accomplished. Lank wondered if just maybe there might be a link between the two cases but how could there be. In his twenty years plus with the FBI, he had always had an explanation for things that in the beginning appeared to be on the weird side. Somehow though, he mused, maybe this was different. There was such a rash of disappearing young women across the whole states, even the world for that matter.

He remembered the reports from New Scotland Yard of the numerous incidents that had not been solved to this date. It did seem like it was a worldwide occurrence and if that was so, then there must be a connection somewhere to explain, even if partial, why so many kidnappings of young girls.

As he pulled into the driveway of his home, Lank spotted his dog, old Duke, lying in his usual place, right in the middle of the driveway just in front of the garage door. Lank smiled as he hit the remote garage door opener with one hand and laughed out loud as 'Old Duke' being startled from a possible dream as the door began to rise up bumping him on its way upward. Upon seeing the car and recognizing his master, he began to wag his tail as he hobbled off to one side out of the way of the car. Lank continued on into the garage and stopped, opening the car door and emerging in his usual way after a hard day at the office. By the time his feet had touched the floor of the garage, old Duke was there with his usual one or two barks that was evidently meant as a "hello."

Lank knelt down beside the dog and begin to rub him behind the ears all the time talking to him in what is known as doggie language by pet owners. After a few minutes of enjoying the welcome, 'Old Duke' went back to his warm spot on the driveway and Lank entered his house through the door into the kitchen. Mary Ann, his wife, upon hearing Lank as he entered, turned from the kitchen range where she was making something good for their supper, and with a big smile on her face turned to him and they embraced with a short hello I missed you kiss.

"How was your day at the office today, dear?" She asked? "I'm sure though it was not as boring as my day has been."

"We have two more kidnappings of young girls to deal with. This one was in the city, and the other in St. Louis.

"Oh my goodness, Honey, what is going on."

"I don't know but it is global now. We have no leads in these cases with the exception of these latest two incidents," Lank replied, wondering just how much information he should be forthcoming with. He had always practiced the old cliché, "just the facts madam."

Lank could already see it was going to be one of those mornings where the only facts he could muster was that the kidnappings were real and the majority were of young women. He would know more though after his interview with the young officer that had supposedly witnessed the young girl vanishing. It was still on the front of his mind about what he had witnessed on the interstate this afternoon. How was it possible the driver of the car had seemed to vanish into thin air? Lank's thoughts, though scrambled as they were, seemed to be heading in a direction he did not wish them to go. He shook his head as though to arrange his thoughts back to normalcy and asked Mary Ann when would they eat.

"It won't be very much longer. Go talk with Jenny. She is in the study doing her homework."

Lank nodded his head and walked through the living room to his study which was an added room they had built a couple of years ago. He noticed as he entered the study Jenny was sprawled on the sofa with books and sheets of paper strewn upon the floor, evidently deep in her homework, as evidenced by a lack of reaction as he entered the room.

"Hi Jen, whatcha up to?" Lank asked as he made his way to his desk.

"Oh, hi dad. I'm trying to get my homework done early so I can go skating with Cyndi," Jen responded.

"You kids are lucky. When your mom and I were in school, we had tons of homework every night. We didn't have time for anything else."

"I know. That's what mom keeps telling me. I'm just about through with it though, only have my math problems to do."

"Ok, then I won't bother you. I have to write up a couple of reports and we can be done before mom gets supper on the table." Lank said as he pulled his chair out from the desk and sat down, and finally upon finding his pen, began to concentrate on the reports he had to get done.

Lank was just putting the finishing touches, as he liked to call them, on his two reports when Mary Ann called from the kitchen, supper was ready. He nodded to Jen and both began to pick up their papers and tidy up a bit before heading toward the dinning room. Lank and his daughter Jen were both big eaters. It was noticeable they had put on a few extra pounds over the past month. Jen seemed to be holding her own though, probably the exercise she was getting through school activities was keeping her trim.

He sure wasn't getting much exercise sitting behind a desk most of the day was his thoughts as he pulled his chair out from the table and began to sit down. He noticed they were having meatloaf with mashed potatoes and plenty of gravy with a big pile of Texas toast with butter and garlic spread on it, roasted of course.

"Honey if you keep putting such fine meals on the table before me, I for sure will have to enroll in an exercise class." This was his way of complimenting Mary Ann on her fine gourmet cooking. After a lot of small talk, mostly about Jen's day at school, the meal ended and as Jen help her mother clear the table and clean up, Lank retired back to his study. He still was not able to clear his mind enough to begin to put this big puzzle together. He needed to contact London, Paris, even Russia, to find out if they had made any progress on solving these mysteries.

Chapter Three

The Director of DHS had appointed Lank as deputy director of The Department of Homeland Security some two and a half years ago. Of course his real duties behind the title of Deputy Director of DHS was his duty as Special Advisor to the President on Bio-terrorist affairs. His office was located in the United nations Building in New York. Although Lank hardly spent much time in his New York office, being on special duty for the President of the United States, he was on the road out of state most of the time.

After enduring at least thirty minutes of traffic backup along the freeway he finally was able to pull into his assigned parking space. Of course he thought to himself this was nothing new at all. He had to fight traffic every morning he came to his office. Lank entered the building from the main street side and continued on toward the elevators. At least one elevator was still on the ground floor so he would not have to wait.

As he entered the elevator he happened to glance back to-ward the street entrance and caught a glimpse of James Gurley, as he was hurrying toward the elevators. Lank kept the door open as James quickly approached and entered. He acknowledged the greeting from Lank and exclaimed slightly out of breath.

"Well good to see you Lank. I was hoping you would be here early today."

"Yep, that's me, early bird Charlie. Why are you here so early today, something come up?" Lank asked.

"No, not really, I wanted to check with you about the acci-dent and the disappearance of the young girl you witnessed. The Attorney general wanted an update on the situation." James was the liaison officer between DHS and the Attorney General of New York, an important link that Lank had used many times in the past. They engaged in non-specific talk for a few minutes until the elevator reached the ninth floor and stopped. They both waited patiently as the elevator doors finally opened and they emerged onto the long hallway that led to Lank's office.

Lank walked ahead of James on the way, they strode toward Lank's office, where, upon entering, Lank's eyes were automatically drawn toward the fax machine sitting on the small table adjacent to the larger table that held his coffee machine and condiments. He briskly walked over to the fax machine with a nod to James to have a seat.

With a sigh of relief he noticed a stack of papers that had come overnight. Lank deftly picked up the stack and began to scan through them. The first page was from the FBI director of south region offices. Nothing important, some memos on training required annually. Lank quickly tossed this one in his in basket on his desk and turned his attention to the rest of the stack. His eyes narrowed as he noticed the title page of the fax he held in his hand.

"Woman Vanished From Sight As Witness Looked On."

It was a copy of an article in the London Daily Mirror paper. Lank sidestepped the stool that was sitting in front of the fax machine and moved toward his desk. As he moved past James he dropped the remaining fax articles on his desk. Just as he was pulling his chair back from the desk in an attempt to sit down the phone rang. He picked the receiver up on the second ring and spoke a crisp "hello" into the receiver. The voice at the other end was definitely British as Lank heard the familiar "Allo old chap" as Inspector Frank Brokain began to speak.

"How are things going in the States mate?" Lank listened politely as the Inspector dispersed with the niceties and began to be forthcoming with the information Lank hoped would help him in his ongoing investigations. It was at this point that his secretary entered, and noticing Lank was on the phone, she immediately began to straighten up the papers on her desk.

Lank, with a casual glance toward James, acknowledging he was there, continued to listen to the Inspector from London. The conversation was mostly one sided as Lank only briefly interjected a "yes" or "I see" in the appropriate places. Finally it was

Lank's turn to talk and as James listened to the conversation he was obviously interested in what he was saying.

"Inspector Brokain, there has developed an interesting turn of events in our investigation here in the states. I don't know, and from what you have told me, I'm assuming you are aware of the fact that now, not only have we encountered abductions, but now we have witnesses that swear they saw the young woman vanish from their sight. Yes, One minute they were in plain sight and the next they were gone. Inspector, I witnessed a scene that is almost as bizarre."

Lank went on to tell the Inspector about the incident he and Officer Joe had experienced. When he got to the part where the girl was not in the car, Inspector Brokain interrupted him.

"You mean the girl just walked away from the accident."

"No Inspector, she did not have time to go anywhere because I was no more than a couple of minutes behind her before the accident happened."

"She could have been picked up by someone, could this be possible?"

Lank responded in a polite but firm voice. "I don't think so, Inspector, I was on the scene almost immediately and I did not see any cars either way until Officer Joe came by."

"Hmmm, well maybe the woman ran off and is hiding somewhere in the underbrush."

"Not probable as this is mostly flat farmland along this particular part of the roadway."

"Ok, noted. Tell me about the other incident, the witness observing the vanishing of a girl."

"I only have secondhand, but reliable information on this one. I have the results of the interview with the officer in about thirty minutes from now so I will know more about it then."

The Inspector was, to say the least, very interested in this possibility. His voice as he spoke into the receiver was aquiver with excitement.

"Now that is something I'm very much interested in. Lank please fax me the details of your interview with that young man. I'm thinking we might be onto something here but I can not speak directly over the phone with you."

Upon hearing this information from Inspector Frank Brokain, Lank figured the inspector had other information that he wanted to share with him.

"Inspector do you think it might be beneficial if we were to meet in person. I can take a flight to London tomorrow morning," Lank was hoping for somewhat of a tie in with all these vanishings reported, especially the eyewitness accounts of a person disappearing into thin air.

"That would be helpful because there are other aspects to this case that we need to look into," Inspector Brokain stated with a hint of relief in his voice.

"I was hoping you would agree to that. You are absolutely right, there are a lot of unusual things that have happened. I'll give you a call when I arrive there in London," Lank responded in a somewhat relieved tone in his voice.

After a few more casual exchanges over the phone they both said bye and Lank placed the receiver back on the hook. He stood there for almost a full minute digesting the exchange of information that had just taken place between the two. Finally, with a shrug of his shoulders, Lank was ready to begin his conversation with the liaison officer, James Gurley.

"Just what did you find out Lank?" James asked in a voice that belied his pent up emotion.

"Not a whole lot, but the young lady's name was Betty Francis Moulton. Her listed address was 305 Queens Drive, Apt 305, Queens, New York, NY."

"Married?" James asked.

"No. She was employed by a brokerage firm and lived at home with her mother," Lank stated.

Somewhere, somehow a small bell was trying to ring in Lank's mind but for the life of him he could not imagine why. Was it because of something Jeff had said or maybe what he had read in some of the reports? After a few more minutes of talk, James exited his office and ambled down the hall to the elevators. Lank picked up the telephone receiver and dialed Jeff in St. Louis. Lank greeted him with a gruff hello as Jeff came on the line.

"Hi Lank, I'm on duty at the VIP airport right now but I was just rereading the incident report the state trouper, Paul Treadway, submitted. He sure seems positive about what he saw," Jeff stated.

"You ready to critique what he had to say?" Lank asked.

"I don't have the time right now Lank, do you think he was sincere, I mean, in telling what he had witnessed. Maybe he forgot something that we need to know."

"No, I'm sure he was trying his best to give a detailed report as much as he could," Lank stated.

"You are probably right. I tend to worry too much," Jeff said.

"Ok. Jeff. I'm off to converse with our old friend from England."

"You mean good old Franky boy," Jeff chided him.

"Yes Frank Brokain. You know the Queen promoted him to X.400 Communications Officer in Charge. He has his own little network going, world wide I suppose. Oh by the way while I'm there I'll fill you in on what I can pick up on from Inspector Frank Brokain," Lank mentioned in a somewhat controlled voice as he was still mulling over the conversation himself.

"Good, I was hoping you would hear from old Frankie. I'm all ears," Jeff exclaimed.

Chapter Four

Lank's mind went back to the report of Jeff on the young trouper that had witnessed the disappearance of the young girl right before his eyes.

Jeff had been unable to shake the young trouper's statement no matter what he threw at him. In the almost two hours of intense questioning he had stuck to his story of stopping the young woman for a speeding violation on State Road 35. While he was in the process of writing out the ticket he had heard a popping sound and upon looking up from filling out the report he was surprised to see no one in the car.

When Jeff had queried him about the possibility of the woman slipping out the passenger side of the car he had responded with an emphatically no. He went on to explain there was not enough time and on top of that she had her seat belt fastened and it was still fastened after she had disappeared. The passenger door had never opened. She had just disappeared without a trace.

As hard as it was, Jeff had agreed he thought Paul Treadway was telling the truth and it did happen just the way he had described it. Now what was a man to do about this turn of events? Lank was deep in thought about it when his stomach let him know he was hungry.

Lank wanted a burger and fries. There was a popular burger joint about a mile further down the highway, at the next exit where he pulled off and rolled into the parking lot. Lank exited the car and ambled up toward the door of the burger joint.

Upon placing his order with the attractive young lady at the counter he had only a few minutes to wait before his order was ready. It was at this time as Lank was carrying his tray back to the table when a loud popping noise was heard coming from the vicinity of the cash register. Lank directed his attention toward this area and noticed the attractive young girl was not there.

It was about this time he also noticed one of her colleagues standing with his mouth open looking toward where the girl had been standing. Also a customer to whom she had been taking his order was looking around in bewilderment not knowing what had happened.

Lank, with the fresh awareness of his duty as an officer of the law identified himself and quickly took control of the situation. He began systematically to sanitize the area thereby preventing anyone from leaving. He began to question the employees as to what they had seen or heard. Lank found out the name of the girl that vanished was Marie Gonzales. When it came to the employee that Lank noticed was standing with his mouth open, Lank wanted to know if he had actually witnessed the disappearance of the girl.

"What is your name?" Lank asked.

Without any hesitation at all he answered. "John Tyler," while still staring at Lank's identification badge and credentials.

"What did you see happen right now? The girl at the cash register, what do you think happened to her?"

"I don't rightly know, sir, I was just going to asked her a question and she just disappeared right in front of my eyes. What happened to her, where's she at?" John Tyler asked with a confused look on his face and obviously scared.

Lank, taking in the fact of this most unusual occurrence, assured the young man he would find out and began to question the other employees not in the kitchen when the girl disappeared from the cash register. He was kept busy getting names and addresses of the customers and was now concentrating on this one disappearance and was unaware of anything going on unusual.

The one customer who had been ordering at the time of the occurrence was an elderly gentleman and had remained calm during all of the questions. Lank approached him and ask for his name and address.

"Ted Hinds, I live at 1021 South Poplar."

Lank then asked him to give his account of what had transpired. His account matched the employee who was looking at the girl when she disappeared.

After about thirty minutes Lank had all the information he needed for his report and allowed the customers to leave and new customers to enter the establishment.

On the way back to the his office Lank went over what had happened and what the witness had observed. Lank had not witnessed the disappearance of the girl. He could not question the fact it actually happened. However, he needed to know why this was happening and what was the purpose. There has just got to be a logical explanation was on his mind as he returned back to the office. No doubt there would be glaring headlines in the newspapers tomorrow morning.

Lank turned into his parking space and begin the trek to his office. His mind a whirl, he strode down the hall to his office. His secretary, Janet Porter, met him at the door of his office and presented him with his tickets to London. She was as usual upbeat and full of spunk as she greeted him with a big smiled as she handed him the envelope containing the tickets.

"Jan I'm all set then for a flight this morning?" Lank queried as he took the envelope. He could not have asked for a better secretary than Janet, Lank thought to himself as he anticipated her answer.

"That's right. You leave from the International airport at exactly eleven thirty five this morning. You need to leave now if you want to be on time." I have all ready informed your wife, Mary Ann and she is meeting you there with your bags.

"Thanks Jan, Then I'm on my way. I need to take that folder that I left on your desk last night with me."

"Right, it's all prepared and in the order you requested."

Jan immediately picked up the folder from the corner of Lank's desk giving it to him on her way to the office door.

"Lank have a good trip and if you need anything done at this end just give me a call."

"Thanks again Jan. I have a meeting with Inspector Brokain just as soon as I get there, matter of fact he is having me picked up at the airport and brought straight to his home."

Jan hesitated at the door and spoke with concern in her voice. "Sounds like he might have some additional information that would help you in all these disappearances."

"I certainly hope so. Jan you will have to check with Jeff and fax him our report on the incident that took place this morning," Lank advised as he tucked the folder Jan had given him into his briefcase. I'll check with you just as soon as I can."

"Ok I'll see that it gets to the Jeff in St. Louis," Jan replied as she waved goodbye to Lank as he exited from the room.

The ride to the airport was uneventful and Lank used the time to go over the past few weeks' events in him mind, trying to make some sense, or at least a semblance of a pattern, in all these disappearances. He had reported all his findings to the Director of Homeland Security last night via secure telephone.

The director, whose name was Larry Duiggs, assured him the whole world was looking into this situation and that the President had been advised and wanted the results of Lank's meeting with Inspector Frank Brokain in London on his desk before Lank returned from London.

Lank was anticipating something positive to come out of the meeting, although he could not even venture a guess at this point as to what it might be. Well he mused, as the limo came to a stop in the waiting zone of the airport, at least the ball was rolling now and maybe it would not be too much longer before the ball was in their court.

Lank directed the baggage handler which flight he was on and continued to the correct gate, bypassing security by showing his Special Id along with an iris scan. The officer on duty recognized him but still Lank had to go through the appropriate security procedures.

Upon checking in with the attendant at the gate he heard his name called and turning around noticed Mary Ann and Jen approaching him. He smiled as he embraced both of them, openly appreciative of his position that allowed them to be expedited through airport security to be able to see him off. One thing about his marriage to Mary Ann, some twenty years, was the fact that it was and had been a good marriage. Not to say they had not had their share of mishaps and misfortunes in their years of marriage, they had, but had managed to weather through all of them.

Then there was Jen. Jen, he guessed, was a typical teenager, succumbing to peer pressure more than once. Nevertheless, she had been strong and direct in her approach to life, using the morals he and Mary Ann had instilled in her as she grew in statue and wisdom. All in all, Jen had her head on right and most of the time listened to her parents. Lank knew he was a lucky man and really felt bad about his many trips across the States and abroad at times, but it came with the job and both Mary Ann and Jen were understanding of which Lank was very appreciative to no end.

They only had fifteen minutes till departure time and used that time to engage in small talk. Lank was glad that he did not have to go through the baggage inspection lines, his baggage had been cleared by the Director of Homeland Security, even Mary Ann and Jen had been cleared to wait in the waiting room with him. Ah, he thought to himself, rank has its privileges, and he was glad for the little perks afforded him.

The flight attendant asked for everyone's attention and made the announcement the plane was ready for boarding. After a final hug and a tearful goodbye from Mary Ann and Jen, he boarded the aircraft. The flight attendant directed him to his seat in first class. He kept an eye out as to whether the plane would be crowded or not. Lank was lucky, when the door to the plane was finally closed, only about half of first class seats were taken. He really disliked being cooped up in small cramped compartment area, especially on a plane with a twelve hour trip ahead of him.

The flight was completely uneventful to Lank's relief. Not that he wanted something to happen. He was glad it did not. They had a thirty-minute layover in Shannon where the passengers were allowed to disembark and stretch their legs somewhat in the terminal. Upon arrival at London's Heaththrow airport, Lank was met by Inspector Frank Brokain and greeted with a warm welcome.

Lank and the Inspector went a long way back in their friendship. Lank knew Frank when he was just a "Bobbie" working his beat on the streets of London. Lank had been in the exchange officer program and was assigned to the same unit Frank was in.

They had become good friends over the years with one or the other visiting in their homes. Mary Ann really liked Frank's wife, a pretty little blond that belied the clichés of the many blond jokes, as she was very intelligent and forth coming with her knowledge, having a master's degree in English/Lit. Jacquelyn, or Jackie, as she preferred to be addressed as, taught at the university in London.

"Did you have a good flight from the colonies mate?" Frank asked in a jovial manner. He had always, as far as Lank could remember in their relationship, referred to the states as colonies. Lank smiled as he remembered the many times he had, in a good nature way, tried to correct Frank's knowledge of the states. After a few years and getting to know Frank and his family in an intimate way, he came to know this was just Frank's way of letting him know how much he really liked him.

Upon arriving at Frank's home, which was located in a suburban neighborhood on the western side of London which made it a fast trip from the airport on the M4 motorway. Jackie was waiting for them. She came running to meet Lank and with tears of genuine joy, began to hug him and ask a thousand questions. Lank had a nice feeling in his heart knowing what good friends Frank and Jackie had been to him and Mary Ann over the years.

They began to migrate towards the front door of the house and upon entering into the living room; Lank began to unwind somewhat from his flight over. He knew from previous trips over the Atlantic about what jet lag can do to your biological clock.

Jackie began to mix drinks for them knowing without asking what Lank would want. She was adept at making a friend feel at home.

"Lank why didn't you bring Mary Ann with you? I would have loved to see her again," Jackie asked as she handed Lank his drink.

"Well she wanted to come but with Jen still in school and all the activities she is involved in at school, not to mention Mary Ann's social clubs she has to attend, there was just no way she could make it this time. She sends her regrets and hope you will understand," Lank responded.

Oh sure, I can understand, I have just about the same problems here but I sure have missed her."

"She has missed you too. How long has it been since we all were together?" Lank asked.

Frank who had been standing by the bar mixing his own drink joined in the conversation.

"About a year and a half, wasn't it Lank?"

"Yep, I think it was in the month of January, wasn't it Frank? When you and Jackie were in New York and we came out to meet you."

"That's right Lank, I remember calling Mary Ann and how excited she was upon learning we were coming to New York for a visit," Jackie said.

"Yes, I remember. If I had not of been able get out of Washington that day, I would never have heard the last of it." Frank at this point in time seemed eager to get Lank off to himself as was noticed by the tone of his voice, cautiously begging for an end to this chit chat.

"Lank come on down to my study, I have something I want to show you."

Lank quickly agreed and with a "We won't be long Jackie" as he followed Frank down the hallway and to the steps going down into the basement where Frank's study was located. Lank remember the study well. He and Frank had spent a lot of time together in this study. Lank remembered it had a lot of hi-tech stuff and communications devices that kept him in immediate contact with European and American law enforcement agencies.

As they entered into the study Frank began a steady discourse of explaining to Lank what each piece of equipment did. Lank's ears perked up when Frank began to show him the satellite phone with encryption devices incorporated in the link between him and Interpol Headquarters located in Lyon, France.

"Frank, speaking of Interpol, I'm sure they are on top of all these disappearances, but I'm just curious as to how much information they have."

Frank's demeanor began to change as he moved closer to the desk that the satellite phone was installed on.

"Lank, I know how much you have in your files on all these disappearances, but you have no idea what Interpol has."

"Oh, I'd sure be interested to learn what they have because I tell you Frank, we in the states are caught blind by all this. We have no clue as to what is going on."

"I know and that's why I wanted you over here because I know you have the ears of DHS and the president too, for that matter. It's just that Interpol has such a huge file dating back ten years or more."

"Well I'm here now and I'm all ears," Lank said with obvious anticipation couched in his voice.

"Well, Ok take a seat and I'll break out the file we have with Interpol on all these disappearances. I feel sure you will be greatly impressed and somewhat taken aback," Frank responded with a slight quiver in his voice. Frank was thinking to himself about how much information they did have compared to what Lank possessed. He was glad they were such close friends because what he was about to show and reveal to Lank was mind-boggling.

Frank set down in front of the computer and began bringing up the files from Interpol. The first one was dated on 10 August 2000. It was a report from a small town in Germany just outside of Frankfurt depicting an incident where a young girl by the name of Lise Meitner, only eighteen years old and from a prominent family, had been abducted as she was shopping in a local store. Only one witness came forward that had actually seen what had happened. The witness stated he was no more than three feet away when there was a loud pop and the girl in front of him just disappeared into thin air. None of the larger news media picked up on the witness's story as they only reported on the abduction. The report stated that within two weeks prior to this incident there had been a rash of young women being abducted all across Germany.

Frank began to bring up the second file when Lank interrupted him.

"Frank, I'm curious as to the witness that heard the popping sound just prior to the young woman disappearing. Did he repeat his story to any other media outlets?"

"Not in so many words, that is why I suppose it was never picked up on by some of the other media."

"What do you mean, did he change his story?' Lank asked.

"No, but he began to keep a closed mouth and would not talk with any reporters about it."

"What happened, do you think he was approached by someone to keep quiet?" Lank ask.

"Yes, that is exactly what Interpol thinks, but the sad thing about it is, this witness, a Ludwig Van Schmidt, simply disappeared himself. Interpol has tried to find him and has not had any luck whatsoever," Frank exclaimed.

"OK Frank, you were about to bring up the second file."

"Right, now this file contains some additional information on the first incident, in addition to a linkage between the first and second disappearance."

Frank was right, the second file did contain a lot of information. Information that was vital to any investigation but from what Lank could determine it all came to a dead end. The German guy Ludwig just disappeared from the face of the Earth. Lank's mind quickly turned over the probability of the witness being abducted himself. When he voiced his suspicions, Frank quickly responded.

"I don't know, it is just like all the other disappearances, no witnesses."

"I gathered that was the way it was. Frank, could we open up the investigation again on this Ludwig Van Schmidt. I would like to talk with his families, friends and neighbors again.

It may be someone will come forward with something they did not think of in the first investigation."

Frank smiled at the professionalism in Lank's voice. He had turned back to the computer and brought up another file that was labeled with a special code word.

"Lank, this file is highly restricted but you are cleared for viewing, I made sure of that before your arrival. This file contains the information you thought we might uncover in a second investigation," Frank stated.

"Hey that's just great. "Her majesty's Service is one jump ahead of us as always," Lank exclaimed.

Lank's ears really did pick up on this bit of information, He took a deep breath and waited for Frank to finish bringing up the file before leaning over and actually began to read the file.

The file listed the relatives first and there was a short paragraph of what they told the investigator. Nothing new here, as it was pretty well the same as contained in the original file. The next few pages were devoted to interviewing neighbors. One neighbor two doors down from the witness stated he had been with Ludwig the morning he was supposed to have disappeared. They were in the neighbor's living room having refreshments. The neighbor had left the room for just a few minutes to attend to something his wife had asked him to do. Upon returning back to the room, Ludwig was not there, not a sign of him. The neighbor had wondered what had happened to him and why he was gone. He supposed he had just left and probably gone home. This was the last time Ludwig had been seen.

"Well Frank, I think we have another abrupt disappearance on our hands. I think Ludwig Van Schmidt went the same way as all these young women have gone,"

Lank's statement was more in the form of a question than anything else, wanting confirmation.

Frank was nodding in agreement. He took a deep breath before he began to address Lank and what he had just said.

"Yes, not only you and I think this way, but so does Interpol. Although this does pose somewhat of a problem as far as our theories go."

"You mean this is the first time we can correlate a disappearance of a male into our theory of why these disappearances are happening in the first place?" Lank asked.

"That's right Lank. I'll tell you what our theory is in these disappearances."

"Oh you have a theory, I'd certainly like to be privy to it."

"Well not so much a theory I guess, but at least it is something of a bite that has been thrown our way."

"OK let me have it."

Before Frank responded he turned back to his files and brought out some newspapers clippings that were obviously connected to the disappearances. He began to hand them one by one to Lank and watched as he began to read them.

The first one was from the Global National and was almost a year old. The headline read:

"YOUNG WOMAN VANISHES IN FRONT OF WITNESS."

The article went on to relate the disappearance and the facts associated with it. Near the last part of the article Lank's eyebrows were raised as the gist of what he read began to sink in. It was what the witness had purported to have said that interested Lank more than the article itself. The witness to this disappearance saw the same things, as other eyewitnesses had, only this time there been something different.

The witness, a Mr. Larry Culvert, told the interviewer that he had noticed the time on the clock in the store and had set his watch because it was a few minutes slow. He had just finished setting it when he noticed the second hand was going backwards. He was astonished as this was an expensive watch.

It was at this time while engaging in conversation with the young lady who was the clerk waiting on him, he noticed she seemed to be frozen in time and then after a few seconds, he supposed, she just upped and vanished from where she was at.

Larry Culvert was the pastor of First Baptist church in Borough Green in Kent, England and was well respected in the community. Still though, the reporter was somewhat skeptical of his account.

Attached to the clipping was a report from New Scotland Yard as to the authenticity of the witness's account. The statement went on to say, "Although it is highly improbable that anyone could disappear into thin air and coupled with the statement the Rev. Mr. Larry Culvert made concerning the improper workings of his timepiece at just prior to the young lady disappearing, made it even more highly improbable.

The rest of the report was more concerned with the internal distribution of copies to all effected personnel.

Lank dropped the clipping and report on the computer desk and with a wave of his hand indicated he was at a loss for words.

Frank, who had been watching as Lank read the clipping and then the report from New Scotland Yard and looking directly into Link's eyes said in a no condescending way.

"Lank I hope you are coming to somewhat of an understanding of what has been happening here. I know I have a glimmer of an idea but I'm going to hold on to it for the present. I want you to look at the rest of what we have and then you tell me what you think."

"Right, Frank. I'm looking to seeing more of what's in the rest of the reports."

With that, Frank handed the third file into Lank's outstretched hand. Lank began to read the report and while he was reading, Frank was busy again on the fourth report, highlighting certain parts so as to cause these portions to leap out at Lank as he was gleaning through them.

Lank read silently and when he had finished reading the last page, he looked up and with a whimsical smile on is face, he exhaled a pent-up breath and stated with a noticeable tremor in his voice.

"Frank I think I'm beginning to see where you are going with this. I just don't know how you or I could explain our position to the powers that be."

"I agree with you, but just hold on until you have read this last report. I think it will either confirm or deny our thought processes on this." While Frank had been speaking he had collected together the pages of the fourth report and handed them to Lank.

Lank took the pages of the file and strolled over to the only couch in the office and sat down before he began to read the first page. He had read with intense interest and when finished was silent for a short period of time, evidently collecting his thoughts on this report.

The file again was a collection of newspaper headlines and stories about the rash of disappearances of so many young ladies. Also there were a couple of critiques from Interpol and New Scotland with a copy forwarded to the Secretary of DHS in Washington D.C. and a copy being sent to HMSS office.

The first critique was an attempt at defining the position of Interpol concerning these disappearances of so many young women. Only a hint in the direction Lank was leaning in viewing the problem was being stated here. It was as if they knew more than they were willing to say, or, maybe they were afraid of being ridiculed if they actually voice their opinions.

The second critique was more specific and to the point. It for the first time mentioned two possibilities. One possibility referred to a supernatural happening that at the present time was unexplainable. Lank immediately thought of what he had learned in his Sunday school class during his growing up years.

The rapture, if he remembered correctly, was for all born again Christians and not selected on gender only. It was supposed to happen all at once, in a twinkling of an eye, not over a period of time and only young women taken. He was quick to conclude in his mind this was not the rapture mentioned in the Bible.

The second possibility mentioned was just a passing thought of someone within the agency attempting to put on paper. It went on to explain the idea of being translated. Translated being explained as dislocation of a person or thing from one place to another. The transference of a person or material over a distance within the time frame of less than a nanosecond was the nature of the project. It relied heavily upon experiments conducted at various colleges and universities.

Although none of the experiments were successful, there was one at Columbia University in New York State that came close, according to the physics instructor, Professor Gerald P. Manning. He had stated he thought they were only a few years away from a major breakthrough in Molecular Transference as the project was so named.

Chapter Five

Lank had been on his return trip back to the states only a few hours but it seemed a lot longer than that. His mind was still whirring with all the new information Frank had made available to him. The interview with Professor Manning at Columbia University as reported in Inspector Brokain's files had been rather enlightened, but also exciting.

The words of the professor were still fresh in his mind as he thought upon the substance of what was relayed to him. Lank decided he would interview Professor Manning in the next few days when he returned to New York.

Lank did obtain an interview with the professor a week later after his arrival in New York. Professor Manning had outlined the project he had been conducting over the past five years. The project consisted of trying to find a way to use the "Displacement of topological shortcut" theory. The construction of a TSMD, Time Space Manipulator Device, was where they had placed all their energy and expertise. In a nutshell, what the professor was telling Lank was their work involved sending matter through a wormhole allowing transit faster than light, the FTL concept.

Lank had studied physics in his last semester in college but nothing this deep. He had understood the concept of what the Professor had been telling him but that was as far as it went with him. If this were possible and someone had invented a TSMD, then could it be possible to transport humans into the future. He had posed this very question to Professor Manning and the answer he got was a very resounding yes. Professor Manning had made it clear in his response that he definitely thought it possible. He went on to explain the parallel universe theory and what it would mean it a person could travel through time.

Lank was impressed with the level of expertise the professor had shown and the preliminary experiments he had accomplished so far in his building of a TSMD. The Professor had told him of the experiments conducted at the Valley Lab located in Los Angels that had involved finding a solution to keeping a wormhole open long enough to permit an object, space ship, to traverse the entire length of the worm hole. Because of the warping of time within the wormhole, the ship would exit out of the wormhole at precisely the same time it entered the open end of the wormhole.

Lank must have had a dumbfounded look on his face, because Prof Manning brought the explanation down to a level that allowed him to get a picture of how the wormhole worked. He went on to explain by giving an example. If you can visualize a long cylinder with the circumference slightly larger than a tennis ball and if you fill the tube full with tennis balls, what happens when you push another tennis ball into the tube. The Professor answered his own question while Lank was getting a picture of the tube filled with tennis balls in his mind.

He had explained to Lank that it was quite obvious that with the manually pushing of another tennis ball into the front end of the tube would cause the last tennis ball to exit the back end exactly in the same proportion to the tennis ball being pushed into the tube from the front end. This is exactly how the wormhole works thereby providing a way of traveling faster than light. The Professor was not through with his explanation, obviously enjoying himself.

"You see, Mr. Miller, we have already demonstrated this concept and we know it is possible to travel faster than light. We have introduced two radio frequency signals into a wave-guide. One signal designed to travel straight through the wave-guide being measured as to the exact time it took to travel through the wave-guide. Now another radio frequency with the same charactrics such as frequency and amplitude, and power, was sent at the same time the first signal was introduced into the same wave guide, however this second signal was sent bouncing off the walls of the wave guide from side to side until it too exited the wave-guide. The time it took this second signal to go completely through the wave-guide was compared to the first signal.

It was shown that both signals, which had entered into the wave-guide at the same precise moment in time, now had exited the other end of the wave-guide at precisely the same time. One signal going straight through the tube and the other signal bouncing off the walls until it too exited, proves beyond a shadow of a doubt that it is possible for radio frequencies to travel faster than light."

Lank nodded his head and asked.

"Because radio waves travel at the speed of light and if one, because of the longer distance it had to travel came out at the same time the first one did, it had to go faster than the first one, right Professor Manning?"

"That's it in a nutshell and this is what the Valley team based all their time travel experiments on."

"Professor Manning, just how far along are the Valley team?" Lank asked.

"I wish I knew myself, but you see the government shut off all media from them. They even have military guards surrounding the buildings the experiments are located in. However, I'm not ignorant as to what they are attempting to do, and I've built most of my experiments on their ideas. I'm just taking them to the next level. So far the government hasn't bothered me. I suppose because I am not that well known."

"You mean, yet, don't you Professor," Lank responded with a smile lifting the corners of his mouth.

"Probably, but I haven't published my experiments as they did," The professor announced. The interview soon ended on this point. Back in the present time Lank and Janet, who had come to pick him up at the airport on his return trip from London, walked with him to the baggage claim area. Lank decided to go by his office before he went on home. Jan said that was fine with her and seemed glad to have him a little longer before he went home to his family.

"Any thing important or pressing Janet?" Lank asked as he poured himself a cup of coffee.

"No Lank, I've got everything caught up. I hope you enjoyed your visit with Frank and Jackie."

"Oh, very much, nothing has changed with those two you know."

"You ready to take me home, seeing I don't have my car handy."

"Of course, if you are ready, then I am ready too."

He and Janet continued talking on the way home. Lank filled Janet in on some of the specifics and promised to have the report ready for faxing to DHS first thing in the morning. Janet was a clerk in the FBI and had been assigned to Lank as his personal secretary. She held full clearance and was kept up on all the investigations going on concerning the kidnappings of young women. Upon arriving at his house, Janet eased into his driveway acutely aware of 'old dukes' habit of sleeping right in the driveway. However, today he was nowhere in sight.

Lank opened his door and waved to Janet to come on in for a visit but Janet assured him she had a pile of work ready for her back at the office and really did not have time. Lank thanked her for picking him up and with a wave of his hand in a gesture of goodbye he stood in the driveway and watched her back out and disappear down the street.

Neither Mary Ann nor Jen was at home. Lank wondered what had come up to prevent Mary Ann from meeting him at the airport. He went on in through the garage door into the kitchen and headed for his study. Maybe this was a god send so he could get his report ready and have Janet fax it on to DHS tonight, then tomorrow it would be there and be freshly read by his boss as he briefed him on his London trip.

Lank was just putting the finishing touches on his report when he heard a car drive up and in a few minutes Mary Ann and Jen came into the kitchen. They gave a squeal of excited laughter when they realized he was home both running and embracing him at the same time. He was glad to see them also.

"What came up today to keep you from meeting me?" Lank asked.

"Well we had forgotten about Jen having a special recital at school and I so wanted to be there. Also I guess it must have slipped my mind because when I finally realized you had asked to me to pick you up at the office it was too late. That's why I asked

Janet if she could pick you up," Mary Ann said in a slightly embarrassed voice.

Lank picking up on the quiver in her voice immediately put his arm around her and whispered in her ear that it was all right. This seemed to sooth her feelings as they settled down in the den. Later on that evening Lank called his courier and had him pick up his report and take it to Janet's home. He was so glad to get it out of his hands knowing that tomorrow he had to brief Director Farshaw at the capital building and then later on that afternoon they would have to brief the President at the white house.

Chapter Six

John Farshaw was a man destined for great things, or so he liked to think this of himself. He had been appointed as Director of Department of Homeland Defense by president Tom Langley two years ago after the previous director had resigned amid a month long onslaught by the media against his character, brought on by his inept ability to get the job done. Especially when he had allowed the top terrorist to escape a huge net designed to capture him.

Lank guessed it was the fact that the Home Land security Director, while this plan had been put into effect, had been on vacation on the French reverie and was out of touch as to what had been going on. This was the straw that had broken the camel's back. He had never been able to recover his political composure.

The senate had no trouble confirming John Farshaw's appointment to the Directorship of Home Land Defense probably more than anything else, he was a man of action, and could be counted on to get the job done in the quickest amount of time. His past record as Attorney General of the U.S. displayed some remarkable aspects into the insight of his character. A couple of entries into his public record caused some eyebrows to be raised but in the end though, he was confirmed.

Lank had respect for the man but also was wary of his tactics in accomplishing a job in the past. However, that was neither here nor there as the man was his immediate boss only as a cover, as Lank answered only to the President of the United States of America. He kept his thoughts to himself for the present.

"Good morning Lank, good to see you again, have a seat," John Farshaw said as he motioned Lank to take a seat.

"Thanks, good to see you again too. How are things treating you?" Lank asked in his best genuine tone of voice, hoping that the director had read his report so that Lank would not have to bring him up to date.

"Fine, Fine. Have a good trip to London Lank? I have read your report and I'm more interested in what you didn't put in the report."

Lank smiled and responded, he hoped in a nonchalant manner.

"Yes, there are thoughts in my head that I did not put in the report. Thoughts that are so far out that I am almost afraid to mention them."

"I am aware of the mysterious aspect of these cases and don't feel like you are the only one with such thoughts. Just go ahead and unload," His boss told him as he settled back in his office chair.

Lank began with his interview of Professor Manning and his experiments with time travel. John Farshaw's eye brows definitely raised at this bit of information. Lank went on to tell him the gist of what he had learned, then he began to voice some of the thoughts he had kept repressed until now.

"You see John, I'm very reluctant to bring these thoughts out in the open. I can see no other logical explanation of what has been happening in these young women disappearing the way they do."

"You mean somehow these disappearing young women are being snatched into the past," John remarked in an offhand way.

"No, not the past, the future. Professor Manning thinks it must be the future that they are being sent to, why, I don't have the slightest," Lank told John.

"Professor Manning thinks time travel is possible?" John asked, with no hint of disbelief in his voice.

"Yes he demonstrated to me with one of his ongoing experiments that time travel is possible, as a matter of fact, Einstein and other notable scientist believed it is possible."

"Your absolutely right Lank, I'm sure time travel is possible. You are aware of the Los Angels Valley Quantum Physics Laboratory. Their experiments in this field are years ahead of what you have seen here," John said as he looked right at Lank.

"Yes, somewhat, I was not able to interview anyone from there, let alone view or learn about what they are doing over there."

"That's right, you would not be able to. Neither you nor I have a "need to know". The military has that place locked down. However, I have a few friends in high places that are privy to what the Valley folks are doing."

"Any bits of information, off the record for sure, you would care to share?" Lank asked, hoping John would share with him.

"Well Lank, what I reveal to you must not leave this room, understood."

"Certainly, my lips are sealed."

"There was a breakthrough in time travel about six months ago. The Valley Lab guys were able to send a dog somewhere. At the time they were not sure where the dog went, into the future or the past. Later experiments suggested that the dog went into the past. So far they have not been able to send anyone into the future."

"How do they know if the dog really did go into the past?" Lank asked.

"It was the dog that told them where he had been and what time period he went to."

"The dog told them?" Lank asked with amazement in his voice.

"Yes, it really was the dog. You see the dog was able to kill and bring back a specimen with him when he returned. The specimen was a rodent that has been extent for thousands of years."

"I see, and by all this they knew what time period the rodent was from by focalized bones, they then were able to arrive at a fairly close approximation of the period, right?" Lank waited for confirmation of his analysis of the situation.

"You got it," John replied.

After some minutes had passed, John asked Lank if he was ready to brief the president. Lank knew they always briefed the president in the Oval office in the white house only if the president notified them and specifically asked to be brief.

"The president has reviewed my report then, I take it,"

"Yes. It is set up for three pm this afternoon. We have a couple of hours to kill before we have to be there. What say we grab a cup of coffee in the commissary," John suggested.

Chapter Seven

The limousine that carried John Farshaw, the director of DHS, and Lank F. Miller, pulled into the driveway that let up to the guard gate. After some coded conversation between the driver and the guard shack they began to move towards the white house. They were stopped once more and thoroughly scrutinized, both them and the car, before they were allowed to park.

Their marine escorts ferried them through the processing room on to the oval office and told to take a seat. The wait was only a few minutes before the president entered. Both Lank and John stood up as the president approached. With a wave of his hand he directed them to sit back down.

President Gordon was a tall man, well over six feet, lean in form and no sign of a potbelly yet. Lank knew for a fact that the president had a hefty exercise program that he religiously adhered to. The president dragged a chair from behind his desk and placed it in close proximity to them.

"Good to see you again John, you too Lank." Turning toward Lank, the president addressed him first.

"Lank I have read your report and have found it very interesting. Your conclusions are pretty much what I have heard introduced from NSA, and the CIA. Your report fills in between the lines and I'm glad to have you on board."

The president turned back to John and asked him his views on Lank's report.

"Mr. President, From all the accounts of missing young women there has to be something to tie them all in and I totally agree with Lank about this time thing. It fits."

"There is one excerpt of your report that I find quite interesting," The president said.

"What is that Mr. President?" Lank asked.

"The fact is the Los Angels Valley Quantum Physics Laboratory team has been under the auspices of the army. I don't have any other information about the Valley team experiments or how successful they were."

"Mr. President, I tried to contact someone from there but was unable to gain any information at all," John Farshaw volunteered.

"I know John, I was told by the Joint Chiefs of Staff I didn't have a "need to know". They wouldn't give me any additional information other than it was a military program and was in the interest of the U.S.A."

"That seems a little out of the ordinary doesn't it sir?" John asked.

"I think so, but my hands are tied right now, just as they were tied when I wanted to visit Area 51 at Roswell."

The interview with the president went on for an additional ten or fifteen minutes more before wrapping up. The president finally bade them goodbye and motioned to the marine guards that were standing just out of ear shot, but ever ready to come to the aid of the president, to escort them out to of the white house.

On the way back to John's office Lank thought about what the president had said. He could not imagine the president of the United States of America being forbidden to enter certain places under military command. Why good grief, the president is the commander in chief of all the military, why wouldn't he have the need to know. Maybe area 51 really had something to hide, for that matter maybe The Quantum Physics Laboratory at Los Angels had something to hide also, Lank thought, maybe the president voiced his thoughts only to be asking for help. Lank didn't have any answers and it was obvious John didn't either.

Lank promised himself he would keep these thoughts to himself for the moment. He had formed somewhat of a comradeship with the president over the years. If President Lewis P. Gordon ever confided in him, then Lank was bound to assist in anyway he could.

John had been silent for most of the trip back to his office, wondering what kind of a connection between that lab at Los Angels and the disappearance of young women could there be. The time angle seemed the most logical, giving the fact that he had been privy to the successful conclusion of the dog sent into time. John was very aware of the advantages of having friends in high places. Well maybe not friends, but people in high places that owed him a favor.

Lank decided to head towards the airport after he dropped John off at his DC office. He mentioned this to John and he agreed, asking what time his flight was supposed to leave.

"At seven pm and if I hurry I will be able to take a shower and get a bite to eat at the VIP lounge at the airport before my flight leaves."

"I was wondering if President Gordon was going to hold us over and you might miss your flight back to New York," John mentioned as they began to pull into the capital parking lot.

John exited the car in front of the capital and Lank directed the driver to take him to Washington Dulles International airport. The driver nodded and pulled away from the curb. The trip to the airport was uneventful and time seemed to pass swiftly. Upon arriving at the loading and unloading curb, Lank thanked the driver, whom he did not recognize, and began the short walk to the VIP lounge.

Lank, upon being cleared by the palm reader, nodded to the bartender, whose name was Lewis Pradder, a good friend of Lank's from their days as members of the Navy's illustrious seal unit. Lank and Lewis had been on many Naval intelligence missions for the NSA, CIA and of course for the FBI.

Lank approached the bar and spoke quickly to Lewis in a quite tone. They had to appear as casual acquaintances because of their previous involvement with the super secret agencies. Both had agreed it would be better if they went this route rather than broadcast the fact they were close friends. It had come in handy several times in the past. After a few brief sentences between them, Lank strode toward the back door of the VIP lounge. The back door opened into a second lounge where Special VIPs were able to congregate while either waiting on a flight or arriving in Washington. The man at this bar was serving only one customer who Lank had no idea who he was or what firm or business he represented.

Lank settled down at the end of the bar several barstools away from the lone customer who was engaged in a conversation with the bartender and waited. He did not have to wait long as he noticed the lone customer had decided to leave, giving the bartender a chance to approached Lank.

"Hi Lank, Haven't seen you in a while, you see Lewis in the VIP lounge?"

"Oh yeah, I saw our old friend. I didn't have a chance to talk with him though, as there were a lot of people there," Lank ventured.

"Yeah, I'm sure he would like to get with us and shoot the bull about old times."

Lank was very appreciative of the friendship between Lewis Pradder, himself, and Raymond Beatey, the bartender of the VIP within the VIP lounge. All three had been the closest of friends during their times with the SEALS. There had been many missions the three had been on and some close calls during some of those missions. The three men had a lot of respect for each other. Both Lewis and Raymond were CIA agents planted here at the airport to act as a kind of safe house for other agents.

"Lewis, I just came from briefing the President on this rash of disappearances of young women. I want to run something by you and see what you think about it."

"Sure Lank, shoot," Lewis said.

"Well the president made a statement that kind of worries me. He said he was told by the military he did not have a "need to know" when he tried to visit area 51 out at Roswell and also when he tried to visit the Physics lab building in Los Angels. You know the army has the Quantum Physics Lab shut down, don't you."

"No, I did not know that. What do they have going at that lab in Los Angels?" Lewis asked?

"Experiments in time travel. I understand they have successfully sent a dog into the past and retrieved him along with an extent rodent."

"Hmmmm, is that right." Lewis said with a puzzled look on his face.

Lank quickly brought him up to snuff on his interview with Professor Manning and their linkage of the Physics Lab at Los Angels experiments to the abductions of young women.

"Could it be possible that they are further along than what you suspect Lank?"

"I feel sure they are, why else would the army have them locked down," Lank responded quickly, sensing Lewis was very interested in what he had found out.

Yeah, that figures, that's a quantum physics lab, is it not Lank?"

Yep, but I can't find out anything about what they are working on, just suspicions."

"What do you propose Lank?"

Well Lewis, I have to take a shower and put on a clean suit. I have a plane to check in about thirty minutes."

"You on your way back to your office in New York?"

"Yes, I have a few things to tidy up before I can get a handle on all these abductions," Lank informed Lewis.

"Ok, when will I see you again?"

"I don't know as of now, but it will probably be in a few months," Lank said as he finished his drink and began preparations to leave the VIP lounge.

"Right, hey Lank, I just thought of something, Doesn't Doctor North work at the lab there in Los Angels in quantum physics?"

"You mean the same Dr. North that was working on a design to raise the threshold of power available for NASA on the shuttles?" Lank asked.

"Yes that's the one. Quite an intelligent hombre, I'd say."

"You're right of course, he was super intelligent. If He is working at the valley lab, than for sure there is something futurist going on, I'd say."

"Ok Lank, I'll clue Ramond in on what you have told me. Let us know if you are planning anything old man?" Lewis mentioned as Lank was entering the shower room, he quickly picked up a spare suit and a clean white shirt in his locker.

"Roger, I'll keep you informed. I know you will be ready if we have a mission develop," Lank quipped over his shoulder.

Chapter Eight

It had been six months since Lank had left Lewis and Raymond in D.C. and he could hardly believe that he still did not have a lead in all these abductions. Since he had talked with them there had been a rash of increases in the abductions. So many in fact that, the Director of Homeland Security, had set up a meeting with President Gordon. They had the meeting with the president in his oval office, as usual, there was nothing new to pass on the president.

This had been two days ago and Lank had not noticed anything unusual in the countenance of the President at the time. However Lank was surprised when he got a call from President Gordon to meet him at the white house. The meeting had been set up for ten thirty this morning and Lank was directed not to let the Director of Homeland Security know of the meeting. He understood fully after President Gordon had briefed him on just how far the investigations of the abductions had come.

He was informed about suspicions in high places that believed the abduction might somehow be of an alien nature.

The president had given Lank a few minutes time to take in this controversial statement.

When Lank did not respond right away, President Gordon began again, and it wasn't till he had finished his thoughts that he sat back and with an obvious feeling of relief, waited on Lank to agree or disagree.

"Mr. President, Do you give any credit to these suppositions?" Lank, finally after taking a deep breath, had asked.

"You mean the alien angle Lank?"

"Yes, That's exactly what I mean."

"Absolutely not, but I do keep an open mind."

"You still have our theory in mind Mr. President?" Lank asked, hoping for an affirmative answer.

"Yes, even more now that this additional information has come to light."

"I still think so too. Mr. President what do you have in mind? You mentioned getting my team ready for a mission. That won't be a problem. We are ready to roll at your word."

"Good, I knew I could count on you. You see Lank I can't trust anyone else being privy to this mission. I can't let the Director of Home Land Security in on this because I know he has friends in high places and I know for a fact he is in the habit of trading information, especially if it would be advantageous to him.

Lank was not a bit surprised at hearing this from the president. He always had something in the back of his mind concerning the director of Homeland Security. He had heard rumors that were not helpful in presenting an honorable image to the American people, however the Secretary of Homeland Security, Larry Duiggs, had recommended him. The President had appointed him and the senate had confirmed him, barley, but they did confirm John Farshaw.

President Gordon, after allowing Lank a few minutes to digest what he had laid out, finished his request for Lank to have his team ready for a major mission, a highly secret mission no less. When Lank had assured him he could have his team ready within twenty hours notice President Gordon seemed to be genuinely relieved.

After the meeting had adjourned he had hailed a cab back to his hotel, checked with the desk and having no messages, took the elevator to his room on the second floor. He cautiously opened his door with the key card and paused ever so slightly before entering. This old ingrained habit of his had come in handy on more than one occasion, most likely saving his life a time or two. Upon entering the room Lank noticed right away the room was not as he had left it. Allowing for the maids cleaning the room, something in the back of his mind told him, other than the maids had been in the room.

He quietly surveyed the room with a practiced eye, noticing first that his luggage had been opened and gone through. The little piece of string, barely noticeable, was missing from the zipper on the luggage. He had placed this string purposely on the zipper so when the bag was unzipped the string would fall out onto the floor. Also his spare suit wrapped in plastic wrap provided by the hotel dry cleaning service was lying on the bed with the coat front buttons lying face down. It looked as if some one was anxious to vacate the room before being exposed and had hurriedly thrown it there.

Granted it could have been the maids or even the dry cleaning man that had gone through his luggage. It was always good to check everything first though just to be sure. Lank had some of the files in his luggage but they all seemed to be there. In any case there was nothing incriminating in his luggage. The other possibility was a bug in the room. He gave the room a quick going over but was unable to find anything. Shrugging his shoulders he picked up the receiver and after dialing an outside line called the airport and confirmed his flight. He then dialed the front desk of his hotel and asked for a wake up for six thirty the next morning. This would give him plenty of time to hail a cab and make it to the airport.

After this call, he placed a call to Lewis. When Lewis came on the phone, Lank quickly filled him as much as he could over an unsecured phone line. Lewis quickly grasped the urgency in Lank's voice and quickly informed him all was ready. In a cryptic voice, Lank got it across that it was necessary for Lewis and Raymond to meet him in his New York office. This was said in an effort to thwart anyone eavesdropping. Lewis and Raymond had been informed a few days earlier over secure lines of where they were to meet Lank. After a few more cryptic comments, Lank hung the receiver up and undressed, preparing to take a shower before hitting the sack for a partial nights sleep.

Chapter Nine

The three men sitting in a rented bass boat in the middle of the lake pretending to fish were oblivious to the unwelcome spying eyes. They did not know it but they had been under those same watchful eyes since they had left Washington D.C. Two men in well-dressed suits had dogged their every move, from Washington D.C. to this lake in the Ozarks in lower Missouri. They were crunched down behind some dense underbrush on an island about a couple hundred feet from the three men in the boat. They had a parabolic antenna connected to an ultra sensitive electronic radio receiver. So far all they had heard were fish stories and some sports talk, but truly like professionals, they listened intently to every word heard.

Just a couple of boats were in the vicinity of the boat under surveillance but were not under any watchful eyes. About an hour had passed and nothing of any importance had been heard. As the sun climbed up into the clear blue sky, things began to come alive on the ground. First the constant buzzing of mosquitoes seemed to increase from momentarily distractions to actually becoming a headache with their constant slapping at them. Two crows became interested in what the two men were doing, especially the sun reflecting off the parabolic antenna. They would come within ten feet of the men and then retreat cawing loudly.

The three men in the boat noticed the crows and their antics but apparently did not equate the antics of the crows with anything out of the ordinary. They were intent on fishing with only a few comments being exchanged between them.

Finally, one of the men suggested turning the radio on. The other two agreed and suddenly a loud blast of rock music emanated from the radio on the boat making it impossible to distinguish anything being said by the occupants of the bass boat.

The two well-dressed men, known as suits by CIA agents, now minus their coats and ties, obviously in torment by the onslaught of bites from the swarms of mosquitoes, were very annoyed at not being able to hear what the three men in the boat were saying. Nevertheless, they stuck to their job and continued to keep the antenna on the boat not wanting to give up at this juncture however disappointing the results were.

After approximately an additional hour had elapsed, the three men in the bass boat turned off the radio that was blasting the loud rock and roll music across the lake and fouling up the interception plans of the two men on the island and began preparations to leave. They had reeled in their lures, laid their fishing equipment in the storage area and started the motor. The boat left a wake as it began to plane over and quickly disappeared in the distance heading back toward the dock.

The two men left on the island, quickly gathered up their sensitive equipment and hurriedly placed everything in the boat that was partially hid by the underbrush. They backed the boat out far enough from the bank of the small island so as to use the forward gear and quickly revved the motor up and headed off in the general direction of the dock.

One of the men began dialing a number on his cell phone and when he got an answer he began to speak briskly into the phone, having to talk loudly because of the noise of the boat motor.

"They are coming back to the dock now," He exclaimed in a matter of fact voice. "I'll check back with you later."

After listening for a minute more and glancing at the other occupant of the boat he stated with a somewhat agitated voice that nothing was accomplished.

"Yes, almost as if they knew we were there watching and listening to them," With that, he quickly closed the lid on his cell phone and turned to the man operation the controls of the boat.

"General McPhee is not going to like this at all. I'm sure they made us," He said.

The other man nodded in agreement and with words somewhat of a consoling manner tried to reassure the first man.

"We can only do so much you know. We don't have super powers."

"Yeah I suppose you are right. Let's hope the guys on the bank will have better luck."

Chapter Ten

After parking their car in the parking area adjacent to the boat ramp the three men in fishing garb, approached the rental office. All three men were well over six feet in height and were what the Marines would say lean and mean. They ambled slowly over to the main office intent on nothing in particular it seemed to anyone that might be watching. The entrance to the rental office was through a doublewide glass door. After gaining entrance for all three of the men, one of them approached the desk where a good looking young lady with blond hair, straight from the bottle, he supposed, whose named tag proclaimed her to be Judy.

"Hi Judy, my name is Lewis Pradder. I have a bass boat rented for today."

The blond lady from behind the desk surveyed Lewis for a moment in time before glancing at the other two men that had entered with him. Finally looking down at her scheduling book and using her pencil to trace down the ledger looked up and said.

"Oh yes, I have you right here Mr. Pradder, a party of three, right?"

"Yep you got it." Lewis told her. "Is the boat ready to go?"

"Sure is, gas tanks full, comes with fishing tackle too, just as you requested."

Lewis turned to Lank and Raymond and directed his next few words in fun at them.

"Lank you and Raymond won't need any fishing gear, you can just watch me reel them in."

"Raymond mumbled something under his breath while Lank just grimaced at Lewis.

Lewis was told the boat rental was already taken care of when he had offered his credit card to pay for the boat. All three exited the rental office and directed their paths toward two boats still docked in the slips. Two other slips were empty. None of the men said a word as Raymond unhooked the boat from its tie down while the other two stepped into the boat. After Raymond had stepped into the boat and had lodged himself on the only other available seat Lewis started the boat motor and slowly eased it out of the slip and out into the main channel.

Lewis headed the bow of the boat out toward the other side of the lake, which probably was in the neighborhood of being a least a mile away. As if on cue none of the men said a word until they had rounded a small island close to the far shore where Lewis cut the switch and coasted toward what looked like a good fishing spot.

The three men began to unlatch the fishing rods from the storage area of the boat and attach lures from out of the tackle box. Finally Lank motioned with his hand in the old familiar signal that indicated they were being watched and listened in on. Both of the men nodded their heads in agreement.

After about fifteen minutes of fishing, Lank landed a big mouth bass that was at least a three pounder and after netted it with the small net, he placed the fish in the live well. He couldn't help but rub it in. It was always important to bag the first fish, or the first of anything for that matter, among friends.

It wasn't long before both Raymond and Lewis had caught fish too. Finally Lank fumbled in his small bag he had brought along with him bringing out a small radio, suggesting they listen to some music as he turned on and cranked up the volume. He tuned it to a hard rock station on the am band. Only then did he address the other two men. It wasn't too difficult to talk over the music. They had learned to watch each other's lips and with lip reading were able to converse quite adequately.

"Lewis, Raymond, did you noticed the boat anchored in the underbrush on the little island we passed on the way over here?"

"That's not all I noticed either. Did you get the reflection off of something, probably binoculars about a hundred yards to the right of the island?" Raymond asked in a mater of fact voice. "Yep I suppose we are under constant surveillance, don't you think?" Lewis stated.

"You know Lewis, I spotted a couple of CIA men on the plane to St. Louis. I wonder how they knew you had rented a boat for us today," Lank queried them.

"The usual, don't you think, phone bugs of course. I don't know how many times I have found bugs in my office either on the phone or placed around the office. I even found a few in my car," Lewis said.

"Well we have to discuss our plans on how to carry this mission through to a successful completion. You know this is wholly directed by the President and is to be kept mute by us," Lank began.

"Yes, I gathered that much from what you were able to discuss over the unsecured landline." Lewis mentioned, looking at Raymond as he spoke.

"Let me be up front first. The president has authorized a payment of a half million dollars in each of our account. Of course our expenses will come out of the fund allotted to the Secret Service," Lank informed the two men, knowing they would never have asked about the finances.

"Never crossed my mind," Lewis volunteered.

"Me neither," Raymond piped in.

"I just wanted you to be clear on that," Lank told them.

After a slight pause and looking around surveying his surroundings, glancing at the one island in the middle of the small lake where they had spotted the boat amidst the underbrush, Lank continued with his discourse.

"You see guys, this plan is in our making. We have a free hand. The Secret Service has been deliberately kept in the dark concerning this mission. I want both of you to realize this mission is in our laps. We are it," Lank cautioned them.

Both men nodded their heads indicating they understood. Lewis spoke for both of them when he said.

"Right Lank, this is nothing new for the three of us, only a bit more complicated than some of our other missions we have been on, considering this thing is a worldwide event."

"I was sure both of you would see it that way. Now we must plan our strategy while we are here because once we leave here we should not be seen together again until the final phase of the mission is started. This is what the president has asked us to find out for him," Lank said as he watched their faces intently.

"He wants to know exactly what is going on. This will involve getting inside the compound, photographing documents, and if we can enter the backdoor and find out as much as we can from their computer networks would be a definite plus."

After another thirty minutes or so, they turned the radio off and returned their fishing equipment to the storage compartments. When everything was stored away and placing the plug into the bottom of the live well, Lewis started the motor and they quickly swung around the tip of the island heading toward back to the rental office.

Keeping the biggest part of the island between them and the half hidden boat and its occupants all the while watching to the left as another boat was on an intersecting course with them. It wasn't long before the other boat the same color and identical markings pulled up along side of them, matching their speed. Lank and Raymond quickly stepped out of their boat and into the other boat. When Lank was firmly seated, Raymond quickly took over the controls of the boat while the other man transferred himself over to their boat relieving Lewis, who stepped into the boat and seated himself in the seat next to Lank. They all had to smile as the man in their boat quickly inflated two rubber manikins so that it looked like there were three men in the boat.

Raymond quickly steered the boat into a left turn and headed back towards the island. They passed well to the left of the island always mindful of where the eavesdroppers were at on the island. It wasn't long before they noticed a boat heading toward the bank where the boat rental office was located. They watched as their original boat pulled into the dock followed a few minutes later by the second boat containing two men.

"I would give anything if I could be a fly on the wall and watch the expressions of those two when they see the rubber manikins," Lewis said as Raymond let out a loud hardy laugh.

Chapter Eleven

Jeff Thompson had been mildly surprised at the phone call three days ago on the secure landline. It had been Lewis Pradder, a long time friend of Lank's and his. Jeff had not heard from Lewis in over a year now. They had exchanged pleasantries for a while but Lewis soon delved into a long line of requests, reminding Jeff that all he was telling him had to be in the strictest confidence. Upon getting assurances that he understood, Lewis laid out the requests.

"First of all Jeff I need to have a secure environment where Lank, Raymond and I can discuss our plans. Do you have any suggestions?"

Jeff thought a moment, remembering an almost forgotten incident where the four of them while on a secret recon mission had parked their boat out in the middle of a lake and finalized their plans. He mentioned this incident to Lewis.

"I don't know Jeff, with all this modern technology I'm afraid we could be picked up on satellite."

"I thought of that but I think it will work. All you have to do is take a radio along and tune it to the am band. That's where you will find all kinds of loud rock and roll music, which will effectively drown out any attempt to decipher your words."

"Yep, that will probably work quite well. Can you set it up for us by renting a boat for the three of us along with three rod and reels and a tackle box? Also I want to add one thing more to our plans, I want you to rent a boat and hide yourself conspicuously on the lake."

"I understand, you want to do the old switch on anyone that might be tailing you," Jeff said.

"Roger Jeff, I think we might just need an additional trick up our sleeve."

"Lewis, I know exactly where we might be able to pull this off. We have a lake just northeast of us over in Illinois, you know just across the Mississippi river. It is called Horseshoe Lake and it has one big island out towards the middle. I will set my boat on the far side in a small cove concealed and will wait for your signal before coming for you. I'll get out there early and watch for any one suspicious."

"Ok Jeff. Set it up and give me a call as to the time and place where we will be picking up the boat.

Jeff had gone to the little rental office located just off 111, which was located on a long peninsular that jutted out into the lake. He wanted to rent two boats. Upon being assured that they did have several boats that were available for rent, Jeff requested that they be fully gassed up with three fishing poles and a tackle box in each boat. He requested the boats for Saturday, this weekend, to be picked up anytime after six o'clock in the morning.

He signed the rental agreement and paid in advance and after arriving back at his office, he had fired up the old encoding machine that he used when he wanted to have a secure line. He had called Lewis and gave him the information about this coming weekend and the times to pick up their boat.

Lewis thanked him and told him they would look forward to working with him again. Jeff figured it was for some kind of computer hacking because that was what he was trained in. Lewis told him he would be briefed shortly afterwards on the mission and to sit tight.

The weekend was not slow in coming, here it was early Saturday morning and he was in the boat he had rented sitting in a small cove just south of the big island. He had noticed while he was waiting, a boat with two men come towards the island from the rental office and pulled their boat halfway up into the bushes. The two men in business suits unloaded what looked like some kind of detection gear, which included a small parabolic antenna. Jeff pegged them right off as being military, probably from NSA. He watched with interest as they began to set up their equipment, careful to keep it hidden from view from anyone on the lake. Jeff grinned as he watched the two men swat at mosquitoes between trying to set up their equipment and watching the lake.

It wasn't long before he caught a glimpse of a boat leaving the rental office. He began to hear the sound of the boat motor long before he was able to recognize its three occupants. He watched as Lank manipulated the boat carefully around the island and come to a stop about a hundred yards on the east side of the island. Jeff smiled again as he guessed that Lank had spotted the boat that was concealed on the south end of the island and had deliberately kept the island between them and the two men on the island.

It wasn't long before they had their fishing poles out, and for all account and purposes commenced fishing. Jeff watched as Lank reeled in what looked like a nice large mouth bass, followed a short time later by Raymond and Lewis catching their share also.

Suddenly the whole lake seemed to come alive with loud rock and roll music making it almost impossible to compose thoughts let alone talk. Jeff noticed the two men on the island began to try to redirect their antenna in order to better pick up the conversation emanating from the boat under surveillance, apparently without any luck.

It wasn't long before Lewis started the motor and began the trip back towards the far side of the lake where the rental office was located. He had kept the speed down to just enough to keep the boat planed over giving Jeff enough time to catch up with them.

Quickly catching up with them, all the time keeping the island between them and the two men on the island, Jeff pulled alongside Lank, Lewis and Raymond. They exchanged eye contact and began to transfer themselves to his boat. After the transfer was complete, Jeff quickly stepped into their boat with him a small plastic bag. He reached into the bag and pulled out two manikins which he used his small portable air pump and quickly inflated them. He had noticed a smile on all three of the men's faces as he steered his boat away from them and headed off across the lake with what looked like three men in the boat.

Lewis pulled the throttle back on the motor and headed to the east end of the lake to a place where they could not be seen by the two men on the island.

The three men and their boat proceeded toward the far end of the lake while all the time watching for the appearance of the two men that had them under surveillance. It wasn't but just a few minutes before they noticed the two men emerging from their concealment on the island and heading straight across the lake towards the rental office.

"What a rude awaking they are in for," Lewis said.

"I agree, Lewis, I think someone is going to get an ass chewing for fouling up an assignment," Raymond tooted. They waited for about fifteen minutes before heading themselves across the lake to the rental office.

Upon arriving at the boat slip they noticed all slips were full now with the exception of the one slip available for their boat. Jeff was long gone and they could see the two men in business suits getting into their car and spinning out towards the pavement of highway 111. They had accepted the fact their quarries had beat them to the shore and were long gone. Of course the rubber manikins were not visible in the boat either as Jeff had remove them prior to turning the boat back in to the rental office.

The three men parted company after they had driven back to St. Lewis. Lank took a return flight back to New York, Lewis and Raymond decided to remain in St. Louis and catch Jeff up to date on their mission plans. Jeff was the only one with computer hacker experience and he would be needed for sure, once their mission got fully underway.

Chapter Twelve

Six weeks had passed before President Gordon had requested his presence in the white house. His secretary had called him from his DC office and gave him the information. Finally, Lank thought to himself, the ball was going to get rolling. His appointment with the President wasn't until eight thirty this coming Wednesday so he had plenty of time to get all his information he had acquired together. Of course Janet, his secretary would have his files all separated out and neatly stacked.

Lank would be acting as a courier and would have his brief case handcuffed to his arm all the way to the white house. No one could take for granted anything any longer in this crazy mixed up world. Lank determined to spend the next day with his family and would pick up his briefcase that contained his files on the way to the airport. Lank considered himself lucky, Janet was a fine secretary and very knowledgeable of how things worked in the Secret Service, being a Secret Service agent clerk herself.

Lank phoned Mary Ann and informed her of his flight to Washington D.C. next Wednesday and his intention of spending tomorrow with her. Jenny would be in school but hopefully he would be able to spend the evening with her and Mary Ann.

On the drive to his home, Lank thought about all the reports and media accounts of missing young women and was demanding at least some semblance of an end to what was really happening.

His mind went over and over without deciding anything, finally his thoughts turned to what might be in store when he had his appointment with the President. His official title was "Special Advisor to the President on Bio Terrorism". But to the world he was a director of all the sub regional offices within the United States with special connections to the European police agencies.

His mind conjured up all sorts of anti climax involvements that could happen.

As Lank pulled into his driveway he noticed old duke was lying in his usual place, right in front of the garage door. Lank eased the car up to within a few feet of the dog and smiled in anticipation as he leaned on the horn for a few seconds. His anticipation was not denied him for at the sound of the horn old duke jumped to his feet, hair rising up on his back and a growl emanating deep from within his throat. Lank tried to imagine what the dog was dreaming about when he was so rudely awakened. What ever it was, it was long gone by now. He was standing there with a silly look on his face, but his tail was wagging, either in acknowledging his master's presence. Or maybe he was pretending that he wasn't really asleep but was ready to defend his assigned territory.

Lank's amusement was short lived when he noticed Mary Ann approaching with a stern look on her face.

"Lank, you ought to be ashamed of yourself, scaring old Duke like that. You might have scarred him emotionally, or caused him to have a heart attack," Mary Ann chided him.

"I have always wanted to do that and this was just too good of an opportunity to pass up."

"Well he looks alright but I will just bet you Lank, you won't catch him asleep in front of the garage again," Mary Ann said.

"Probably not," Lank mentioned, as he reached down to stroke the dog's ears. 'Old Duke' languished in the attention he was getting and quickly forgot about the episode of the blast from the horn.

"How did your day go hon?" Lank asked Mary Ann.

"Ok, nothing out of the ordinarily happened. I took Jen to cheer leading practice this afternoon and we just got home a few minutes ago."

"Good, I'll be able to spend some time with both of you before I have to leave for Washington D.C. Wednesday morning."

"Well you haven't had to take a trip since you got back from St. Louis so we will enjoy while we can."

"Right, lets go in the house and see what Jen is up to."

Lank put his arm around Mary Ann as they strolled toward the front door.

Chapter Thirteen

Lank was deep in thought process concerning his few days he had with Mary Ann and Jen in their New York home. He had always relished his time spent with his family and was dismayed at the prospect of having to be away from them for extended times.

When the sign came on over the cabin door of the plane informing passengers to fasten their seat belts for the approach to Washington National airport, Lank was snapped into the present world and his appointment with the President tomorrow.

As the plane descended into its final approach to landing Lank began to think about what kind of mission the president had in mind for their team. Lank knew some significant data but had not been made aware of any of the final details. He was sure that Lewis, Raymond, and Jeff were ready and chomping at the bits to becoming involved again in what they were trained to do. Well after tomorrow he would know what they were required to do.

When the plane had come to a complete stop, Lank unbuckled his seat belt and made his egress from the plane on to the tarmac. He then made his way toward the terminal while observing the surroundings around him, as was his custom, noting the airport workers engaged in their various duties. Nothing seemed out of place and all appeared as the normal activity going on at a busy airport.

Once again Lank headed for the VIP lounge in the hopes of seeing Lewis or Raymond on duty. They were assigned by the CIA but occasionally were transferred to the President's special security operations. Lank had been with the FBI until he volunteered to join the secret service and was ultimately assigned to the Presidential Security Council as special advisor.

Lank was met by a special security officer at the gate to the entrance of the terminal and ushered through a door to bypass security checks. He thanked the security officer and made his way through the terminal to the VIP lounge. He placed his right hand on the palm reader and when recognized, he made his way into the VIP lounge. Yes Lewis was there behind the bar wiping a glass with a dry cloth. Upon seeing Lank across the room striding toward the bar with a brief case handcuffed to his arm, Lewis couldn't help himself. He let out a loud guff haw and motioned to Lank to have a seat at the bar.

"Well look what the buzzards drug up and the cats wouldn't eat," Lewis yelled out from across the room.

"Yeah, I probably look like one too," Lank responded. "How are you doing Lewis?"

"Fine, fine Lank. Been waiting to hear from you."

"Right now I'm looking for a drink, just to tide me over, you know," Lank said, noting Lewis recognition of the coded signal within the statement that let him know something was up and he needed to talk with Raymond and him. After Lewis had made his drink and set it in front of Lank, he swiped the bar with his rag and only then did he lean over and engage Lank in conversation.

"Lank, its sure good to see you again, you're a sight for sore eyes, you know."

"Well it's good to see you too." Lank responded and after a slight pause he continued. "I have that date tomorrow morning that I have been looking forward too now for some time."

"Oh, do I know her?" Lewis chided him with a slight smile curving the corners of his mouth.

"I don't know, you might," Lank said and then continued in a slow and measured voice that was intended to clue Lewis in. "I'll know more tomorrow evening Lewis, anyway I need to wash up before I leave here."

"Right, ok, you know where the john is." Lewis said, obviously catching the clue that was couched in the Lank's response.

"See you around Lewis," Lank said as he slipped off the bar stool and headed for the door in the wall that was to his left. A palm reader controlled this door, like the main door to the VIP lounge. Lank placed his right palm on the glass and after his identity was confirmed he pushed the door open and entered into a room similar to the outer VIP lounge. Only the bartender was present. After looking up from the book he was reading and glancing toward the door, he recognized Lank, and with a quick flip of the book toward the end of the bar, he patiently waited until Lank had settled himself on the bar stool at the bar. He spoke with genuine pleasure in seeing Lank again.

"Lank, boy it's so good to see you again. How have you been?"

"I'm making it," Lank said after shaking Raymond's hand vigorously. "Heard any good ones lately?"

"Naw. Just the same old ones that keep cropping up."

"Yeah I know, I've heard them all too," Lank came back to him with the coded answer that let Raymond know that something big was in the works.

"Oh, well I guess we will just have to make up our own jokes, huh."

"Maybe I'll hear a good one tomorrow morning," Lank exclaimed. "If I do I'll tell it to you so you can pass it own."

Lank and Raymond conversed in clipped and coded sentences for a while, long enough to agree on a time and place to discuss the upcoming mission. Lank was glad that all four of them would once again be working together. They made a good team, good at what each individual's talents were. Of course all details of the mission had to be kept secret, not only from the criminal element, but from our own government.

Lank remembered the Watergate scandal during Nixon's presidency and all the Senate investigations and the ultimate price that had been paid. This was why Lank and his team had to be super sensitive to any leaks. They had devised a way to cover their tracks by eliminating any record or logs showing any involvement in the past, present or the future of any malicious behavior. So far all their precautions had worked just fine.

Lank was sure that Jeff would use all his hacker knowledge gained through his membership of IBM's Global Security Analysis Laboratory, known simply as GSAL, to erase any evidence of tampering with net security working systems.

Then Raymond was adept at using his extensive knowledge of gaining entrance to any place at any time. Yep, good old Raymond had got them past many a supposedly secure place in the past. Of course the team could not be effective without Lewis and his expertise in "foot printing", that is, gathering information essential to obtaining a complete profile of an organizations' security system. He was the one that provided advance knowledge before any mission was executed. He did this by being on the scene months in advance doing what he did, which was scouting the place finding out the weaknesses and the problem areas, devising a plan to overcome any problematic situation.

Chapter Fourteen

The president had laid out in the open what he wanted to know and when he wanted it. Leaving no detail unnamed, naming names that he suspected were involved, he had been adamant in his desire to find out what was being kept from him and the possible ties with the thousand of case files concerning the missing young women. Finally, when he had concluded his request, he looked Lank straight in the eye and told him that under no circumstances could he ever acknowledge his offices' involvement.

Lank assured the president his lips and the lips of his team were forever closed and under no circumstance would anything ever be leaked.

"I know I can count on your team to bring this mission to a successful conclusion. Furthermore, I know how you operate so I won't be asking how you go about it, just knowing it is in your hands is enough for me," The president stated with a small smile curling up the corners of his mouth.

"Mr. President I can assure you, the mission will be accomplished and with no linkage to you or your office. I speak for the other members of my team, as you already know, we work under cover with only one desire, that is, to pledge our allegiance to our government and its elected representatives." Lank knew this sounded corny but it was the truth.

Now armed with the special requests of the President, Lank was ready to meet with his team and devise a plan as to how to pull it off. He knew it would take several months before they could put the plan into action. First there had to be the gathering of information that could be useful in the executing of the mission. Lewis was the man for this job. He always worked alone on this and was very thorough and adept at laying out a plan that would secure the involvement of the other team members. Lewis would not be satisfied until he had gathered the last remaining detail and briefed the team members.

Lank knew what he had to do and was already devising how, when, and where, he would gather his team and brief them on where the mission was to go and how to accomplish it. His first duty was to call Raymond and informed him of the meeting. Raymond would gather Lewis and Jeff and relay to Lank the place and time they would all be together. Of course this would all have to be done in the strictest confidence over secure land-lines. Raymond and Lewis in a place that was as secure as they could make it would set up the meeting itself. Even then there was always the possibility of someone eavesdropping.

Lank knew Jeff Thompson was their key man in this mission. Not only because of his immense computer knowledge but because he had many times in the past opened doors that would have obviously been unopened to the rest of the team thereby putting the mission in jeopardy.

Lewis Pradder was just as important as any other member of the team, only he had the knowledge to open physical doors to gain entry to a place. This included all kinds of locks, including electronic locks, optical locks, palm reading locks, even the newest fingerprint scan locks that could detect if the body tissue in the finger was alive or dead.

Raymond Beatey was a people man. He had the ability to put people at ease in his presence and elicit important information from them without their even suspecting what he was doing. Lewis was indeed a very valuable man to have on the team. His unique abilities had made it easier for the team to draw up a working plan before the mission had gotten underway.

Lank had led this team many times in the past on some hair-raising missions. He had put their lives in danger numerous times in the past. One thing Lank could count on with his team was simply their willingness to put their lives on the line without a moment's hesitation. He had been proud of their accomplishments and was looking forward to getting started on this mission. Lank was sure once he informed the team of what the president wanted them to do they would start the ball rolling. Sometimes it might take six months before everything was in place before they could even think of beginning the operation.

Lank, with a soft smile on his face, mused at himself as he thought about the times he and his comrades had been in danger and how they all had responded quickly and forcibly to ensure the safety each team member.

As Lank drove the last few miles to his DC office He was looking forward to calling Raymond and letting him know that President Gordon had authorized the mission and to start the ball rolling. Raymond would know exactly what to do and when to do it. Because of security reasons, Lank would have to remain removed from association with the team until the final stages were in place. It was of the utmost importance Lank could not be even suspected of involvement at this time. They would keep him informed at ever step of the way and at the correct time he would join them and do his part.

Upon arriving at his office Lank checked his in basket and tossed most of the mail in the trashcan. He briefly scanned the remaining mail and selected two messages that had to do with the disappearance of the many young women. Since it was after hours, his secretary had left for the day. He quickly typed up a short message to her, letting her know he had been in the office. He stuffed the two messages in his inside pocket of his jacket and used the telephone on his secretary's desk to make his call to Raymond. It was just another ploy to try and keep the other guys off balance. They would not be expecting anything of importance to be mentioned on this landline. Of course Lank knew it was bugged but he and the other team members a long time ago had worked on a simple but efficient way of using coded messages. It depended on the date and time and who was talking for the coded talk to be effective.

Raymond answered right away knowing from the caller Id that it was from Lank's DC office.

"Hello, this is Raymond what can I do for you?" was the curt opening statement.

"Raymond, this is Lank. I know the hour is late but I was hoping you would be available. Something has come up and I wanted to converse with you on the possibility of you taking control. Well anyway if you can let me know when you are ready, then we can go from there.

"Oh you mean you want me to do all the work, don't you Lank," Raymond quipped.

"Well, I guess, at least the biggest part of it. I have an engagement on that date and just can't get away."

"Ok, I guess I can handle it. I'll call you when I get it all set up."

Lank used a coded sentence to see if Raymond understood what it was he was requesting of him. When Raymond responded with the correct response Lank quietly expelled his breath. After a few more exchanges between the two, consisting of mainly personal information, Lank and Raymond said their good byes.

The weeks ensuing seemed to just fly by, especially seeing the rash of abductions had increased to over a hundred a day throughout the world. The London office had tried to keep abreast of it all but simply was unable to do so. Lank had many messages from Frank concerning Interpol dealings with, or lack of dealing with the ongoing situations.

The Berlin Niedersachsen newspaper had carried a story that had gained international acclaim throughout the world. This paper gave a report of another eyewitness account of a young lady suddenly disappearing. It seems this witness had been talking face to face with the young lady when there was loud popping sound and she just disappeared. The eyewitness, a young man by the name of Johann Behrens, had stated he did not know what happened and was very concerned as to the whereabouts of the girl. The young lady was his fiancée.

The witness went on to say he remembered a man that had approached the girl a few days before and sold her a necklace. The necklace was unusual in that it looked nothing like he had ever seen before. The design was of a long oval shape, about an inch long and gold in color, with the hook attached to one end and the chain going through the hook. The reason it was unusual, the witness stated, was that it was always warm to the touch even when left out in the cold. He and the girl thought nothing of it except to comment on the warmth to their friends. When the girl disappeared the necklace disappeared with her. Johann Behrens had described the necklace to the reporter who had included a drawing of it in his report.

The little thing in Lank's mind again rose up to alert him to something he had seen before. Yes, that was what his mind had been trying to tell him. He remembered now, the girl in the burger joint had been wearing a necklace with a golden medallion, exactly as described in this German newspaper. Lank wondered if any of the staff or customers had seen the necklace and if any of them had it now. He made a mental note to check with all the witnesses and workers who might have had an opportunity to either observe or maybe have picked it up. Of course if the necklace disappeared with the girl then it would be to no avail.

Maybe the girl that had smiled at him on the highway had a necklace like that. He did not remember seeing any necklace in the car, but then again, he had not been looking for it. He made another mental note to check with the wrecker company that had hauled the car away to see if they had any record of it. Lank doubted it but he wanted to investigate each and ever avenue. Also he wanted to check with her parents and the relations of the girl in the burger joint to see if she had a necklace with a medallion that matched the others.

Chapter Fifteen

Almost three and a half weeks had passed since he had placed that coded telephone call to Raymond. A lot of things had transpired since then. Lank had checked with the local wrecker company that had hauled the girl's car away. The driver of the wrecker told Lank he had not noticed any jewelry in the car. Lank had been in touch with the girl's mother and she had remembered, after being shown a drawing of the necklace, that their daughter had indeed possessed one just like it. She had worn it for about a couple of weeks before she disappeared. They told him that they had not received anything from the wrecker company or the police about the jewelry.

Lank had further checked with all the witness that had been in the burger joint at the time of the young girl's disappearance. None of them had ever seen the necklace, not even any of her co-workers. She could have taken it off and left it in her purse or pocket, only Lank doubted it. If his theory were correct she would have had to be wearing it.

With this new information and his theory about it, Lank decided to report his findings to Frank in London. He had his secretary Janet place the call to Frank. It would be early in the morning there, but Lank deemed this important enough to wake his good friend up. When the call was completed Lank heard the voice of Frank spout out his usual "allo mate". When he understood it was Lank doing the calling, his tone of voice shifted to that of surprise and joy.

"Hi Frank, I'm sorry to ring you so early in the morning but I think I have found something that might be a valuable lead."

"That's good news indeed Lank. Let me get some light on in here so I can see whom I'm talking too. Ha Ha," Frank joked, then went on. "Alright let me have it."

Lank went on to tell him about the report of the necklace with the golden medallion in the German paper and how it had reminded him of the same necklace he had seen here around the neck of the girl who had disappeared in the burger joint. Lank went on to relay what he had found out about the girl's parents asserting their daughter had a necklace just like it.

"Ok Lank, please tell me you have the necklace in your hands?" Frank asked, with genuine excitement in his voice.

"Sorry Frank, but I don't. It could be someone in the burger joint found it and kept it, but if my theory is correct, she would have had to be wearing it when she was taken. I suppose the same is true about the girl in the car that I witnessed. Then the wrecker driver or any of the employees working at the wrecker yard would not have found it." Frank stated with some remorse in his voice.

"Do you have any idea as to what the necklace is?" Frank asked.

"I have a theory Frank, but at this point in time, it is only a poor theory at best."

"A poor theory is better than no theory at all Lank."

"Ok, here it is. I believe it might be the device that when triggered by a remote sending unit in close proximity, propels the girl either into a parallel universe or propels her into time, either in the future or the past, I don't know which," Lank when finished, patiently listened intently for Frank's response.

Franks response was not long in coming.

"I do believe you have stumbled onto something exciting mate," Frank began. "I'll start an investigation from this end into the German newspaper. I'm curious as to what happened to the German Johann. Give me all the details and I'll get a copy of the news article and get Interpol on it right away."

Lank and his friend Frank, shot the bull for a few more minutes and finally with Frank assuring him he would find out all he could on the necklace and get back to Lank the phone call ended.

After Lank had hung the receiver back up he turned to Janet, and with controlled excitement in his voice he addressed her.

"Well Janet I do believe we have some solid leads to go on now."

"I certainly hope so," Janet exclaimed with the usual perkiness in her voice when she talked to Lank. "I know you have worked long and hard on this and maybe this is the one piece of evidence you will need."

"It is the only piece that seems to be common to at least three incidents," Lank told her.

Lank was in the middle of pouring himself another cup of coffee when Janet caught his attention, motioning toward the blinking red light partially hidden behind a makeshift table that was used to store miscellaneous objects on. He indicated with his eyes for Janet to go ahead and make the connection while he returned his attention to finishing pouring his coffee.

In a few minutes Janet had made the connection on the encryption device so the call would be sanitized. She held the receiver out to Lank and he spoke into the phone. Just as he supposed, it was Raymond.

"Hi Lank, I have everything in place now," Raymond said. Lewis will need a couple more weeks to get his end going."

"How about Jeff, How's he doing with his part? Lank asked.

"Jeff has got what he needs and is raring to get on with it."

"Ok, What date do you want to start on?" Lank asked.

"It looks like one week from today would be the ideal time. That is Memorial Day weekend and a lot of soldiers are going home for the weekend," Raymond stated. "I feel sure there will only be skeleton crew on duty."

"Right, well I guess I will see you at the safe house and go over the details prior to launching. It might be better if I arrive a few days early, you know to kind of confuse our shadows as to what we are up to."

"Yeah, and bring the rest of our equipment and drop it off at the usual place." Ok?" Raymond said.

"You got it. How about I show up next Tuesday around six pm."

"Sounds good to me, we will be waiting on you," Raymond responded.

"Right," Lank answered and with that and broke the encryption machine.

Turning to Janet, he said. "Janet, looks like I'm going to be busy for at least a couple of weeks. One of us will try to check in regularly with you here in the office."

"I know you will, always have in the past," Janet said with obvious emotion in her voice. Remembering a few times in the past when they had been late in checking in due to being pinned down somewhere.

"You remembering the time we were almost caught in Baghdad, aren't you?" Lank asked.

"Yes." I suppose, but you know me, I'm just a sentimental old fool," Janet answered, holding the emotion in her voice in check for the time being.

Lank sensing the need for reassurance walked over and put his arm around Janet and gave her a big hug. "Try not to worry about us. We have been a good team. We have always come back so far and this will be an easy job, seeing as it is not even out of the States."

"I know Lank, but I still worry about all of you"

"Well you know we do appreciate your concern for us and knowing that someone is concerned makes us even more careful," Lank told her.

With those few words said, Lank parted company with his secretary. As he left the office his mind was racing. Going over and over his plan of operation concerning their mission. Lank knew he had to have a SOP in place before he could plan the mission. He would update the last Standard Operation Procedures and build his plan around it. He had a couple of days to compose and finalize it before he had to join the other members of his team.

The president had laid out what he wanted accomplished. Now it was up to Lank to draw up a plan of operation that would minimize the danger. Although their objective was within the borders of America, Lank knew the precautions would have to be, out of necessity, the same.

Chapter Sixteen

Lank's flight to the LX airport had been uneventful. He had debarked the plane and gone through airport security with no hitches. Lank's courier credentials were scanned and his briefcase that was handcuffed to his left arm was x-rayed, but other than that, he was ushered through with a minimum of disruption.

He checked in with the car rental agency and after picking up the rented car, headed for the safe house, located on a fifty-five acre farm south of Los Angles. Lank was sure the safe house would be under observation, but that did not matter as, his plans had already been formulated and each member was aware of what he was supposed to be doing.

It was a two-hour trip to get to the safe house. The place was located about a mile off the paved road, down a long curvy dusty road, in a clump of trees and well hidden from casual view. Lank had been here several times in the past bringing organized plans before a mission could be started. The last time was when the mission required them to go to Cambodia. That time they were gone for the better part of six months with no knowledge of news from home. Every thing had to be done in secret and their even being in this communist country could not be revealed. Their job had been to rescue a pilot that had been shot down.

It had seemed as though the enemy had been one step ahead of them. When they were sure of the pilots' location and were on the verge of launching a rescue mission, the pilot would be moved to somewhere else. It had been touch and go for months before they were able to rescue the pilot and bring him and themselves out of the country into a safe area.

Lank's thoughts turned to Jeff and his part in this mission. Jeff had excelled in computer technology from the beginning.

During his final year of college the CIA had recruited him where he had been able to fine-tune his expertise.

There must have been a mental link between Lank and Jeff because at this very instant Jeff was laboriously checking the results of his hacking into a computer system that was regarded as highly classified by the government. Fully aware he had to carry his weight, so to speak, in this mission. Lank expected him to be able to hack into this system and not leave any evidence of anyone unlawfully entering. Of course, that was the easy part. He wasn't a member of GSAL for nothing. Jeff had burned many a midnight candle learning his trade.

So far this computer network system had been relatively easy for a man with his knowledge. Not to brag of course, but he had pre-planted a Sniffer program into the military network which enabled him to record unencrypted computer traffic as it passed by, including the key strokes of passwords as they are typed into the computer by the operator. Knowing the passwords, allowed him to set up a root account file where he was able to access the whole system.

Now it had only been a matter of time before he was able to put in place one of the more adaptable advance programs. With an advance program such as the one he had secretly installed in the computer network he was hacking into, enabled Jeff to break into more sensitive administrator root accounts. Jeff remembered, smiling, as he had been able to install backdoors or Trojan horse programs into the system with relative ease.

There was no way an operator would stumble onto any of these programs during daily operation. However, once it was suspected a hacker had gained access, it wouldn't take a trained computer technician long to flush the program out in the open. Jeff was hoping he would be able to get into their system and get what he came for. He then would be able to use the "cover tracts," a program that eliminated any record or logs showing their system had been hacked into. He had been downloading programs now for the past two days.

Deciphering what was on the discs would take several weeks if not months so that was why it was necessary for the team to gain access to the building housing the network. For sure that would be dangerous. Raymond and Lewis would be the ones that would have to figure out a way to accomplish this task.

Speaking of Lewis and Raymond, Jeff wondered how close they were to having a final plan for the successful completion of this mission.

As Jeff's thoughts were turned to the other two members that the mission depended upon, Raymond and Lewis were discussing this very plan.

Both men were hunkered over blueprints of a large building located just off campus grounds. They had uncovered the fact that the Army had signed a five-year lease on the building a little over three years ago. What made it suspicious was the fact several college professors of physics worked there. From the chatter heard from college students about what was going on in the building had directed the attention of Lewis and Raymond to concentrate on this building. They knew, from what Lank had passed on to them, some kind of experiments with time travel were being conducted.

It was their job to get inside the building and photograph anything they found. There were always classified publications and with Lewis's expertise in breaking any combination any time or anywhere, nothing would be denied them.

Both men had worked hard to devise a workable plan on how to gain entrance to the building. Once inside they would have to play it by ear, utilizing their hard earned knowledge from past missions to help them, hopefully it wouldn't be too difficult.

They would have to deal with guards, but the way they operated, it was very doubtful if any of the soldiers would become aware of them. The goal of this mission was to get in, do what was necessary and get out with no one suspecting a thing.

Raymond noticed the time and with a grunt said. "Lewis we need to wrap this up. We have to go and meet Lank you know."

"Roger on that. It will be good to coordinate all our plans. You know I'm looking forward to this one. I'm curious as to what is going on in that building, ain't you?" Lewis asked.

"Sure but we have to get the go ahead from Lank on this one. We don't want to get in a predicament like we got ourselves into in Baghdad," Raymond said.

"Yeah I remember that. Kind of got sticky there for a few days didn't it."

"Well yeah, but we assumed some things on our own and you know what comes from assuming, don't you?" Raymond asked out of the corner of his mouth.

"Sure, it made an ass out of you and me, didn't it?" Lewis came right back.

"Ok, well lets get on over to the safe house. I bet Lank is there already waiting on us."

"Your right. Lets tidy this place up and go see."

Lank was sitting in an easy chair in the safe house reading the local newspaper when he heard Raymond and Lewis coming in.

Both men were moving lightly on their feet. Lank smiled as he remembered the training each of them had had in moving silently.

A few seconds had passed before Raymond and Lewis sighted Lank, and when they did, they let out a loud whoop and closed the distance between them and Lank swiftly. Raymond grabbed Lank's hand and with a tight squeeze let Lank know how glad he was to see him again. When Lank had shaken both their hands, he headed toward the table gesturing they should take a seat at the table.

When the three had settled themselves at the table, Lank opened the conversation with his usual statement.

"I guess you two have been enjoying yourselves while you have been here in southern California."

"Oh yeah, having the time of our lives," Lewis spoke up.

"That's right and too bad we have to go to work now and miss out on all this nice sunshine," Raymond quipped.

"Sorry about that boys, but you know that is how it is in our business," Lank reminded them.

"Yeah we know," Lewis said and then asked. "When do we get to go to work on this one Lank?

"I figure this Sunday morning at precisely one in the morning," Lank said and continued speaking. "This is Memorial Day weekend and we know how the military operates on holidays."

"That's right Lank, there will only be a skeleton crew on duty and none of the professors or their staff will be at their desk, right?" Raymond answered for both him and Lewis.

"That's right Raymond and the less we have to deal with the better it is for us," Lank said, and after a brief moment, he then asked if they had put the final touches on their plan of operation.

"Right down to crossing all the t's and dotting all the i's," Lewis said.

"Good, then it's all set. We need to take a drive by this afternoon and you guys show me where you want me placed as lookout," Lank said to both of them.

"What's wrong with right now?" Raymond asked.

"Not a thing Raymond, if you two are up to it I'm ready," Lank said as he rose up from the table.

All three piled into Raymond's car which was a late model SUV and soon was on their way toward Los Angles city limits.

Two hours passed before they realized they were nearing the campus of the college. When the university finally appeared Lank was surprised at how large this university was. He had envisioned a university about the size of some of the A&M colleges he was acquainted with, but this university could be compared with any major university across America. The only difference was in the name. This University was not that well known and the reason, it could very well be; it was considered a military university.

Raymond slowed down at the next intersection and made a sharp right turn onto a tree-lined street. It looked like any sleepy street anywhere in USA. Two intersections later still skirting the university campus Raymond slowed down once again and directed Lank's eyes toward a large three story building on the right just ahead of them.

"Lank that's the building. From the blueprints we have, the best way to enter it is from the rear," Raymond told Lank.

"Yep, there is a door that opens into a hallway that harbors a stairway to the top two floors. We will be able to access the top two floors from this door," Lewis mentioned to Lank.

"How about the guards, where are they stationed? Lank asked.

"Normally there would be three guards on each floor but from overheard conversations of some of the guards that pull duty this weekend, there will only be one guard on each floor," Lewis told Lank.

"Right Lank, and all the desk and offices are located on the first floor. This is where we will find hard documents. On the second floor is where all the computers are located."

"The third floor is where all the hard core equipment is located, where the experiments are conducted."

"Ok, what about the roof and the basement?" Lank asked both of them.

Lewis piped up, ahead of Raymond on this one. "On the roof, Lank, is located all their antennas. Some very weird looking antennas I must say."

"That's right and the basement, from what I can salvage from all the chatter we have intercepted, is where all the big generators are located. Re-enforced concrete two feet thick for the walls and four feet thick on the floors where the generators are sitting," Raymond volunteered.

"You have done good, team. I've talked with Jeff and he is still downloading files but he should be done by the time you gain entrance to the building and will extract all his hidden files he used."

"Yeah Jeff is good at hiding his tracks, isn't he Raymond?" Lewis said jokingly.

"You ought to know, Lewis, he saved your ass a time or two," Raymond said, looking at Lewis as he spoke.

"Let's not go there, if you don't mind guys," Lewis responded with a somewhat impetuous smile covering his face.

"OK fellows, correct me if I'm wrong, but my observation point would be at the far end of the parking lot here behind the building, right?" Lank asked.

"You got it old man. You see that big oak tree to the right of the building; well on the other side of the tree is a small off pavement trail. You can back your car into that little trail and no one driving by, or for that matter parking in the parking lot, will know you are there," Raymond said to Lank as they slowly drove past the building and on down the street, picking up speed as they traveled.

They drove on back to the safe house and after discussing their plan, making sure each understood what was required of him and with a triple handshake they departed to their cars. Lank was the first to drive away. He would stay at the safe house tonight but first he needed some things from town to tide him over until the start of the mission. Lewis and Raymond followed, and after turning right onto the paved road, soon disappeared down the road.

Early Sunday morning seemed to come before Lank thought and he soon found himself parked behind the brick building behind the big tree that was just off the parking lot. He had arrived early and noticed there were still three cars parked in the parking lot. He mused to himself, must be the soldier guards for the three floors of the building in front of him. He adjusted the radio headset that all three wore and would not use except when it was necessary to break radio silence.

At exactly one o'clock Lank noticed a dark figure slowly inching his way toward the building. The figure would merge into the shadow of a small building and then reemerge for a few minutes, just long enough to confuse anyone that was actively looking for an intruder. Soon the figure disappeared completely into the darkness of the shadow cast by the main building.

Lank kept his eyes peeled for the other intruder but was unable to pick him up. Lank reached into his bag and extracted a pair of infrared binoculars. He directed his gaze through the binoculars slowly back and forth around the perimeter of the building but still was not able to pick up the other man.

Lank thought to himself that maybe one of the team had not made it or was late. He watched patiently for the next two hours with nothing to arouse his suspicions. Finally close to five o'clock he noticed a figure emerging from the back door. The figure was unidentifiable even with the infrared binoculars.

Lank was not sure if it was Raymond or Lewis that had emerged. Lank was becoming somewhat concerned about the missing team member but as it was getting close to dawn he decided it was best that he pack it in and head toward the safe house.

Lewis had his gear with him and positioned himself in the shadows of the small outbuilding. Unnoticeable to anyone that might be watching. He saw that Lank had not arrived yet. That was part of the plan. Lewis was to go in first and unlock the doors and slowly enter. He was to set off the sleeping gas on the first floor and when the guard was fast asleep he was to proceed to the second and third floor. The sleeping gas would keep the guards asleep for at least five hours. They would start waking up an hour before they were to be relieved by the oncoming watch. Lewis disengaged the lock on the outside door and quietly entered the hallway.

By prearrangement he left the door unlocked. He slipped the gas mask over his face and made sure it was tight. He noticed the guard was about half way down the hall. He had a cup of coffee in his hand and had his back toward Lewis. There were no other persons on this floor as far as Lewis could see.

Lewis reached in his bag and brought out one of the canister of sleeping gas, which was a form of fentanyl, with a flip of his thumb punctured the top and the gas began to be expelled. He stayed out of sight until the canister was empty and then took a quick look down the hallway. The soldier was sprawled out on the floor, the coffee had spilled onto the floor and had made a dark stain on the white tile surface.

One down and two to go, he said under his breath as he slowly climbed the stairs to the second floor. Lewis very carefully poked his head around the wall to see where the guard was. Oh no, he thought to himself, where could that soldier be.

He waited for a few minutes and then took another look down the hallway. Still there were no sign of the security soldier.

Lewis was about to take matters into his own hands when he suddenly heard the slamming of a door and then the faint foot-steps of someone coming down the hallway. The footsteps steps continued on for a few minutes and then stopped. No further sounds were heard from the hallway and this prompted Lewis to look once more down the hallway. The guard on duty now was sitting in his chair looking directly down the hallway towards Lewis, who was crouched just out of sight on the stairway.

There was nothing Lewis could do now but wait a few more minutes and see maybe if the guard would change his position. Five more minutes passed before Lewis took another look and this time the guard was still sitting facing Lewis, but now his head was flung back on his neck and he was asleep.

A break, Lewis thought as he pulled out another canister of sleeping gas and set it off. He watched as the gas traveled down the hallway and engulfed the guard.

Two down and one to go, Lewis thought as he looked at his watch and noted the time. Raymond by now would be on the lower floor doing his thing with his camera. Lewis knew he had to get the guard on the third floor asleep very soon so he could help Raymond by unlocking all the safes.

The third floor was the easiest. The guard was already asleep. Lewis didn't know if it was a natural sleep or sleep induced by the gas seeping up from the lower two floors. He couldn't take the chance though as he pulled out the remaining canister and set it off in the hallway of the third floor.

He remained long enough on each floor as he descended to make sure he had accomplished his mission. He was relieved as he entered the hallway of the first floor and saw Raymond taking pictures of all the things in sight. Raymond noticed him and with a wave of his hand indicated to Lewis the safe was next on the agenda.

As Lewis approached the safe with the tools of his trade he noticed a large safe situated behind a large picture. The picture had been swung open a foot or two so the safe could be visible. He cast a look at Raymond who shrugged his shoulders and continued on taking pictures. A momentary lapse of security, Lewis muttered to himself as he deftly and quickly opened the safe for Raymond to photograph the contents, one document at a time. This would take a lot of time but once the safes were opened Lewis could assist in photographing too.

It didn't take long for Lewis to open all the safes and then start photographing the contents himself. It took almost two hours of steady snapping the shutters before they had photographed the important pages. They then skipped the second floor as it contained the computers. Jeff would have taken care of this floor with his hacking into their work.

On the third floor they were surprised to see all the state of the art equipment neatly stacked in bays. The bays were all lined up against the back wall of a windowless huge room. The first piece of equipment that caught their eye was a huge circular pad on the floor. It was approximately ten feet in diameter. The material of the pad was made from material neither Raymond not Lewis was familiar with.

Embedded in the pad were three circular imprints about a foot in diameter each and arranged equally around the pad about a foot in from the outside rim of the pad. The pad was surrounded by a glass enclosure with three tubes protruding from the top like showerheads. Wires were coming from the showerheads and running to a bank of electronic equipments. On one of the pieces of equipment was a frequency counter that Lewis recognized right away. The frequency was set to 121 GHZ. This was definitely worth a few pictures so Lewis flashed away.

The other banks of electronic equipment were unknown to each of the men. All of the electronic equipment was wired to a bank of wires that went up through the ceiling to the roof and other banks of wires went down through the floor and probably went to the basement that housed the generators. They would check out the basement on their way out.

When all was photographed they walked up the stairway to the roof. The roof door gave Lewis a little trouble but on his third attempt it opened for them. Emerging onto the roof, an array of sophisticated antennas glared at them. They recognized some of the antennas but for the most part they were of some design he was not familiar with. It didn't matter, Lank would know someone that could figure out what these antennas were being used for. After the photographs were taken, both men walked past the guard who was still sprawled in his chair with his head thrown back.

Raymond paused long enough to straighten out the guard's head to a more comfortable position.

Lewis wondered if the guard would have appreciated the effort if he had been aware of it.

The basement was full of expensive four phase generators. Raymond wondered why so much power was necessary. The generators all emptied into a power grid of transformers that would boost the voltage tremendously. Both men became engaged in photographing the nomenclature of the generators.

When this job was done Lewis motioned with his hands that Raymond was to go first and Lewis would lock everything back up and secure the place. Raymond nodded his head and picked up his gear and exited out the back door. He glided silently past the outbuilding and down the street to where he had parked his car on a side road.

Lewis went to each individual safe he had opened and rearranged the contents back to its original position before moving onto the big wall safe. The big wall safe did not reveal much information to them, maybe it was used for something other than storing information.

The last thing he had to do was to remove the picture of what the surveillance camera was viewing while he and Raymond were in the room. He had almost made a mistake when he first attempted to turn the cameras off. Just in time he noticed that the surveillance cameras were wired to sound an alarm if they were turned off. This necessitated a change in plans. He had to take a picture of the area the camera was trained on and then insert the picture in front of the camera.

This way the person that looked at the film from the camera would only see a continuing picture of the room. With the camera's view blocked by the picture, Lewis and Raymond had the run of the place unbeknownst to anyone.

It was a simple procedure to remove the picture from in front of the camera, allowing the camera to view a live shot of exactly what it had been viewing with the picture in front of its lens.

Lewis was surprised that no surveillance equipment was employed on the roof. He had made a special effort to try to locate a camera or some kind of recording devices, but had not found any. Lewis made his way back to the roof and used his steel cable with its small electric motor to lower himself down from the end of the building farthest from where Lank had positioned himself.

Raymond had at least a thirty minute head start on him but no matter, they would all meet back at the safe house in a few hours and hand over what they had acquired on this mission to Lank who in turn would take it back to Washington DC for final analysis.

PART TWO

The Abductees

Chapter Seventeen

The young woman, who looked chic and uptown in her manner-isms, was apparently shopping for herself today. She had just left one of the more elegant department stores in town, heading in the direction of a parking lot where she had parked her car. Suddenly she turned around at the sound of someone hailing her and with one hand shielding her eyes from the glaring sun looked to see who it was.

"Betty, Betty," a voice came from the entrance to a gift shop that she had just passed.

The young woman who we now know as Betty directed her gaze toward the owner of the voice that had hailed her. It took a few moments to recognize the voice and when recognition oc-curred, Betty hurriedly backtracked her steps and with great en-thusiasm said in a voice filled with emotion.

"Mike, oh Mike, what are you doing here?" Betty said as she quickly embraced Mike.

"Well I'm just passing through but I'm sure glad I saw you," Mike said and then blurted out. "How are you Betty? Do you still live at home with your parents?"

"I do. Yes I still live with my mom, my dad died two years ago Mike. "And you. How about you?" Betty asked.

"Betty, my dad was also killed in a car accident last year, mom is still trying to get over him."

"I'm so sorry Mike, how is she doing?" Betty asked in an emotional voice.

"She seems to be coping, but there are days, you know," Mike said in answer to her question.

"Mike if you have time, maybe we can pop into the cafeteria and have a cup of coffee or something?" Betty asked in an expectant voice.

When Mike did not answer right away, Betty thought she might have offended him, but after the pause Mike readily agreed and they started toward the cafeteria that was just down the street.

Mike steered Betty towards an empty table and as they sat down, Betty thought about the last time she had seen Mike. She remembered Mike from high school and their senior high school prom. Mike was her date for the prom and was very attendant to her needs. She remembered being in awe of him because he was a very popular guy, what with being a star on the football team and all. Betty could still feel the thrill in her body as she reminisced the past. She was suddenly brought back to the present with Mike asking a question.

"I'm sorry Mike, what did you say?"

"I was asking you if you are still in college."

"Yes I'm still in college. I'm working part time at a local brokerage firm here in town. But I'll be graduating from college this coming May. Boy will I be glad when that happens," Betty said.

"Good for you. I tried college for a couple of years but dropped out when dad was killed to help mom with all the expenses," Mike said with a down cast look on his face.

"Are you going to go back and get your degree Mike?" Betty asked in a voice that was filled with sympathy for him.

"Not in the immediate future. I have a good job right now and mom still needs me around."

"What kind of work do you do Mike?" Betty asked.

"I kind of stumbled onto this job. Basically it's a traveling job, delivering packages and items for the army."

"Sounds like a good job, especially since you are working for the government," Betty said.

"Yes, that reminds me, Betty you want to ride over to the army navy outlet store?" Mike asked in a hopeful voice. "I was on my way there to make a delivery when I saw you."

"Betty took a quick look at her watch and then asked Mike.

"Is it that army navy surplus store over on Chestnut Street Mike?"

"That's the one, on the east side of town, want to go with me?"

"Sure. I guess so. I have a little spare time right now."

They rose up from the table and dumped their empty hot cups in the container that was conveniently placed for just such a purpose. As they left the cafeteria, Mike informed Betty that his car was just around the corner from here.

When the car came in sight Mike indicated to Betty this was his car.

"Man your government job must pay good Mike. This is a beautiful car."

"I like it," Mike said. "And it is all mine, just paid it off a couple of months ago."

Mike held the door open for her and as Betty seated herself, Mike shut the car door and slid in behind the wheel. It wasn't long before they arrived in front of the army navy store.

Once inside the store they were met by a man who upon seeing Mike, came from behind the counter with extended hand quickly grabbing Mike's hand.

"Hi Mike good to see you again."

"Yeah, you too, Will." I've got a delivery for you" Mike said as he handed Will the package.

"Thanks. Let me see what the army has sent me this time." As Will began to open the package, Betty was busy looking at the jewelry in the display window of the counter.

Will finished unwrapping the package and began to inspect the merchandise. Immediately, when he recognized the type of jewelry the army had sent him, his countenance changed from that of a jovial person to that of a serious minded individual. He knew what this type of jewelry was made for.

He got paid by the Army for each one he sold and it wasn't nickels and dimes either. Of course there were restrictions on the sale. The army had definitely told him under no circumstances was he to sell this type of jewelry to anyone other than young women between the ages of eight-teen and twenty-five.

The army had insisted that he keep the price low but to keep perfect records as to whom he sold to. He was to have a record of the address, telephone number and birthday of each person who bought one of the necklaces. This type of necklace was not to be on display but was to be offered to a customer that met the criteria that was laid out in his instructions.

As Will thought about the contents of the package Mike had brought to him, he turned to Betty who was looking at the jewelry on display.

"Miss, I see you are interested in the jewelry. If you will permit me, this has just come in. These necklaces are very rare in that only a few have been made. I could only purchase ten."

Mike came and stood beside Betty as Will draped one of the necklaces over his arm. Betty immediately liked the necklace with the golden medallion and asked Will how much they were. Knowing they were probably out of her reach financially.

The necklace was itself a beautiful piece of artwork. The medallion was hung on a beautiful gold chain and the chain was itself something out of the ordinarily. The medallion was gold and was about an inch long, probably a quarter of an inch in circumference. Beautiful was hardly the word to describe something like this.

Will held the necklace out to Betty. "Here Miss, hold it in your hand. It creates a strange sensation, kind of like a warm feeling when held by a beautiful girl like yourself."

Betty took the necklace and noticed right away what Will had said was true. It definitely did radiate warmth when held next to her skin.

"Oh how beautiful it is. You are so right. It does feel warm against my skin. I can't afford something like this though, I'm just a struggling college girl that has to still live with her mom." Betty said with misgiving in her soul.

Mike had never seen the contents of anything he had delivered to the stores across the state before and he showed interest in the design. He watched as Betty kept stroking the golden entity.

"Miss these are not as expensive as you might think. You see they are a promotional item. Not yet in full production."

"How much?" Betty asked with a catch in her throat. She had a couple hundred dollars in her checking account but couldn't afford to spend much of it.

"Miss, I'll tell what I can do. I can offer you this fine necklace at a ridiculous low price if you agree to wear it at all times and talk it up among your friends," Will said.

Betty thought to herself this would be a good deal but she was sure the price would still be out of her range.

"I can let you have this one, if you agree to the instructions the company has laid down. The price will be twenty-five dollars."

Betty turned to Mike and with a smile lighting up her face, asked him what he thought. Mike looked at the necklace and felt the face of the necklace and he felt the warmth himself but didn't comment on it.

"I think it is a good deal Betty. I do know a lot of companies when first putting an item on the market will offer huge discounts."

Betty turned back to Will and with firmness in her voice told him she would like to take the necklace. Will placed the necklace around Betty's neck and began writing up the ticket. He asked for Betty's full name and her address and telephone. He took the check Betty filled out and wished her all the best with the necklace.

Betty thanked him and as Mike said his goodbyes to Will they left the store. Mike began the drive back to her car.

"Betty I hope you will be happy with your purchase. It looks like a good buy to me."

"I'm sure it is, and I do like it very much. It feels so good around my neck, nice and tingly."

"I wished I had more time to stick around but I have to deliver other products and I'm on a strict schedule," Mike relayed to her.

"That's ok Mike, It was good to see you again," Betty said.

"Maybe the next time I'm in town we can get together or something."

"That would be fine Mike. Just give me a call."

"I'll do that Betty. I'm glad you like the necklace.

"I do. I must say though I've never had a piece of jewelry that is so unique."

"Ok, bye for now. Take care Betty," Mike said as Betty pointed out her car.

Mike pulled in behind Betty's car and wished Betty good luck again as she removed herself from his car and started walking toward her car.

Back at the Army and Navy surplus store, Will had just finished talking with a man whom he had never met, but talked to on the phone each time he sold one of these unique necklaces.

This man, whom Will had never met seemed pleasant enough and was prompt in sending money to him each time he had reported a sale. Will did not understand why these necklaces should be so important. Yeah the money was good, five hundred dollars each time he sold one. Will rationalized within himself; it was no concern of his what the importance was.

Just as long as he was paid with no questions asked. Will did wonder though why the man was very implicit in getting the name, address and telephone number of the purchaser.

Each package that Mike brought to him contained six of those necklaces. It usually took him a few weeks to sell all the necklaces because he could not put them on display and had to hand pick his customers before he could show them a necklace.

Two or three thousand dollars a couple times a month sure came in handy, especially since he was paid in cash and would not report it to IRS.

Betty had finished her shopping after being dropped off by Mike and was returning home. She was anxious to show the necklace to her mother. As she pulled into the driveway of her mothers home Betty was not aware of the black Lincoln town car parked across the street from her home. A lone man sat behind the wheel. He was well over six feet tall and well dressed. Well past middle age though, as evidenced by his balding head and wrinkles on his face.

If someone had a close up view of the man, he would appear to be in his eighties or nineties. He had kept himself in good condition, wide shouldered and trim, more like a military man. On the seat beside him rested a rather large piece of electronic gear. If a person was looking intently at this object then he might be able to make out the small metal nomenclature tag that declared this particular item was a TSMD.

He had observed the young woman and recognizing her from the description given to him by Will, the manager of the Army Navy store. Mentally posting a picture of the car and license plate, the man would leave and come back in the early hours of the morning. He had a job to do and it must be accomplished in total secrecy.

The man did return, precisely at three am. He pulled into a vacant driveway just a couple of homes away from the house he had been parked in front of last evening. He waited fifteen minutes before reaching over and picking up the object beside him on the front seat. Although it was eighteen inches long by ten inches wide and six inches high, it was not heavy at all.

The casing was made from titanium, which was lightweight but strong metal. A telescoping antenna was folded down behind the case. The top of the case would rise up and reveal a keyboard. From this keyboard certain programs could be activated remotely It was designed to be operable if in close proximity to the person it was intended to effect. Therefore it had to be no further than the trunk of a car or under a bed or some other close by location before it could program the medallion, usually a couple of hours would suffice.

The man lifted the article from the front seat of his car and carried it to the driveway of Betty's home.

Her car was just where she had left it. He chose the trunk to open, knowing that most security alarms for cars would not be activated if the trunk was opened. He very expertly opened the trunk in under two minutes. He then placed the electronic item in her trunk underneath the trunk lid just out of sight next to the back seats. He extended the telescoping antenna to its full length but only in a forty-five angle as the TSMD operated in FM mode. He then raised the lid to expose the keyboard, after quickly inputting a few numbers, he flipped a switch on the side of the keyboard that activated the device.

He then quickly closed the trunk without making an audible sound and returned to his car. After he had slid in behind the wheel, starting the car and slowly picking up speed down the road, knowing he would have to return soon and remove the electronic device after it had programmed the necklace around the girl's neck.

Chapter Eighteen

Betty woke up early the next morning and after taking her morning shower dressed herself and made her way toward the kitchen. Her mom was already seated at the kitchen table with a cup of coffee. As Betty entered the kitchen her mom looked up and with a cherry greeting asked how her night was.

"Great mom, I don't think I knew anything all night. I must have slept like a log," Betty responded in cherry voice also.

Betty becoming aware of the warm feeling of the necklace around her neck reached up with her hand and lifted the medallion away from her body. She leaned over showing the necklace to her mom.

"Mom, looked what I bought myself yesterday at the Army navy store."

"My it is so pretty Betty," Her mom commented. "Gold, isn't it?"

"Yes and it stays warm to the touch, isn't that something."

"Hmmm let me feel of it," Her mom said as she touched the golden medallion. "Hey, you're right Betty. It is warm. You think it might be because of your body heat."

"No it was warm to the touch when I was looking at it in the store."

"That's seems so strange, doesn't it?" Betty's mom said almost as an after thought.

"Well I don't know how it is always warm, but I like it and want to wear it," Betty said in an effort to convince her mom that there was nothing wrong with it.

After a few days of wearing the necklace Betty could not bring herself to take it off, even when she showered. Little did she

know but now the medallion hanging around her neck was programmed.

Yes it had been programmed and the electronic device had
been removed from the trunk of her car. It was only a matter of
time now till activation would be done.

Two weeks and one day after Betty had purchased the necklace she found herself driving herself to college at Columbia. She
had to drive to a little shop in Queens on an errand for her mother.
Betty thought to herself about the trip. It wasn't that she minded
doing this for her mom, but she had skipped lunch already and
now this would now mean she would be late getting home. Really
though, it probably was her fault. You see she had a call from
Mike who was on his way through the town and wanted to see her
again.

Betty had thought a lot about Mike since she had seen him
the day she had purchased the medallion. For him to call today
really lifted her spirits. They had agreed they would meet in front
of the mall, which both was familiar with.

The car in front of her was doing the speed limit but Betty
became a little impatient and decided to pass him. She signaled
her intention, although there were no other cars in sight behind
her. As she pulled alongside the car she could not keep herself
from glancing at the driver. He looked to be in his middle thirties,
sharp, good looking too. Betty smiled at him as she passed and a
little tingle went through her as he smiled back at her. She had
outdistanced the car and as there were no other cars either in front
of her or behind, she slowed back down to the legal speed limit.

All was well, Betty was feeling good, and she had a date for
tonight. Just maybe there might be possibilities somewhere down
the road, who knows.

The first indication that something was wrong came in the
form of a loud popping noise then suddenly everything went
black. Betty felt herself being propelled through something that
looked like a long curving tunnel. On and on she traveled, aware
of only her immediate surroundings, which were only the clothes
she had on. She thought about the necklace and raised her hand
up to clasp it.

It felt warm in her hand. That was far as her thoughts got, for at that precise moment in time the tunnel opened out into a huge circle of light. She felt solid ground under her feet for the first time since she had first heard the loud popping sound. As her senses began to settle down in some kind of order she became aware of her surroundings. The first thing to return to somewhat of a normalcy was her eyesight. Now she could see and noticed she was in a huge room with all kinds of electronic equipment. Betty had an opportunity to view around the room and right away noticed it did not have any windows.

Looking down at her feet she noticed she was standing on some kind of pad that was circular. The pad was about ten feet in circumference and had three bright shinny metal plates on it. She was in the middle of the pad with the plates circling her.

Betty was still unable to move, transfixed in time, when she began to hear a low hum that slowly increased in frequency to a high pitched hum. It was at this time she became aware of a figure that stood by her side, reaching out and adjusting some of the controls. The room began to dissolve from in front of her and suddenly she was on her way through another tunnel similar to the one she had just come through.

Betty had no fears at all of what she was going through, only a sense of peace and tranquility that encompassed her body. She never knew when she had exited through the tunnel, only the wakening in a strange bed in a place she did not recognize.

It wasn't long before a figure of a man came close by and spoke to her.

"How are you doing Miss Betty Francis Moulton? His voice was firm but sounded old in her ears.

"Where am I and what happened to me?" Betty asked with a quavering voice.

"All in good time my dear. We want you to rest now and in a few hours all your questions will be answered?"

"How ....?" Betty started to ask but was interrupted by the man at the foot of her bed.

"Don't worry now, all your questions will be answered. The sleep inducement shot we gave you will start to take effect in a few minutes."

Betty's thoughts were on how odd the voice of the man sounded. She could not place the accent. Her thoughts became scattered and abstract from her body as she drifted off to sleep.

When she awoke she found herself alone. Betty looked around the room only now comprehending her surroundings. The room was quite large and contained two beds, hers and one empty bed.

Her gaze was drawn to the far end of the room when the only door to this room began to open slowly. An odd looking old man dressed in what looked like a jump suit walked softly across the room and stood beside her.

"Good morning. How are you today Miss Betty Moulton?" He said in a voice that was at least a few octaves above what she considered a man's voice.

"I feel fine right now. I want to know what happened. Did I have an accident?" Betty blurted. Actually she would feel much better if she had some answers.

"Don't worry Miss Betty Moulton, you will know everything in a few days. There are other young women coming that we must also advise."

"Other women? Where is this place I am in?"

"Come with me and I will show you your quarters," The man said, ignoring Betty's question.

Betty pulled the sheet back and noticed she was dressed in a nice looking pair of silk pajamas. She swung her legs over the side of the bed and when her feet touched the floor, stood up. She followed the man across the room and out the door into a hallway. The man continued on down the hallway with Betty closely following behind. He stopped in front of a door and spoke a command. The door began to swing open. They entered into a very large room that contained a long table with an adequate number of chairs pulled neatly up to the table.

A courtroom was Betty's first thought, Oh lord what have I done, was her first thought. The door they had come in opened once again and a group of young women entered, looking as bewildered as Betty thought she must have looked upon seeing this room for the first time. The old man, yes that was what he was, an old man, motioned to all of them to take a seat at the table.

When they were all seated another old man appeared in the doorway and approaching the head of the table, sat down in the only chair available. He surveyed the women around the table, each in turn, finally addressed them in a high squeaky voice.

"You all are here I admit, in all regards, against your will. However, I hope you will understand why it is necessary for you to be here in this capacity. I will now show you the history of this planet. It is not what you think the history of your planet is, but the history of our planet," He stopped here and looked intently at the group of women.

"I will show you what happens when something of the nature that happened to this planet. Please place the headset on your heads," As he spoke, a wide movie screen appeared before their eyes. They watched as the history of this planet unfolded.

Betty was not alone in wondering if they had somehow been transported to another planet. She had heard of time travel but shoved it to the back of her mind as only science fiction. Her attention returned back to the screen.

The voice on the screen in front of her eyes informed her of the consequences of living as if nothing would ever fail. The movie, and Betty guessed that was what it was, on the screen drew their attention to the plight of a segment of society that only showed old men and old women. It went on to explain how, unbeknown to the powers that be, their society was doomed. Somehow someway, Betty and the rest of the group of young women began to understand now the situation that faced this planet.

Anyone would have to have sympathy for them. Betty noticed right away there were no children in the scenes now showing as there had been in previous scenes. She wondered why. What could possibly be the reason there were no children. Her understanding was enlightened as soon as she thought of a question. That was amazing. She could have used such a device in her classroom work at college.

It was not hard to understand now why there were no children and the adults looked so old. As the movie progressed it, became obvious there were no women either. Something had happened to the women, which caused them to be barren.

There were sperm banks but since the women produced no eggs than there would be no children.

The rest of the movie explained all the attempts to help women ovulate. Nothing worked. Finally in a desperate attempt, the scientist turned to time travel and invented a device that would send things through a wormhole to their planet. Where they went was to a parallel world that had not reached the point in time they were in.

Time travel consisted of sending someone back to the time when women were fertile, identifying each potential woman that qualified as a candidate by accessing her history, her medical records and then placing a DTS (Displacement of Time Syndrome) on the person, programming the device with the TSMD (Time Space Manipulator Device).

The group of women clearly understood all the technical information being provided. They understood about the DTS, that it reduced a subject or thing to its basic molecular information and sent all the molecules through a wormhole using the FTL principal. The other end of the worm hole had its vertex connected to a larger mechanism that could send objects or people interplanetary, using the faster than light (FTL) principle.

Betty understood what was being presented to them. This planet was in dire need of young women of childbearing age to furnish eggs to be fertilized by the sperm of men. Most of the men were not much interested in having sex with women. Luckily, there were sperm banks that held the sperm of young virile men that could be used.

The rest of the tape, if it could be called that, showed where the women would live, what they would be doing for relaxation. All the sightseeing trips they could go on. Really a nice structured lifestyle was being presented to them.

When the tape was ended they were told to remove the headset from their head. Another old man had replaced the old man who had addressed them in the beginning; only this one had to use a cane to get about.

The old man, who introduced himself as Ladle, motioned to them to follow him. On their way out Ladle told them their names would be on the door of their apartments. They would be encour-

aged to visit one another for a few days, then they would be inter-
viewed one at a time. At that time they would be presented with a
bank account that they could use for their personal pleasure. The
money placed in the account would be quite adequately.

Chapter Nineteen

Betty watched for her name as they progressed down the hall. A lot of the apartments were already occupied by other women that were not in their group evidenced by the fact that none of the girls found their name on the doors of this set of apartments.

Finally, one by one the young women found their names on the doors and left the party to enter their new home. Betty found her name on the door about halfway down the long hallway. She was really surprised when she entered her apartment and noticed how nice it was. A lot of the things sitting around the apartment were strange to her but something told her she would be happy with them. First of all, the living room sported a couch made of the softest material Betty had ever seen. Accompanying the couch was a recliner that lowered itself when she approached it.

A screen on the wall was obvious a TV set of some kind although Betty could not find any remote control that operated the set. Oh well, she thought. I'll learn how to operate as time goes by. Briefly a thought entered her mind. What about mom, when will I be able to see her again. For some reason Betty was not too concerned about being abducted.

It was a necessary thing to do as evidenced only old people were left of this world. Why was she not worrying about herself. She was slightly annoyed with herself for not having more anger at those whom had abducted her. Really though she would miss her mom, but that was the only person back in her world that mattered.

It was at this time a woman entered her room after knocking lightly on the door. She was obvious old, as depicted by her physical condition; but still she had an inner spirit that was the drive that moved her.

"Miss Betty Moulton I have been appointed as your guide to show you around our facilities," She mentioned, almost as an afterthought."

"Now, you mean right now?" Betty exclaimed.

"Yes, right now. You need to know your way around here as quickly as you can."

"Ok just give me a few minutes to get myself ready. I won't be long."

"Certainly." The old woman said as she waited patiently for Betty to get ready.

It did not take Betty long. She had only to grab a scarf to throw over her shoulders. The scarf was from the contents of her apartment, which was completely furnished in every detail.

The old woman after noticing Betty was ready, led the way out into the hall and toward the exit door only a few doors down from her apartment. Betty was led out the door and into a sunny patio and on to the other side. They went through a door that opened into a huge room.

It was very pleasingly decorated exhibiting a warm welcome to all that entered. Groups of women, who all appeared to be around Betty's age, were gathered around the many nice areas provided for just such an occasion.

The old woman guided Betty to one such group and after getting their attention; she introduced Betty to the group.

"Girls, this is our newest guest, Miss Betty Francis Moulton. Would you make her welcome."

The girls, about fifteen of them, each gladly gave her a hearty welcome.

"Hi Betty, Glad to see a new face. Come on over here and sit with us. We will bring you up to date. My name is Marie Gonzales. I have been here about a month. You might say I'm new here too."

The rest of the girls each introduced their selves. They wanted to know how she was abducted, where did she work, did she have a boy friend back home.

Betty eventually answered all the questions put to her. Only to listen to the stories of the girls she had just met. Some hours later, the girls asked Betty to join them as they went to the cafeteria to eat their dinner.

Betty sat down at the table beside a girl who had told her she was called Lise Meitner. Betty remembered the story she had related concerning her abduction. She was engaged to her boyfriend Ludwig, something or the other, Betty could not remember his full name. But Lise had known him most of her life. Lise spoke lovingly of Ludwig with a far away look in her eyes.

The meal was very palatable and nutritious. After the meal Lise suggested they go and meet some of the other girls.

"Some of the girls have been here two years or more. They were all abducted as we were," Lise informed Betty as they left the cafeteria on their way to meet the other girls.

Lise led Betty to a door that opened to the outside world. Betty could see what looked like a garage with a bevy of small cars, at least she thought they must be cars, all lined up neatly forming a long line on each side of the parking garage.

Lise took Betty by the hand and touched the first car they came to and the door began to open automatically. Betty was instructed to enter the car while Lise continued on around the car to the driver side. When Lise was seated she commanded the car to take them to the rec hall. Seat belts began its trip around their bodies and fasten itself around them.

"Wow." Betty exclaimed with excitement in her voice.

"I felt the same way the first time I rode in one of these. I guess you noticed everything is automatically, no steering wheel, no gears to shift."

"Amazing, don't you think so Lise?"

"Oh yes but just you wait, you will see and experience much more amazing things then what you see here," Lise said.

After a drive of twenty miles or so they came to a small town. It looked just like any other town in the USA. The only difference being, all the people that were visible were old. There were no children at all.

Betty felt an eerie feeling go up her spine as they slowly traveled down the wide avenue towards a distant building that looked all the world a courthouse.

"Lise, what is this place?" Betty asked as the car deftly pulled into the large parking area in front of the building.

"It's where you will be indoctrinated," Lise said.

"Indoctrinated? What do you mean?" Betty asked in an incredulous voice.

"Well you need to know how these towns are run. You don't see many people around, and the ones you do see are very old. It's easy, all you have to do is put another headset on and you will experience a live introduction into their way of running their country," Lies informed her.

"Oh, I never thought of it that way. What's going to happen Lise, when all these old people die and there is no one left but us?"

"Well there are a few still left that are a little younger then what you see here, not many though. But that is one of the purposes in bringing us here in the first place. Of course, you are aware that we are here also to replenish their population," Lise promptly reminded.

Betty thought about all this and wondered if she would ever see her home, mom, or even Mike again. Her thoughts were quickly interrupted as they approached the front door of this large building by an elderly, but firm voice, coming from a speaker to her right.

"Good morning Lise, Good morning Betty. Please enter and follow the blue arrows to the indoctrination room," The voice instructed them.

Betty gasped, "How did it know my name?"

"You are known all over this planet Betty. You will understand when you have been indoctrinated."

The indoctrination room was directly ahead of them as they walked toward it. When they were only feet away from the room, the door opened and once again they heard the voice instructing them to go in and take a seat. Betty and Lise entered and seated themselves in two of the many seats that were built into the wall. Each seat was connected to what looked like a virtual reality machine, complete with a large headset with what looked like a small TV screen in front.

Lise turned to Betty and said. "I have already been through this one. I will wait for you. It won't take but about thirty minutes."

"You knew all along where we were going, didn't you Lise?"

"Yes I did but there was no ulterior motive involved. You will have to bring many of the Breeders, that is what we are known as by the locals, here for their indoctrination," Lise informed her.

Betty reached for the headset and put it over her head. As the faceplate came over her eyes she heard once again the welcome she had heard many times before through the headset speakers.

The scenes coming before her eyes captivated her attention. Once again the history of this planet was displayed in front of her eyes. This time though, there was a further revealing of her purpose in being brought here.

For the first time she learned how the dying race on this planet proposed to renew their planet with babies born to the women that were brought here by abduction. It was emphasized why it was necessary to bring in women from a different world to accomplish the task.

The scene shifted to a hospital room with bed after bed filled with young women, pregnant in different stages, some ready to give birth. A panoramic view showed young mothers with their children romping and playing in various parts of the planet. The children seemed to be about equal in number of girls and boys. Betty was told these women had been brought to this world in the last five years for the purpose of having children in an effort to repopulate this planet.

No harm will come to any of the women or their children she was told. It was explained once again how when it became obvious women were not producing eggs, the sperm banks were increased and fill to full capacity with the hope that the scientist would find the reason the women were barren and be able to rectify the situation. However it soon became obvious to the scientist that this was beyond their expertise and the race would die out in the next fifty to seventy-five years.

The attention of the powers that be on this planet turned to perfecting their time machines in order to kidnap women from a different time of this planet. However they ran into a lot of difficulties in trying to bring women into the future from the past of their own world.

By reverting their attention to parallel universes they were able to devise a way to travel between two worlds. In so doing we established a contact with another world, your world, enabling us to work closely with teams of their scientist. Working together we were able to build a terminal that would receive the person that was transported from one location on your Earth to the terminal where the DTS was removed. This kind of time travel involved sending an individual, known as the encoder, through the vortex to the parallel world and with the utilization of the programmable necklaces provided to women the encoder had deemed viable to this dying planet.

A system was devised where the encoder would distribute the necklaces to a point of distribution and then would be further distributed to different points on the planet by a local who would be paid very well.

A group of the younger men, a relative term considering the average age of the men on this planet, would be the encoders and follow the necklaces, programming them to act as DTS. They would work closely with the military of the United States army, keeping secret from everyone but those involved.

We have been doing this now for seven years, the first baby born two years after the first woman brought here has developed into a fine young lady of five years old.

The voice went on for several more minutes showing clips of the children playing together, the women socializing and living a life of no restrictions, The practically had the run of the planet. Finally the introduction was ended and the screen went blank. Betty removed the headset from her head.

Betty was silent for a minute or two, just fitting in her presence here on this planet with what she remembered of her home, mother, and coworkers at the brokerage firm. For some unknown reason she harbored no ill feelings toward those that had brought her here. Maybe it was the mother instinct that quieted fears that other wise would have overwhelmed her. Betty was abruptly brought back to her present surroundings, by Lise tugging at her arm.

Chapter Twenty

"Betty, Betty." Lise was earnestly whispering in her ear. "Come on, we have another viewing to do before we can return back to out apartment."

"Oh, I guess I was deep in thought," Betty remarked, and then as if an after thought had brought light to her mind, she said. "Lise, I can understand now why it is so important to these old folks."

"I know, I understand also," Lise said as she led Betty back to the car.

The next viewing, as it was now called, took place in an adjacent building. Only this time Betty was informed how she would be artificial inseminated with stored sperm from the sperm bank. However it was her prerogative either to use the sperm bank or mate with an elderly man.

After the viewing was completed and Betty had removed the headset, she was slightly embarrassed as she faced Lise.

"Your face is red, Betty," Lise laughingly chided her. "Can you imagine yourself going to bed with one of these old men?"

"I don't think any of the old fellows that I have seen, could perform very well, do you?" Betty asked in an effort to cover up her embarrassment.

"You might be surprised. Anyway there are a few, very few I might say, who are a bit younger," Lise came back to her.

Two months later Betty and Lise, who have become the best of friends, decide to take a tour along the seashore. They picked out a light blue car and seated themselves in it. A voice from the car's dashboard asked in a slightly quivering voice. "Where would you like to go?"

"We would like to take a drive down the seacoast," Lise informed the strange voice. There was hesitation on the part of the car's enunciator. Then a map appeared on the screen directly in front of them. There was an instruction scrolled across the screen, to touch the screen on the destination where they wanted to go. Lise immediately touched a town that appeared to be about twenty-five or thirty miles from this location. When the car entered the main highway and picked up speed to about sixty miles an hour, Betty began to relax and let the cool breeze from the open car window blow her hair.

She settled back to enjoy the scenery, noticing an absence of any buildings along the highway. The road was all grown up with weeds. Betty was thinking about this when Lise suddenly made the comment.

"Betty, Have you noticed the lack of any cars, either going or coming?"

"I hadn't, but now that you mentioned it, your right, also I haven't seen any buildings either." Betty exclaimed as she continue to look for any signs of life.

"Hmmm, I wonder what that means. In the indoctrination tapes we repeatedly saw all kinds of buildings and old men and old women strolling about the streets of town," Lise made the comments while taking in the views from her side of the car.

"Lise, If I'm not wrong, I think this is Los Angles, California, or at least close to it anyway."

"I think you are right, but where is the town and where are the old men and women at?"

"I don't know Lise, but I am going to try to find out. I'm not going to be slaughtered without a fight," Betty said.

The car begin to slow down and exited off the highway onto a street that did contained some buildings, most of them no more than two stories high. They came to a large brick building and the car immediately pulled into an empty parking space. The car made the announcement, "You have arrived at the destination you chose," as the doors opened wide for them.

Betty and Lise exited the car and began to stroll down the street toward what looked like a family park. Upon getting closer they saw it was indeed a family park but without the families.

However there were ten or twelve old men and women sitting on various park benches placed around the park. Betty and Lise walked past some of the benches and noticed the stares that were directed their way. It made both of them uncomfortable to be under the microscope so to speak.

"Lisa lets sit down beside one of the old men and start up a conversation."

"Ok by me. Maybe we will find out what really is going on here."

They chose one of the younger old men and both sat down beside him on the bench. The man turned his gaze towards them and with a flutter of his hands motioned to them they were welcome.

Betty introduced herself and then introduced Lise. The old man looked interested enough to listen to them. He introduced himself as George Pate.

"Sir, can you tell me what the name of this place is?" Betty asked in a quiet but steady voice.

"You are in Malibu, just above Los Angles," the old man said and then continued in a raspy voice. "Where did you come from?"

"We don't really know, we started out south of here, probably we traveled about twenty miles or so." Lise said, watching the old mans face.

"You probably started out from Santa Monica," The old man called George responded.

"Why Santa Monica?" Betty asked.

"Well that's where the breeder farm is located at."

"Breeder farm!" Both Betty and Lise exclaimed with emotion in their voices.

"Yep, that is where the young girls are taken to. You know so they can replenish the Earth."

"Can you tell me where the young girls are coming from? I mean are they born here or come from someplace else?" Betty asked.

"The young women come from various places on Earth, not this Earth mind you, but from a parallel universe. I would have thought you would have known that."

"We only know what they have told us that this is a dying world," Lise replied.

The old man seemed puzzled for a moment, then begin collecting his thoughts before he went any further in his explanation.

"Yes that is correct. Since all women have become infertile we have been on a downhill slide and can be considered a dying planet," George Pait went on in measured tones.

"Is this the only bre.... Breeder farm?" Betty halting asked.

"No, Breeder farms are scattered all across the planet, I think the oldest one is about five years old."

"Then that means the oldest child would be four or five years old, doesn't it?" Betty asked.

"Yes that's correct," George stated.

"Well, we haven't seen any children yet, where are they at?" Lise asked.

"They are taken from birth and sent to several large nurseries. One of the nurseries is located in Chicago, another in London, Paris, even a couple located in China and Russia."

"Have you ever been to any of those cities George?" Betty asked in an effort to glean more information from the old man.

"Years ago I visit my brother in Chicago and while I did my stint in the service I was stationed in London. Since then, I have remained here in Malibu."

"What happened to all the buildings, Most of the ones we have seen are relative new?" Lise asked.

"Well in 1955 we had a big earthquake, the big one that had been predicted for years. The sea came in and was turned to steam as the fissures emitted gases that spewed into the air. It wasn't long before the whole globe was contaminated with the gas. At the time we did not know what the gas was and never noticed the effects it was having on our young women," George related.

"And the buildings?" Betty asked, taking advantage of the pause in George's recital.

"Ah yes, the buildings," George said, and then began to pick up from where he had left off. "The buildings along the oceanfront all up and down the California coast were knocked down by the earthquake and swept away out into the ocean by the resulting tsunami. It was years before the coastline reappeared. The few buildings you see now were all built in the last thirty years or so."

"The effects on the women, you said, were the effects of the gas what made them barren is that right?" Lise asked being very sincere.

"That's right. We begin to get reports in from hospitals all around the world of a drastic diminish in births. It wasn't a slow thing, it happened all at once. Only a few live births came from women that were already pregnant at the time of the earthquake. After that nothing," George told them with that noticeable quiver in his voice.

"When did your scientist figure out it was the gas that made the women barren?" Betty asked.

"Not right away, they didn't know at that time about the women's inability to produce viable eggs. That came a couple of years later."

"When they did get it figured out, a request went out world-wide to stock our sperm banks to the fullest."

"That doesn't figure, does it? Lise asked.

"It does when you have a plan already in use. You see we had time travel already before the earthquake, and so it was only natural that we go back in time to bring young women here to our time," George said.

"But isn't this a parallel world so the women are not really coming from back in time?" Betty asked anxiously.

"Exactly, it would cause a disruption in our history to bring women from our own past into the present. That is why the time space manipulator device was invented. The other end of the ver-tex of the wormhole has been programmed to open into a parallel universe, which just happens to be your universe."

At this time during a break in the conservation, Lise sug-gested to Betty it was time for them to go. After saying their goodbyes, they made their way back to the car.

The return trip was uneventful, as both girls mulled over in their minds the things they had learned today. Really, their eyes had been opened by George Pait and his knowledge of what had transpired in this planet's past.

"You know Lise, at first I didn't mind too much the way I was brought here, but after talking with George I wonder if there is more too our being here than we have been told," Betty said, more wondering out loud than speaking directly to Lise.

"I don't know Betty how I feel right now. I'll have to sleep on it and we'll see tomorrow," Lise said, continuing with that train of thought. "Time heals all, as the old saying goes."

After arriving back at their apartments they decided to check out the other apartments that housed some of the other women. They walked to the apartment block directly across from their apartments. This apartment building was laid out similar to theirs with one noticeable exception. There were pictures, Laurels, big and little adorned the walls of the community room. There were scenes of the ocean crashing up against the rocks, making beautiful sound effects, so soothing to a body.

The girls could not help but wonder why their apartment only had the wall mounted TV that only showed old movies of the 40's and 50's. A voice from the far end of the room caught their attention.

"Hi there, I haven't seen you around here before," The young woman said. Both Betty and Lise turned around to face the voice. The girl who had hailed them was about their age, tall and slender, with flaming red hair.

"My name is Betty, and this is Lise, we're from across the street," Betty volunteered the information.

"Yes I've been here for about four months and this is going on Betty's third month," Lise put her two cents worth.

"You will probably be moving over here in the next month or two," The girl with the flaming red hair said. "Oh by the way my name is Ann Long and I've been here going on six months, as you can see I'm pregnant."

"Is Pregnancy a requirement for moving into this apartment building?" Betty asked with a little stiffness in her voice.

"Yes it is. Or either of you pregnant yet?" Ann asked point-blank.

"Not that we know of," Lies said laughing.

"You will never know when you are impregnated girls. I tell you they must put you to sleep or something," Ann said.

"Will they tell us before we find out ourselves?" Betty asked.

"Oh yes, they will take you to the clinic and give you an examination. If you are pregnant they will tell you then. I think they are batting a thousand right now."

"Man, getting pregnant without the thrill of sex. What a let down," Lise commented out loud.

"Yeah I agree," Betty said as she turned once more to Ann.

"Ann where do they send the pregnant girls that are showing?" Betty asked. "We haven't seen anyone yet. You are the first person we have seen with child."

I don't know. I haven't seen anyone showing either. I've even asked the old doctor that gave me the examination, but he wouldn't tell me anything," Ann said as she nervously fiddled with the dolly that had been placed on the table beside her.

"Ann would you show us around here in this building? You must know quite a lot of the girls that live here."

"Sure Betty, let me turn the oven down. I'm fixing a pot roast for my dinner, you and Lise are welcome to stay and eat with me. I'll certainly have plenty," Ann suggested as she walked the few steps to the oven and turned down the heat.

Ann led them down the hallway from her apartment and knocked on the door of the apartment next to hers. They heard stirring on the other side of the door and after a slight pause the door was swung open. A girl of dark complexion stood there expectant. When shed recognized Ann from next door, her face lit up.

"Ann what a pleasure. I was just going to call you," The girl said, while looking at Betty and Lise.

Joan, this is Betty and this is Lise. They are from the apartment building across the street," Ann said as she introduced the two girls to Joan.

"Oh you haven't been here too long have you?" Joan asked as she stepped back into the room and with her demeanor inviting them into her apartment.

"No, only a couple of months for me, Lise has been here four months I think," Betty said.

"Have either of you been impregnated yet," Joan asked in a matter of fact voice.

"No, if we have we don't know it," Lise said in response.

"Yeah that's right, you wouldn't know. But you'll know when you begin to show," Joan said.

The girls settled down into a long discussion of how they were being treated by the locals and where they might be going when they're due date came closer. Finally with a look at her watch, Ann exclaimed her pot roast must be about done by now and invited Joan to come along and join her, Betty and Lise, for a meal.

Chapter Twenty - One

The meal, which consisted of roast beef cooked with whole potatoes and onions together in a crock pot was delicious and when
served with side orders of lush young sweet peas, corn on the cob,
all topped off with a dish of ice cream at the end of the meal was
simply out of this world.

"Ann, where did you learn to prepare a meal like this?" Lise
asked as she was finishing the last spoonful of ice cream.

"I guess, mostly from my mother, but with four brothers and
one girl in the family I had to learn pretty quick how to cook big
meals," Ann responded.

"I never had any siblings Ann and my mother wasn't the en-
tertaining type. I don't remember her ever cooking a big meal."

"I never learned to cook very well myself," Joan chimed in.
"I now know where I will be spending a lot of time,"

"Joan you know you are welcome here anytime," Ann told
her.

"Thank you Ann. We mostly ate TV dinners or some little
something mom would throw together," Joan said, feeling somewhat sheepish because she couldn't fix a meal such as the one she
had consumed.

After a few discussions, about nothing in particular, Betty
and Lise prepared to make their departure from Ann's. Bidding
both Joan and Ann goodbye, returned to their own apartments
across the street.

Things went fairly good for the next few months. Ann and
Joan were now showing and were waiting with anticipation as to
where they would be going.

Betty and Lise had become very good friends with Ann and
Joan and several other girls, some in their own apartment building

and some across the street. It was not with any anticipation they were looking forward to seeing Ann and Joan leave. Not knowing where they would be sent off to, maybe not ever seeing them again caused tears to well up in their eyes when they happen to think about it.

The day finally arrived, the day they were hoping wouldn't come, but it did. Betty had decided to walk across the street and visit with Ann. She had finished her morning of sunning while relaxing on the little patio adjacent to her apartment. When she arrived at Ann's door she noticed it was slightly ajar. She looked inside but did not see Ann.

"Ann, you home," Betty hollowed, trying not to be too loud. Getting no answer to her inquiry, Betty was on the verge of entering when Joan's door opened. Joan smiled at Betty and said in a hushed voice.

"She's gone. I heard some movement late last night and opened my door to see what it was and I saw them taking Ann away on a stretcher," Joan told Betty with a teary voice.

"On a stretcher," Betty repeated with some remorse.

"Yes, that is the way we go. I suppose they put you to sleep so you won't resist."

"They must have put something in her food or drink, because I know Ann would have wanted to tell you that she was leaving."

"I know she would. We talked a lot about it before she was taken," Joan said.

"Makes you mad, doesn't it?" Betty said, knowing what Joan's answer would be.

"Yes. It's the, not knowing part, that I become angry with."

"I know what you mean Joan, I feel the same way."

Betty pulled the door to Ann's apartment shut, told Joan bye and returned to her own apartment. She would fill Lise in on this information in a little while, after she had time to maul over the facts herself. Betty realized the rest of the young women were in the same boat. Why wouldn't these old people tell them where they were being taken to? All these thoughts and many more raced through her mind as she tried to imagine what was happening to Ann.

Ann had awakened in a strange place. The last thing she remembered was going to bed after a light snack. Awakening, where, she did not know. Ann slowly looked around the room. It was a room that looked for all the world like a hospital room, White walls, no curtains on the windows.

Giving the room a panoramic sweep with her eyes, Ann was able to see one chair in the far corner of the room. The chair, being occupied by a very elderly person, seemed to be the only attachment the room had to offer, other than the bed upon which she lay. Ann in her attempt to raise herself up from the prone position she had been in awoke the elderly man from his sleep. He lifted his head and spoke in a voice that was relative strong for a man that was as advanced in his age as he seemed to be.

"Miss Ann. I see you are awake. How do you feel?" He asked her.

Ann was slow in answering, composing her thoughts so as to form a collective answer that would convey to this person her displeasure of being taken against her will.

"Who are you and where have you taken me to?" Ann asked in a low voice that did not conceal her anger.

"My name is Alex and you are here in Chicago."

"Chicago, why?" Ann asked quickly.

"Yes you have been brought here to Chicago. It was necessary. You see you are advanced in your pregnancy and we didn't have the facilities in Malabu to treat you that we have here in Chicago."

"Then why the secrecy. Why not just tell me that I had to come here?" Ann asked in a controlled voice.

"This is the procedure we use on all our patients," Alex told her. "We don't want to take any chances on something going wrong."

"Do you take all the women that were as far along as I was here to Chicago?" Ann asked.

"No there are other places that we can take them to," Alex replied.

"What other places?" Ann asked.

"I am not at liberty to reveal those places to you. You must understand we have your total welfare in mind and will not allow you to come to any harm."

"Well so far I have not been mistreated other than being kidnapped from my world against my will."

"Yes, we regret having to do that, but you can see the predicament we were in. I don't think many of the young women on your world would have come willingly, now do you?"

"I don't know, maybe if you explained to them and assured them they would be treated well. Also if you would allow us to return back to our world after we gave birth I think you might have had some success."

"We could not do that. The door only opens one way and it would be impossible for anyone to return back to the other world."

"Then I'm stuck here on your world, right?" Ann asked with a note of annoyance in her voice. "I only wish you would have told me in the beginning."

"I'm really sorry but that is the procedure recommended by our council committee. We can't deviate from it."

"Can't or won't."

"Can't, Miss Ann. The council committee has the final word in any conflict of interest and I must follow their lead," Alex stated as he began to raise himself from the chair. With slow and measured steps he proceeded to the door of the room and when he had opened it he turned and was silent for a moment.

I'll check on you in a few minutes. You will have the opportunity to choose your living quarters soon." With that, he turned and closed the door on his way out.

PART THREE

The Abductors

Chapter Twenty - Two

The small conference room was filled to capacity. All present were scientists and technicians that were deeply involved in the project. The speaker, who at the moment was engaged in a hushed conversation with an elderly gentleman. Finally looking up and out across the room, the speaker obvious embarrassed, called the meeting to order.

"Gentlemen it is with great concern I have called this secret meeting for today. My name is Dr. Alex North. I work here at the Valley Institute in Los Angles. Most of you I have worked with from time to time or in the least, I know of you through your previous work in the infancy of this project. There is an issue of grave concern that has come to my attention."

"Unless we get this issue resolved within the allotted time frame I'm afraid we might lose our advantage. I'll get right down to the natty gritty of what is facing us later on. First I want to spell out the conditions that have brought about this meeting. We have been compromised over the holidays.

"Yes, our security was breached and I'm afraid all our work will be made public soon. I don't know how soon, but our intelligence indicates the president and his men are busy this very minute reviewing the documents that were photographed. Our files were downloaded and stolen by a government hacker. The latest modifications for the TSMD were stolen. It is just a matter of time before the government scientists come up with a workable displacement of a topological shortcut. When they do, they can tie in with the wormhole generated at the Valley Institute of Quantum Physics in Los Angeles."

"When that happens our whole plans for the project will be null and void. I hasten to add, jail time for some if the govern-

129

ment can have their way. General McPhee has assured me they will keep a tight security watch from now on. Right now we are ok. We are continuing to operate as if nothing has happened. I can't guarantee how long we will be able to operate at this level before the lid blows off."

"For those of you thinking to fly the coop before this happens. I must tell we are all in this together. One falls we all fall. What we have been doing is paramount to our future and to the future of others in the parallel world. I can promise you we are working on a plan that will, when the time comes, help us all to escape from being revealed by the government."

President Gordon and his Special advisory on Bio-Terrorist will not find anything when they bring the FBI here. What I need from each of you is a commitment to me and to this project. You will continue to work in this atmosphere. You will be rewarded handsomely and be provided with an escape plan. I must get back to work and I need each of you to go back to work also. I will, you understand, not entertain any questions at this time. Thank you all for coming." Dr. North left the podium and strode toward the elevators to go to the operations room located on the third floor.

"Good morning Dr. North," Lyle Green, one of the scientists greeted him as he strode toward the tri-pod that was the hub of all their secret work.

"Morning Lyle. Everything going ok," Dr. North said acknowledging the salutation with a hand gesture.

"Yes, so far. It looks as of right now, we will be on schedule by tonight," Lyle replied.

"Good, I want to have most of the shipments back through the vortex by tonight. Do you think we will be able to do that?" Dr. North asked.

"Barring unforeseen accidents, we can have it done by tonight," Lyle said with confidence.

"Ok. How about seeing if you can run down General McPhee."

"Sure thing," Lyle replied.

On his way to the hub of operations Dr. North began to rehash the totally unexpected turn of events that had transpired.

Only in the last forty-eight hours things had gotten out of control. General McPhee assured him their little secret would be safe. Ha! Was he ever wrong? He made a mental note to get some answers from General McPhee.

On approaching the hub, Dr. North noticed how busy the technicians were getting everything through the tri-pod. He had instructed them nothing incriminating could be left behind. He marched on by and entered a half concealed office.

It was his office. It was an office where he could be himself. Dr. North needed a respite from the self-control he had to exert to keep up this human composure. He slowly let himself return to his own preferred shape. It was a shape that was so much in contrast to humans. The man that called himself Dr. North slowly admired himself in the mirror. He was a strong looking figure of a man, no, not a man, he had been in the shape of the human Dr. North too long. He was a genshee. He had two thousand genshees working with him on this project. A project his home world considered tantamount to life itself.

The genshee parading himself as Dr. North opened the refrigerator door and removed a plastic bowl filled with a reddish brown substance. The Genshee, whose name was unpronounceable in the human dialect, placed the bowl on the table and with an outstretched arm, thinner than a human's arm, broke off a piece of the food, if that was what it was, brought it to his mouth and with a look of pleasure, tasted for a mere moment before swallowing the bit whole. He emitted a grunt and reached for another bit but was interrupted by the door of his office opening and Lyle entered.

Upon seeing the Genshee in his natural body immediately let himself go also.

"I needed to be back in my natural shape again also. It's so hard to maintain this ungodly human body shape for long," The alien who called himself Dr. North said to the other alien.

"Yes, I was ready to revert back to myself too. It will be good to end this project," the other alien stated as he reclined himself on one of the two chairs in the room.

"We can all rest easier if we can wrap this up and get ourselves through the vortex before the United States government catches on to what we are about,"

Having the ability to cloud human minds so that humans would not be able to see the aliens as they really were, but to see only how the aliens projected themselves when around humans. It was impossible to differentiate between the aliens and humans when they were in this projected mode.

When not in their projected mode as they now were, they would appear to humans as about six feet tall, walking upright on two legs. They were humanoid in appearances but the texture of there body was different. The skins of the aliens were of a leathery texture, brownish in color. The heads of the aliens were where the most difference could be observed. Elongated and slighted pointed on top, made them appear to be serpent like, having slits that contain black eyeballs that were independent of each other. They each had on garb that was of a coarse material, kind of like a jump suit, for a better explanation.

Both of the aliens relaxed as long as they dared before resuming the projected human forms they were previously in. Mingling back in with the rest of the people busy bringing crates to the tri-pod and sending it on its way through the wormhole. It was going to be a busy week ahead of them.

Chapter Twenty - Three

Lank had met with his three friends who had successfully accomplished a raid on the Valley team operations. They had regrouped in the safe house just as they had intended, reviewing all the material they had been able to remove.

"I think we hit pay dirt." Don't you?" Lank asked in a spirited voice.

"Yeah, I'm proud of myself," Lewis said laughing.

"Ha, I thought I was going to have to go back in there and retrieve you again like last time," Raymond came back.

"Just how did you get out?" Lank asked. "I never saw you come out and I waited an additional thirty minutes."

"Its secret know how, don't you know," Lewis, shrugging his shoulders, said with a sly grin on his face.

"It won't be much of a secret when you get caught one of these days," Raymond said.

"Ah I'm just like the Jackal, disappearing into the woodwork."

"You wish," Raymond came back.

"OK, I'll get all this stuff back to Washington. President Gordon already has a team assembled to go over all this evidence. I'll stop off in St. Louis and pick up what Jeff has for us on the downloaded files." Lank told them.

All three of them men stayed and helped Lank package up all the material from the raid. It was packaged in a neat bundle and ready for shipment by secure means to the president's assembled crew.

When Lank arrived in St. Louis airport Jeff was waiting on him to arrive. He had met Lank at the baggage claim area and after shaking hands Lank had claimed his travel bag, Jeff guided him to his waiting car. The driver of the car grunted as Lank and Jeff climbed into the back seat.

"Back to the office, Pete," Jeff instructed as he settled back for the ride and some conversation with Lank.

"Well, Lank, how is everything in California?" Jeff asked.

"Fine, it couldn't be nicer. California is really a nice state."

"I know. Sometimes I wish I had of settled down there instead of here in Missouri." Jeff replied with a wishful tone noticeably in his voice.

"Missouri has its good points too, you know," Lank said, then with further reflection, went on. "Jeff, you have a lot of nice attractions, such as Branson, Silver Dollar City, the Bass Pro Shop to name a few."

"Yeah, I guess that's true. I just get itchy feet sometimes I think," Jeff said.

"You need my job for a month. I guarantee you will be ready to go home and do nothing."

"You couldn't give me your job, no amount of money would I take on your responsibilities," Jeff declared earnestly.

They continue to bat the breeze, ensuring nothing of a classified manner would be divulged, thereby limiting their small talk to items of no consequences. Finally, arriving at the building where Jeff's office was located, they removed themselves from the car and with a "many thanks" to the driver, both entered the building and into the elevators where Jeff punched the sixth floor button.

Neither one felt any inclination to talk while in the elevator. Lank was wondering what was on the files Jeff had downloaded. Jeff kept thinking to himself about whether or not he was able to sniff out all the programs that were germane to the mission.

The elevator eventually reached the sixth floor where Jeff's office was located. When the elevator doors opened Lank held back, allowing Jeff to lead him down the hallway to his office. Jeff opened the third door on the right and held it open while Lank entered the well lit and perfectly designed office. Pleasing to the eye was Lank's thought on it. Jeff's secretary was at her desk scanning the computer, occasionally writing something down on a pad in front of her. Noticing Jeff and Lank's entry into the office, she quickly turned and with smiling eyes welcomed Jeff back from the airport then quickly embraced Lank. Paula was like Janet and Pat, she was a CIA clerk with a full security clearance.

"I'm so glad you are ok. I was so worried," she murmured.

"Never in doubt Paula, never a doubt," Lank responded.

"Yeah with Raymond and Lewis on the job there is nothing you three couldn't get done," Jeff chimed in.

"Don't leave yourself out Jeff. You know how important your part in this mission was," Lank said, as Paula released him from her welcoming embrace. "The job wouldn't be complete without your input."

"I know," Jeff responded. "I just miss the action with you three, like it used to be."

"Well hang in there Jeff. This is just the start of this mission. There will be ample opportunity for action, probably more than we realize or want, before everything is over."

"You men, never satisfied until you are right in the middle of everything," Paula commented.

"Every person's job is important to President Gordon. He is waiting to see what we have," Lank told her.

"Listen, guys," Jeff interjected. "When all this is over I would like for all of us to have a get together here. Lank you remember the lake we went to a while back." Jeff asked.

"Yeah, nice lake."

"Well on the other end of it there is a park with plenty of tables and Bar-B-Que pits. Let's have us a good old family get-together," Jeff said with enthusiasm.

"Sounds good to me. How about you Paula?" Lank asked.

"That would be great. Al would really enjoy seeing all of you again," Paula said.

"How is Al doing Paula? Has he any thoughts about coming back onboard with us?" Lank asked.

"No, and I'm glad. At Least I have him home every night."

"Poor Al," Jeff mocked in teasing Paula.

Jeff turned after that and gave Paula a little hug saying: "You're doing a good thing for Al. I'm glad."

"Lank let me get you all the files I was able to download from the Valley," Jeff said as he walked toward the wall safe hidden behind a false wall. He quickly spun the combination dial and opened the safe. Reaching in he removed a hardback folder that contained twenty-one CD's. Jeff handed the folder to Lank who took it and noticed how neatly each disc was labeled.

"Looks good to me Jeff. When can you get it to Washington on the secure line?"

"We will get it bundled up and it will go out at eight pm tonight along with some other things I need to send," Jeff said.

"That will be good Jeff. Ok I guess I'll grab a bite to eat and then mosey on over to the airport."

"Lank, why don't we both go and grab a steak on me," Jeff said as he took the folder and gave it to Paula, knowing she would take care of it.

"Sounds good to me Jeff, I'm so hungry I could eat the whole cow, I think."

"Paula I'll guess I will see you tomorrow." Jeff said following Lank towards the door.

"Good to see you again Paula, give my best to Al and let him out once in a while," Lank kidded Paula.

"Ahh he gets out now more than he should Lank," Paula laughs.

Both men waved their goodbyes to Paula and strode down the hall toward the elevators. With luck the elevator would still be on their floor. No such luck. They had to wait a few minutes until it ascended back up to the sixth floor.

The bell chimed, signaling the elevator had arrived and then the doors opened. When the doors opened, a lone man smiled at them as he made his way out of the elevator. He was of nondescript, just an average Joe, nothing to mark him any different from any other person. Lank and Jeff both made mental notes of the man's appearance and watched as he went past Jeff's office and around the corner of the hall.

"Ring any bells Jeff," Lank asked.

"No, never seen him before. Probably an ok guy."

"Probably right. Could be we are just looking for trouble."

"I suppose so. Lets get on down to that steak house.

The steaks were out of this world. Just enough pink left to really make them savory. Not much was said between them as they ate their steaks. Only when finished did they engage in any kind of meaningful conversation.

"Lank, how long do you figure it will take before we know what we are up against?" Jeff asked, while wiping his fingers on the napkin beside him.

"I don't really know for sure. I think it might depend on how long it takes to decipher the files you supplied us with." Lank suggested.

"Yeah, That could take a while. I guess it depends on how good the guys are that's working on it," Jeff said.

"I think they are pretty good. I know Professor Manning is one of the best in his field. If anyone can figure it out, the Prof can."

"That's good to hear," Jeff said in a kind of offhanded voice.

"Jeff, I guess I had better get moving if I want to get out of here tonight," Lank suggested.

"Ok," Jeff said, reaching for the ticket before Lank latched onto it. "If you're ready then, let's roll."

Jeff drove Lank to the airport, which did not take as long. The traffic was light and they were on the near side of the airport anyway.

Jeff pulled the car to the curb where the baggage area was located and Lank disembarked from the vehicle. Waving goodbye to Jeff, he made his way into the airport and down the walkway to his flight desk. Obtaining his boarding pass Lank decided to go ahead and go through security. He had no baggage to check so it was an easy shot to walk through the metal detector.

Mildly surprised at the efficiency of the operator, Lank pulled his shoes off when directed. He remembered the shoe bomber on a previous flight and had no qualms at all about this procedure.

After he had cleared security, Lank checked with the flight attendant to make sure his flight was still on time. Being assured it was, he strolled on down to the cafeteria and ordered a cup of coffee. He chose a table that was on the outskirts of the cafeteria area and sat down to a peaceful few minutes.

Lank did not think he had been observed here in the airport but then that was the mark of a good surveillance man, keeping the quarry at ease. He had used many of these same techniques in his past assignments. Nevertheless Lank scrutinized all the occupants with his trained eye who were at the cafeteria. Nothing seemed out of the ordinary. His attention now turned to the waiters behind the bar waiting on folks. Most of them were young kids, however there were two middle age men that had just come out of, what looked like the door to the manager's office, and proceeded to glance at Lank.

They quickly averted their eyes when they became aware of Lank's interest in them. They had obviously shed their ties and coats and looked out of place among the young kids. Lank studied their walk as they left the cafeteria, searching his mind, comparing their walk with known agents of the enemy. When suddenly, it came to the forefront of his mind, he had seen these two before.

Finishing his coffee, Lank strolled back to his gate area and choosing a seat that faced the runway, he sat down prepared to wait comfortably until boarding time. He now remembered where he had seen the two before. It was the same two Iranians who had sabotaged his team's efforts in Baghdad when they were trying to get close to Sadam Hussein's living quarters.

He had been face to face with both of them in Baghdad just before the explosive charge went off. Only the explosive did not go off where it had been planted. The charge had been moved to another location. Since these two were the only men in close proximity to the explosives it had to be them that had removed the explosives to another area away from Sadam Hussien. To be able to accomplish such a task they would have had to been trained in making and exploiting these charges.

Lank had been sitting there for about fifteen minutes looking out at the plane that was being serviced prior to the flight to New York. Into his view came two men dressed in coveralls driving the work trucks pulling baggage.

They drove up close to the cargo door underneath the plane and begin unloading baggage and placing it into the plane.

Suddenly it clicked in Lank's mind. Their walk was the walk of the two men who had been in the cafeteria. The unusual thing about it was the clothes they had on in the cafeteria. It was highly unlikely baggage handlers would be dressed in those kinds of clothes, blue jeans and a t-shirt.

They would have had on the uniforms that baggage handlers customarily wore at airports. Lank watched the two men loading the cargo into the belly of the plane for a few more minutes. He made up his mind and using his cell phone he dialed the code number for security at this airport. The call was answered on the first ring and a firm voice asked.

"St. Louis International Airport Security, May I help you."

Lank gave his name and his coded government identification number assigned him by the Home Land Security. The voice on the other end of the line, after a slight pause, came back on.

"Yes sir Mr. Miller. What can I do for you?"

Lank went on to relay what he had seen and what he suspected about the two men. He was asked what airline and what gate. Upon giving the required information Lank was assured it would be checked out. He would be told a security man would be along shortly and escort him to the airport security operations center.

Only a few minutes had passed before there was unusual excitement on the airplane-parking runway.

Two security cars with lights flashing and sirens going swarmed down on the two men who were still loading cargo into the plane. Shortly afterward three more local police cars came on the scene in like manner. Lank did have a chance to see the two men apprehended by the police. The security officer walked up to Lank and asked if it was Lank Miller.

"Mr. Miller, Mr. Lankford Miller." He said with authority in his voice.

"Yes I'm Lank Miller. He responded.

"Sir, if you would, please come with me."

Lank followed him to a door in the wall. The Security Officer opened the door and motioned to Lank to go through. The door opened only to a stairway that led up to the top of the airport. Arriving at the top of the stairs, Lank was told to go on through. The door in front of him opened into a huge room. Operators sat at scopes monitoring all kind of things Lank surmised.

A Navy Lt. Commander met him before he had reached the center of the room.

"Mr. Miller, How are you sir?"

"Fine and yourself?" Lank returned.

"Just fine sir. I am Navy Lt. Commander John McMasters. We thought it best to bring you on board before the excitement, if any, starts," He explained.

"Yes it will be good if my suspicions pan out in this case," Lank told him.

"We have delayed the flight an hour, which should give us time to search the plane for any bombs or other destructive devices."

"Sir if you wish, you can wait in my office until this thing is over. If you just have to get back to New York in a hurry, I have a navy jet at your disposal,"

"No, I'm not in that big of a hurry. Anyway I would like to see what transpires here before I leave." Lank said with a grin on his face.

"Fine, I'll see you are kept abreast of all developments."

"Good, thanks Commander," Lank said.

The better part of an hour had transpired before Lank was informed of what had happened so far. The navy officer had briefly stuck his head inside of his office where Lank was waiting and informed him the two men had been arrested.

Lank thought about that for a brief time, coming to the conclusion, if the men had been arrested then the security men must have found something incriminating.

Another fifteen minutes or so had passed before the naval officer McMasters came into the room. He took a seat directly across from Lank. Looking Lank straight in the eye he began;

"Two bombs were found in the cargo hold. They were sufficient enough, if exploded, to tear the plane apart.

The two bombs were successfully removed from the plane and defused. A thorough search of the plane was conducted and no further explosives devices were found. The plane will be released shortly to continue its flight to New York. The two men were taken to Police headquarters here in St. Louis for further questions.

"Any clue as to who they were working for?" Lank asked.

"NSA has a file on them. They are members of Iranian terrorist group. The FBI will be questioning them and I suppose will more than likely find out who they were working for."

"I'm just glad they were caught and the bombs removed. You know it would have been my ass blown up along with all the other passengers if I had of been on that plane.

"You are quite right sir. We owe you a debt of gratitude," McMasters told Lank.

"I'm just glad I remembered where I had seen them before."

"Anyway the whole department is thankful you were on the job tonight. I'll have a man walk you back to your gate and once again, accept my thanks."

Lank was happy to be boarding his plane and was so thankful of his training in profiling. Little did the Lt. Commander know, but there were more to what almost happened, then was obvious to the eye. Lank knew this was not just any ordinary attempt by terrorist to blow up just any plane.

He was sure they had him in mind along with any material he would have with him. That is why he had decided to send everything they had collected at the Valley lab by military secure service. The MSS had always protected their material. Lank could not think of a time when anything he had sent via them had ever been in jeopardy.

Lank now turned his attention the amenities offered in first class. The first thing he wanted was just to have a quite and quick fight. He missed Mary Ann and Jen. Oh well, as he had mentioned many times in the past. It comes with the job. He loved his job and would not be doing anything else, although there were times when he had wished he was somewhere else.

Like the time he rescued Lewis and Raymond when they were inside the Vladivostok harbor in their snorkeling gear, placing explosives along the side of a sub docked there. Lank concealed behind a stack of cargo located about a hundred feet away, acting as lookout for them, noticed a couple of Russian sub sailors become excited as they peered over the side of the sub. They had noticed the air bubbles coming up.

It wasn't long before a Russian officer was by their side looking down into the sea. Lank knew he had to get them out quickly and out of the harbor. He quickly took the special radio from his backpack and placing the specially built antenna designed for maximum range through the medium of water transmitted the special coded signal to Raymond and Lewis.

Lank would have no idea if they had received the signal or not until they met at the prearranged place.

In the meanwhile the Russian sub crew were preparing to send down divers. Lank imagine they would not attempt to use depth charges this close in to other ships, however that might be debatable given their past behavior.

Lank eased himself from his hidden vantage point and quietly slipped back into the shadows of the buildings along the port. It would be approximately a quarter of a mile back to their prearranged meeting place and he hope beyond hope those two had slipped out of the port harbor unobserved.

He did not have to wait too long before two shadows emerged from an alley directly in front of him. Lank waited until he was sure it was them before he gave the all clear low whistle.

Upon hearing the low whistle, both men quietly moved to the side of Lank. Removing the rubber mask from his head, Raymond filled Lank in on the details of what they had accomplished. They had been working on the bottom of the harbor directly beneath the Russian nuclear sub.

Plastic explosives buried a few feet into the sand at the bottom of the harbor would result in a massive explosion that would lift the sub completely out of the water, hopefully tearing a hole in the bottom thereby sinking the sub. This was how, after the cold war was over, war was still being raged.

Lank remembered back before the end of the cold war era how the US had played tic for tac with the Russians in disabling each countries subs. It was work, had the news media ever gotten a hold of it, would have placed both countries in an embarrassing situation. Of course the Russian Government would have accused the USA, forcing the USA to reveal what the Russians had been doing to us.

Lank knew his job and that of his team and various other teams, were hidden from the politicians who, if they had even a sniff, would ruin a president and his party very quickly.

Link's reminiscing was brought to an end when the stewardess asked him if she could get him anything.

"No not right now, thanks anyway," Lank answered her. She had smiled and turned to the next passenger with the same question.

Lank's thoughts now turned to the team gathered by Professor Manning at Columbia. He knew they were awaiting the files and documents procured by the raid on the Quantum lab at Los Angels. It would not be an easy task simply because of the huge amount they would have to go through. Lank had no doubts of the outcome, only he hoped they would be able to come up with an explanation as to the huge amount of abductions of young women in the last three years.

Lank drifted off in a nap still thinking about all the disappearing young women and where they were at. It wasn't till the fastened seat belts light came on with the two toned bell accompanying it woke Lank from a much needed nap. The plane descended rather quickly, he thought, and leveled out over the runway. A thud was felt and heard as the plane touched down and continued traveling down the runway finally slowing down before turning onto taxi runway.

Lank had not informed anyone of his flight so he was not expecting anyone to meet him at the airport. Sure enough as he walked through the terminal he saw no one he recognized. Having no baggage he walked out of the terminal and hailed a cab.

He gave his cab driver his home address and settle back for the ride home. It was beginning to become dark when the cab stopped in front of his house. Lank paid him and the cab driver smiled and thanked him for the generous tip.

Lank used his house key and unlocked the front door. Standing in the doorway for a few moments, Lank raised his voice calling out to his wife.

"Mary Ann, I'm home," he called out. In a moment, Mary Ann emerged from the kitchen with her apron on, a swipe of flour on her cheek, looking for the entire world like an advertisement.

"I'm so glad your home, Lank," she spoke in an animated voice, showing her delight he was home again.

"Yeah, me too, it has been a long few days being away from you and Jen," Lank said as he put his arms around her and held her till he was sure she would not break out in tears. It so embarrassed her when she had broken down in tears in the past.

They walked on and entered the kitchen where Lank was sure there would be something good cooking on the stove. Sure enough a big pot was on the stove simmering. From the aroma coming from the pot, Lank knew it was Italian spaghetti, one of his favorite dishes, especially when served with garlic bread.

"Ahh spaghetti with garlic bread," Lank said expressing his delight.

"It's ready, have a seat and I'll bring it to the table," Mary Ann said to Lank while she turned and yelled for Jen to come to supper.

There was a muddle response from the bedroom adjacent to the kitchen and after a few moments Jen emerged with a disheveled look about her.

"Hey, it's dad," Jen exclaimed in a high-pitched voice as she ran to hug Lank.

"I missed you little girl," Lank said as he held Jen back and admired his daughter.

"I'm not so little any more dad," Jen corrected him.

"You are so right, you are growing up in a hurry."

"Jen, grab dad and you all come to the table before the spaghetti becomes cold," Mary Ann told them, bringing the big pot of spaghetti to the table.

Chapter Twenty - Four

It had been five days since Lank had returned home from St. Louis. He had spent a couple of days with his family before calling Janet at the office and telling her he would be in the next morning. She had informed him there were no pressing issues, only something was going on. Janet had told him over the phone the abductions had abruptly stopped.

There had not been any reports of any young women being abducted now for a week. Lank thought about that and what it might possibly mean. Maybe by now Professor Manning might have some answers. He would make it a point to call him from his office in the morning and quiz the old professor's mind.

The last evening Lank spent with his family. They played the monopoly game for a few hours then Jen wanted to play a charades. They had a laughingly good time with that game. Lank was not very good at some of the antics Jen and her mother put on but at least it was a family thing and they all were enjoying each other. The evening was gone before they knew it. When it was time for bed, Jen said good night and retired to her room. She would be up early tomorrow morning getting a last minute studying in.

Lank awoke to the alarm blasting on the nightstand by his head. He reached over and hit the snooze button while rubbing the sleep out of his eyes. Mary Ann was probably already awake. She did not have the ability to sleep late and had always been an early riser.

No different this time. Lank could hear dishes bumping against each other and the smell of bacon permeated into his bedroom.

It did not take Lank long to do his bathroom duties, including shaving and taking a shower, and on to having breakfast with his wife. It seems Jen hitched a ride with her friend Cyndi, wanting to arrive at school early in order to review their notes again before class started.

After he had finished eating Lank bade fair well to Mary Ann, speaking to old duke before backing the car out of the garage. Old Duke had forgiven Lank for putting the fear of god in him a few months ago or maybe he had forgotten all about it. Lank seemed to remember reading somewhere a dog's memory was not too good.

He carefully backed the car out of the garage and into the circular driveway an onto the street before accelerating and proceeding toward his office which was about twenty minutes away, providing traffic was light.

He arrived at his office without incident and parked his car beside Janet's car. Noticing the weather did not look so good this morning. A big black cloud was hanging in the distance to the southwest. Probably going to rain all day today Lank thought as he continued on into the building.

Janet was busy at her desk as he entered the office. Upon seeing Lank she quickly stood up and walked around her desk exclaiming with great pleasure at seeing Lank again.

"I'm so glad you are back Lank. You know how I worry about you when you are away." Janet told him while giving him a hug and patting him on the back.

"I know and I appreciate it. We were ok this time, everything went just as planned," Lank told her proceeding toward the coffee pot. When he had finished pouring himself a cup of joe, Lank turned to Janet and asked her to get Professor Manning on the phone.

"He should still be at home, if not, then try his office at Columbia," Lank told her.

"Ok I'm sure I can run him down," Janet said. "Are you going to be here at the office very long?"

"Yes I will be here for a few hours. I need to catch up on some of the work I have been putting off," Lank said, not really looking forward to sitting down behind his desk.

It didn't take Janet long to find Professor Manning. He had just walked into his office at Columbia when his secretary motioned to him he had a phone call.

"Lank, I have Professor Manning on the line."

"Good," Lank said as he picked up his receiver.

"Hello Professor Manning, How are you doing?" Lank said with enthusiasm.

"Fine Lank, just fine," answered the professor. "How are you doing?"

"I'm ok, Just resting up from my little trip."

"Yeah, I heard about your vacation. California, wasn't it?"

"That's right but I was so busy I didn't get to enjoy the beaches."

"You know I have never been to California, the closest I got was Las Vegas one time," Professor Manning said.

"I would think Las Vegas would be close enough," Lank came back laughing.

"You are so right, lost a bundle that time in the casinos."

"Professor, are you far enough along in the project that it would be beneficial if I came by?" Lank asked with a note of urgency in his voice.

"Yes you probably do need to come by. I was going to call you today and suggest you do just that." The professor said his voice matching the urgency in Lank's voice.

"Ok I'll be by this afternoon, Will you be there all day? Lank asked the Professor.

The rest of the morning went along smoothly. Lank finished up most of the paper work that had accumulated while he had been gone. He cleaned swept his desk with one hand and said to Janet.

"I'm all caught up now. Would you like for me to take you to lunch, maybe the Pizza Place?" He asked as he replaced his coffee cup on the table next to the coffee pot.

"Sure, I would like a some pizza right now. It will be good to get out of the office for a little while," Janet responded.

"Ok lock up the office, put the answering machine on and let's go," was Lank's way of making a quick get away from the office.

Both enjoyed the respite from the office and really did enjoy each other's company. Of course the pizza was simply out of this world. A person could not find a better pizza then what was made here at the Pizza Place. They talked and Lank brought Janet up to par on some of the things that were not in his reports to the director of DHS.

"You know, Lank, I just can't imagine what the reason is for all these kidnappings, or abductions as they are referred to now," Janet lamented.

"I don't know either, but I hope to have some concrete evidence to report to the President the next time he wants to see me," Lank mentioned as a passing thought.

Soon, though, Lank knew he had to get on over to Columbia and converse with Professor Manning. He was sure something had been learned. When he suggested as much to Janet they made their way out and walked to Lank's car. He drove her back to the office and waved good-bye to her as she departed into the UN building where their office was located.

Lank weaved his way back into traffic and headed on out to the University, checking his rear view mirror occasionally, from force of habit more than anything else. He had not noticed anyone tailing since he had returned from St. Louis a week ago, however a person could not be too careful.

Upon reaching the campus of Columbia, Lank drove around to the Quantum Physics Laboratory and parked in the visitors' parking space.

He set the security alarm on his car with a push of the button on his remote and headed toward the entrance of the lab. The information desk was usually filled by a student making a little extra money to help pay expenses. Not so today, there was a man in a suit manning the desk.

"Good afternoon, I need to see Professor Manning," Lank told the man at the desk in a matter of fact voice.

"Your name sir."

Before Lank could answer he heard Professor Manning's voice coming from behind a large crate.

It's ok Dobson, his name is Lankford Miller, he's cleared," the professor directed his statement to the man at the desk.

"Sorry sir, I did not recognize you. Go right on through," he told Lank.

"Thanks," Lank said as he walked toward where the Professor was hunched down over a large box.

"Help me here, will you Lank?"

"What is this thing Professor Manning?" Lank asked as he helped the professor lift the heavy object from the wooden crate it had been stored in.

"Its what I had our lab people make for me. It's an encoder that receives the information the TSMD sends out to it."

"Well Professor, that doesn't tell me a whole lot," Lank said.

"It is a device that receives from a distant point, called the TSMD, through a wormhole and reassembles onto a tripod. The tripod acts as a collection point before sending the information on its way to its final destination. The tripod kind of acts as a relay in time," the professor explained.

"Have you learned all this from the files and documents we got for you from the Valley lab," Lank asked.

"You bet, and then some. There is only one thing lacking we have not figured out yet Lank."

"What's that professor?"

"How to manipulate the other end of the wormhole so we can send the information on the tripod to a designated place in time," the professor said. "We have been unable so far to find the right frequency that will cause it to resonate."

"Have you tried 121 ghz yet?" Lank asked.

"Not yet, we are inching our way up. I haven't even found a harmonic of the fundamental frequency to work with. What may I ask, caused you to suggest that frequency?"

"I don't know, I think I must have seen it displayed somewhere," Lank said as he was trying to remember where he had seen or heard the frequency.

The professor called some of his lab technicians over to finish setting up the encoder.

"Set the encoder to 121 ghz and see what happens," the professor instructed one of the lab boys. He then turned back to Lank and suggested they retire to his office.

Lank followed him back to what looked like a hole in the wall but surprisingly held a desk with a couple of chairs placed behind the desk.

"Professor what happened to your other office, the big impressive one you had when I was here before," Lank asked.

"Piled full of things, I guess, anyway I wanted to be closer to my work," he remarked. "Anyway I want to go over with you as to what we have found out so far."

Lank listened as the Professor went on to explain what he was doing with all the new information. Lank's curiosity was aroused when the professor mentioned something about alien technology.

"You said alien technology was involved. What did you mean?" Lank asked.

"Only that I don't see how it was possible for the valley lab to have developed this knowledge on their own. It involves things I have never dreamed of."

"Like what professor?" Lank asked with a puzzled look on his face.

"Well for one thing, how was it possible they knew how to migrate the other end of the wormhole to any parallel world they desired," the Professor declared. "Furthermore, we have no procedures for the development of the tripod, no such details as were found on some of the files."

"Where do you think the information came from?" Lank asked.

"I did not know then, but I sure as hell know now," he said.

"From alien technology?" Lank asked.

"Where else could they have gotten it from," the professor stated.

The rest of the afternoon and well into the early part of the evening were spent in listening and watching the professor and his crew work on the station, as it was now called. Professor Manning explained how they were setting up a duplicate station here at Columbia using the alien technology, as it was now commonly referred to among the working crew.

Lank decided it was time he should leave. He would definitely be back first thing in the morning. He informed the professor of his intentions and departed the lab.

He had an uneventful trip home, the traffic was a lot less than expected even at this late hour which made it a pleasant trip. Mary Ann's car was parked inside the garage with the garage door still up. Probably anticipating his late arrival. He steered the car into the parking space beside his wife's car. Old Duke came from somewhere outside in the yard wagging his tail wanting his head petted.

"Hey old boy, what have you been up to, you old hound."

Duke let out a half growl, half bark of pure pleasure at seeing his master home. Lank continued on into the kitchen from the garage. Mary Ann came from Jens room pushing the vacuum machine.

Seeing Lank she mumbled something about why couldn't Jen keep her room clean.

"What's wrong now?" Lank asked. Knowing the answer even before he has asked the question.

"Her room was a mess. Her clothes were scattered all over the room. Why can't she just put her dirty clothes in the clothes hamper?" Mary Ann went on.

"You know how these teenage girls are these days, don't you hon?" Lank asked in an attempt to sooth her ruffled feathers.

"Where is Jen at now?"

"She is staying the night at Cyndi's tonight. They have a big day planned tomorrow I think."

"Well if I had of known we were going to be by ourselves, I would have come home earlier," Lank said with a mischievous smile lurking at the corners of his mouth.

"I didn't know until about an hour ago myself. Jen called and said she wanted to stay the night at Cyndi's."

"I'm glad they are such good friends. I really like Joe and his wife Judy. Nice folks, don't you think so?"

"Oh yes, Judy is really nice. I see her quite a lot when I attend Jens school activities." Mary Ann said.

"You know, it has been quite some time since I saw Joe. I must try to find time to see him soon," Lank commented.

"How was your day? Any more abductions?"

"No, not since last week. They just all of a sudden quit happening. I don't know why." Lank answered.

Both engaged in small talk until bedtime and then Lank took a hot shower, which did wonders for his old stiff muscles. Returning to bed and finding Mary Ann already under the covers he slid in next to her. They quietly embraced with passionately kisses, relishing each other's body until the wee hours of the morning before finally falling asleep.

Lank was awakened by the delicious smell of brewing coffee. He made the effort to get out of bed and wash his face before applying lather to his face and shaving. He splashed aftershave lotion on, then finishing dressing before sauntering into the kitchen.

Mary Ann was pouring a cup of coffee for him. He sat down at the table as she brought him his coffee, then a plate with eggs, bacon and buttered toast. Lank enjoyed the breakfast, as he always did. He finished eating before telling Mary Ann his plans for the day. He had wanted to get an early start and be at the lab by eight. That was out of the question now. He still would get there before nine anyway and he guessed that was early enough.

Lank pulled into the visitor parking space at the lab just in time to witness a large van backing up to the ramp at the side of the lab. His curiosity peaked; he hurried on into the lab and sought out Professor Manning.

Finding the professor hunched over some drawings he had spread out over the large table, Lank walked up beside him and spoke his name.

"Professor Manning."

The professor looked up from the drawings and upon recognizing Lank, motioned with his hand for him to have a look at the drawings.

"Lank I could kick myself. You know what this is," He gestured at the drawings.

"No I don't, clue me in," Lank said.

"Well, look here. This is a neuron schematic of the brain's opioid system," professor exclaimed excitedly. "It shows what happens when the synaptic transmission allows the propagation of nerve impulses from one nerve cell to another."

"What does that mean in layman terms professor?" Lank asked.

"Ok, I'll see if I can explain it this way. The transmission occurs at a junction where the axon of the presynaptic neuron terminates at a predestinated location on the postsynaptic. Now when the axon is stimulated by a known frequency it causes the receptors to become dormant, in effect eliminating their effect. Now the presynaptic neuron must find another location to attach itself to. This is where the wormhole comes into play. The TSMD provides a space for the vertex of the wormhole to occur at the precise location of the axon, thereby funneling the whole body into the front end of the wormhole.

It then travels through the wormhole and materializes onto a tripod or gate, if you will, located on a parallel world," The professor explained as best he could.

"Easy to explain but hard to understand," Lank suggested.

"Yes that's correct. You see this is exactly how the TSMD encodes the DTS. This transmitting time/space device works on the same principle the human body nervous system does. I don't understand how it works but I do know the technology is not of this world. We don't have anything to compare with this."

"Professor Manning, I can see this working here, but how can it be applied to someone hundreds of miles away being snatched through the worm hole?" Lank asked.

"Glad you asked that Lank. You see there is a missing piece of gear. A piece of gear that will cause the receptor to become dormant," the Professor went on. "You see those that are transmitted from a distant will arrive here because this is where the receptor has been placed, somewhere between the entrance end of the wormhole and the start end of the wormhole. This end of the wormhole has it termination on a parallel world of the aliens choosing.

"I just thought of something. The girl that disappeared right before I came upon the scene had purchased a necklace with a medallion hanging from it a few weeks before she was abducted and there were reports of other girls having purchasing one also.

Do you think that necklace might be the missing gear? Lank asked.

"Lank have there been any reports of the medallion being warm to the touch?"

"Yep, both her mother and the girl expressed some concern at the medallion being warm."

"It would have to be warm, you see, it's a nuclear transmitter that prevents the neuron receptors from receiving the neurons and redirecting them to the tripod. You know the same way it happens in the opioid system."

"I see. Professor I wonder if we could get our hands on one of those medallions?" Lank asked.

"It would be nice but not necessary. We have the capability right here of being able to transmit all the way through the worm-hole. Only one problem though, we need an exceptional steady power supply. We can't take the chance of losing power or having a power dip right in the middle of a transport. That is why I have ordered a megawatt generator with a built in stabilizer. It should be in that large van parked around to the side of the lab." The professor said looking up at Lank.

"Man you folks have sure been busy last night." Lank stated.

At that moment a lab technician approached Professor Manning with an urgent look upon his face.

"Sir," He began. "Where do you want us to place that large generator?"

"Good deal, I'll be right over there and show you." The professor said.

"Then I'll be off Professor. There are some things I want to find out. I'll check back with you later on today." Lank informed Professor Manning.

With a wave of his hand the professor acknowledged Lank and started off in the direction the lab technician had gone.

Lank wanted to check back with the mother of Betty Moulton and find out just where she had purchased the medallion. That meant a trip up into Queens to where the mother lived. If he could get his hands on one of those medallions, just maybe some of these pieces could come together in his mind. He did not fully understand the explanation given by the Professor as to why it was possible for a person to just disappear with a popping sound.

"It took Lank a good forty five minutes to reach his destination in Queens. He finally found a place to park two streets over, and walked back to the apartment where Mrs. Moulton resided.

Lank pressed the buzzer button for her apartment. A voice came through the speaker asking who it was. Lank gave her his name and the reason he wanted to see her. When the door unlocked, he went on through to the elevators. Mrs. Moulton lived on the third floor in apartment three oh five and was waiting with the door ajar when he approached.

"Good day Mrs. Moulton. How are you today?" Lank said.

"I'm fine. How are you doing?" Mrs. Moulton answered with a question of her own, with that she invited Lank into the apartment offering him the couch to sit on.

Lank accepted, and after looking around the apartment as if to collect his thoughts, he began to speak.

"Mrs. Moulton, I'm interested in the medallion Betty had on when she disappeared. Do you know from whom she purchased the necklace?

"Why yes. Betty was with a classmate of hers from high school the day she bought it. I think she bought it from an army navy store over on the east side."

"What is the name of Betty's school mate?"

"Mike Lisowski. I don't know where he lives. Betty told me he works for the government as a distributor of jewelry. She told me Mike makes monthly trips to Los Angels and back to New York.

"Mrs. Moulton may I take a look at Betty's senior class album?"

"Sure I'll get it for you." She said, rising up and pulling out a drawer in a small table that was placed across the room. She removed the album and walked back and handed it to Lank.

Taking the album from her outstretched hand Lank began thumbing through the book until he came across Betty's class. Scanning the pictures until he came across Mike Lisowski's picture. Lank took a long look at the picture and asked Mrs. Moulton to scan him a picture from the album on the computer that was sitting on a desk along with a scanner and printer.

"Oh that won't be necessary Mr. Miller. Mike gave Betty a picture of himself before he had to leave for Los Angels."

"May I have it? I'll see that you get it back."

"Sure, you can have it. Do you think Mike had something to do with the disappearing of my daughter?"

"I don't know. I'm interested in where he was getting his jewelry and also I want to get my hands on one of those medallions," Lank told her.

"You might be able to purchase one from the dealer of the army navy store."

"Yes I intend to explore that avenue. Well thank you Mrs. Moulton. If I get any leads on the disappearance of your daughter I'll let you know."

"Thank you. That is comforting to know," she said as tears begin to well up in her eyes.

"Goodbye Mrs. Moulton." Lank said exiting the door and walking toward the elevators.

He walked the two blocks to his car knowing what he would do. From his car he dialed his friend at New York FBI station. A clerk answered on the second ring.

"FBI, New York City, how may I help you? The clerk listened as Lank identified himself and asked for Doug Fields, the agent in charge of the office.

"One moment sir," was the answer he received.

"Hey Lank, How are you?" Doug said with enthusiasm.

"I'm doing ok Doug. How about yourself?"

"Oh I'm about the same just getting older. How's Mary Ann and your daughter? You know I haven't seen them in, let me see, over a year for sure I think. Doug exclaimed.

"Well you should get yourself hitched. There's nothing like it. Lank chided him. "I wouldn't have it any other way."

"I know, but you know how it is. I just don't have time to even date, let alone find someone to marry."

"Yeah I know. I guess I was lucky. I think Mary Ann pursued me although she won't admit it."

"That will probably be the only way I will ever marry."

"Say Doug the reason I called you, I need a favor." Lank said and then continued. "I need an agent, young lady, say about seventeen that can pose as my daughter.

"No problem. Let me know when you want her and for how long."

"I'll only need her for a few hours. I'm working on these abduction cases that have been plaguing the world." Lank explained, knowing Doug would be well aware of the abductions.

"Yep, think you might have a lead on it Lank?" he asked.

"I think so. Look Doug do you think you can let me have the agent in the next hour?" Lank asked.

"Sure can, you coming by here or shall I send her to meet you?

"I'm on my way now. I should be there in a few minutes. While I'm there Doug I'll clue you in on some of the things we have uncovered in these abductions cases."

"Good Lank, see you in a bit."

Lank broke the connection and concentrated on the rest of the short drive to the FBI office. The office was located on west Ninetieth Street in a new office building. Lank pulled into the one parking space left in front of the building and preceded to enter the building.

He had been here several times before so he knew the way to Doug's office. Arriving shortly he knocked and entered before Doug's secretary could answer his knock. Lank did not recognize the young lady. He only remembered an older lady doing secretarial work for Doug in the past. Doug came out from his office and came across and shook Lank's hand in a pumping display of affection.

"Hi Lank. It sure didn't take you long to get here. Must not have been much traffic," Doug said as he motioned Lank to come on into his office.

"New secretary Doug?" Lank asked.

"Naw, that's the agent you asked for. Agent Heather Banks. Think she will be alright for the job you have?"

"Looks good to me. I'm sure she will do just fine." Lank said as he sat down in a chair across from Doug.

"Doug I might need an FBI team to assist me. I don't know yet. It all depends on how successful Professor Manning's work is." Lank began.

"Professor Manning at Columbia eh. How's the old professor doing?"

"Right now he is loaded down in work trying to duplicate some equipment that we think was used in the abductions. It involves time travel, or at least travel to a parallel world." Lank explained, all the time watching Doug's expression to see just how much he had heard.

"Yeah I heard that Dr. Alex North was working on some kind of time travel out in Los Angels. Is it the same program Lank?"

"Yes the same program and if he is successful I'll need a team to go through and began rescuing the young women if it is possible."

"No problem Lank, you know that. I've been reading some of your reports Lank, but I did not know how far along the project was." Doug said.

"Ok, I guess then we need to bring Agent Heather Banks up to snuff on what I will be needing from her. Lank said.

"Right." Doug said as he lifted his voice to call her.

"Heather, will you come in here please." Doug said and waited until Heather entered his office.

"Heather stood in the middle of the room looking expectant at Doug. Finally Lank motioned for her to have a seat and introduced himself.

I'm Special Agent Lank Miller, Heather, and I need an assistant for a couple of hours. Want to go out on a mission with me?" Lank asked, watching for any hint of resistance.

Heather looked at Doug and when he nodded his head in the affirmative, she said yes, of course.

Lank explained to her exactly how he wanted her to act while in the army navy store. He told her it was imperative to obtain the necklace with the oblong medallion.

When he was sure she had understood what he asked of her, he asked if she minded stopping by a department store and he would buy her an outfit that would be more in line with a teen age girl out with her father.

Heather readily agreed and appeared pleased she would be working with Lank Miller. She had heard many good things about this man and his crew of undercover agents. Heather knew Lank had direct access to President Gordon any time he needed to see him and this alone stood out in her mind as exciting. Now she was to go on a mission with the great Lank Miller.

"Doug, we must be on our way. Thanks for the loan of Agent Banks. I'll have her back in a few hours."

"Anytime Lank. Just let me know when you will need the assistance of my team," Doug answered.

Lank took Heather to one of the more expensive department stores and followed as Heather looked through some of the more daring teen clothes. Finally holding up a short skirt with a pretty top, Heather waited for Lank's approval. When he nodded his head affirmative, she went into the fitting room and shortly emerged, dressed as any teenager would like to be dressed.

"Now the only thing left to do is to buy myself a pair of shoes and a matching purse." Heather remarked as she watched the expression on Agent Lank Miller's face.

"Ok, lead on," Lank replied, thinking how much Jen would appreciate an outfit like this.

Heather was a fast shopper, especially for a woman, and the shoes and matching purse really set the outfit off. She kind of strutted up to the check out register, or was it just Lank's imagination working overtime, telling the clerk she wanted to wear the clothes out of the store.

"I get to pay for these I guess, seeing I'm the dad," Lank told the clerk, mainly to allay the suspicions the clerk might have about an older man buying clothes for a young girl.

"That will be fine sir," the clerk said as she began to use the portable scanner to scan each individual piece of the outfit.

The total bill was not out of the question. Lank had seen the bills Mary Ann or Jen had spent on clothes. Digging his visa card out from his wallet he paid for the clothes and they departed from the store.

Once in the car and in route to the army navy store, Heather thanked him for the clothes and promised to return them to him when they got back to the office.

"No Heather, you keep them. It all comes out of the budget anyway," He told her. "Now are you all clear on what we have to do when we get there?" Lank asked.

"Yes I'll get that necklace for you, that is if the store has one for sale."

"It won't be on display. I was told he keeps them behind the counter out of sight. You'll have to convince him you really want it."

"I can do it. I know I can," Heather told Lank, looking him in the eye without flinching.

The army navy store was not a large store but still it had plenty of room for all the surplus goods that was acquired from the military. The store was located on Chestnut Street in the east part of town. Not the best locations, but considering what it sold and the type of clientele it attracted, it probably was in the right spot.

There was a long counter towards the back of the store that contained a variety of watches, rings and other type of jewelry. The man behind the counter was a rather heavyset man, around six feet tall, wearing horn-rimmed glasses. He made his way from out behind the counter and approached Lank.

"Good day sir. How may I help you?

"I just want to look over you merchandise. I'm looking for a computer for my daughter." Lank said, hoping this would suffice and let him walk away giving heather a chance to do her thing.

"Sir may I look at this necklace please," Heather said from the counter.

The proprietor immediately went back behind the counter anticipating a sale. He took out the necklace Heather was pointing at and placed it on top of the counter. Heather took her time admiring the necklace but in the end suggested it might not be exactly what she had in mind. This went on for some time until Heather had looked at most of the necklaces. Sensing he might loose a sale the man opened a shelf that was hidden from the front of the counter and removed a golden chain necklace with an oblong medallion on it. Heather was very careful not to be overly thrilled at recognizing this was the medallion Lank had told her about.

"Very pretty. I like it," Heather said stroking the necklace against her throat.

"Yes it is very pretty and I can give you a good buy on this one. You see this is a promotional necklace. The company wants to see how well it is received before mass producing it."

"Sounds good, exactly how much does it sell for?

"You know it is a promotional device so the company wants to know who bought it and the area of the country she lives in." If you are willing to wear the necklace all the time, I am authorized to sell it for only twenty-five dollars.

"You mean I can have this beautiful necklace with the medallion for only twenty-five dollars if I agree to wear it all the time.

"That's right. Would you like to have it miss?" the salesman asked.

"Dad, what do you think?" Heather yelled at Lank who was at the other end of the store.

"Let me look at it first Heather." Lank hollered back at her.

When Lank approached the counter he picked up the golden necklace and gave it a good once over, noticing it was gold and the medallion did really feel warm in his hand. Yes this was the necklace that the young women were wearing when they were abducted.

"How much are you asking for it?" Lank asked the proprietor.

"Only twenty-five dollars with the agreement your daughter wears it all the time for two weeks. Sir this is a promotional item and the company wants to know how well it will be accepted before they mass produce it.

"Sure looks like a good buy for me," turning to Heather he asked her what she thought of it.

"I really do like it dad and it will go well with this outfit. Complete the outfit don't you think dad?"

"Here, put it around your neck and let me see it on you." Lank encouraged her.

"Sure is pretty," Lank said reaching for his wallet and extracting his credit card.

"We'll take it sir," he told the salesman.

When the necklace was wrapped and in a bag, a short agreement form was presented to Heather, after glancing through it, filled it out with her name and address. She signed the form and the man handed the sales receipt to Lank.

They both thanked the man on their way out with Heather displaying her pleasure to her dad for buying the necklace.

Arriving back at the local FBI office they found Doug talking on the phone. Sensing it might be a long telephone call, Lank wave his hand at Doug and thanked Heather for her help. He took the necklace and headed towards his car. Once behind the wheel Lank let out a sigh of relief, thankful for Heather's help in helping him get the medallion.

Now all he wanted to do was get back with Professor Manning and show him the medallion. Maybe it would help in his calculations with his experiments with the time traveling.

Lank headed back to the lab after he had left Doug still on the phone back at the FBI office. He could go over the details of using an FBI team later on.

When he pulled into the lab parking area he noticed right away most of the cars were gone. He did not dwell on it though as he was anxious to talk with Professor Manning. Reaching the front door of the lab he pushed it open and entered. His first glance around the room revealed no one was there. That's funny, he thought, I wonder where everyone is. He walked on back to the little room that Professor Manning called his office, noticing on his way the extra equipment and bays of electronic boxes with different colored lights. Reaching the office and finding the door ajar, he pushed the door open as far as it would go and entered. Lank was not in the least surprised to find the professor hunkering over some blown up pictures of what looked like where a chicken had wiped his feet on a blank page of paper. Little squiggly marks and symbols filled the page.

"Professor Manning, it's me," Lank said, hoping not to give the professor a scare.

"Come on in Lank."

"Don't you ever have to sleep?" Lank asked truly concerned.

"I take power naps Lank. I find a power nap for ten or fifteen minutes every six or seven hours is all I need."

"You've been at this for I don't know how many days now. I would have to have a lot more hours of sleep than that."

"That's right, but you see I have trained my brain to function on less sleep."

Noticing the wrapped package Lank had in his hand the Professor gave Lank an inquiring glanced.

"Oh, that's the golden medallion I told you about," Lank said, beginning to unwrap the necklace.

When he had it completely unwrapped he handed it to the professor. Taking the necklace from Lank he held it in the palm of his hand for a few moments then looked at Lank.

"Yep it's radioactive alright. Did you feel the warmth?

"Yes I noticed it and thought as much.

"It isn't enough to harm you though, maybe over a period of time, but not for as long as these women were wearing it," The professor told Lank.

"Well what do you think about it?" Lank asked.

"I know what it is used for but I have not figured out yet why it works the way it does. It might be good to have though, we will see."

Lank did not have time to query the professor on that statement. The professor continued on.

"We are sufficiently far enough along now to test this apparatus. That is why I sent most of the lab boys home for some much needed sleep. I plan on firing this thing up tomorrow morning bright and early. You may want to be here Lank."

"Yes I do. You are not going to send anyone through yet are you Professor," Lank asked, worried he would not have time to brief the president.

"No I want to make some trial runs first. It will be a couple of days before I'm ready to send anyone through."

"I'm still set to be the first one through, right Professor?"

"If you insist Lank. I'll try to give you every safe guard I can think of to try to keep you safe," the Professor said.

"Ok, then I'll brief President Gorden tomorrow and I will check back with you when it is time for the activation."

"You leaving now then Lank?"

"Yes I really need to get home and rest up. Who know what lurks on the other side of the worm hole," Lank said laughing.

"Ok see you then."

Chapter Twenty - Five

Dr. Alex North was in a long tense conversation with Lyle Green when General McPhee arrived.

"Dr North, you wanted to see me?" the general asked.

"Yes General," Dr North said, directing his words to the General.

"Any word on how far along Professor Manning and his crews are at Columbia," Dr. North asked with a keen interest.

"My last report I have on their progress states they are still studying the files and pictures acquired from their raid."

"Well that is a bit of good news. I'm wondering if they got enough to really build a duplicate."

"I guess we will find out soon enough," Lyle Green commented.

"Gentlemen my contacts within the Columbia lab will keep me informed. We will know when and if they are ready to slip through the wormhole." General McPhee said.

General McPhee was not aware he was addressing two aliens from a distant galaxy. He thought they were legitimate doctors involved with trying to help those poor people on the parallel world whose race was dying off. He understood the problem with the women being unable to produce eggs any longer. He did not know the reason and he assumed the two doctors did not know the reason either. General McPhee had been through the wormhole several times and knew first hand the trouble this world was in.

He remembered seeing only old men and women, no children. The world was a mess with no young men to do the heavy work. The city of Chicago was where the surrogate mothers to be, who had undergone gestational surrogacy at the clinic in Los Angels prior to being sent here.

He had only been to the Chicago clinic once about four years ago. He remembered seeing a lot of pregnant women but come to think of it he had not seen any of the children. Probably kept them in a separate clinic.

He had other troubles on his mind. He was still upset about the lab being violated by special agent Miller and his band. General McPhee could not rationalize why his government would be against trying to help another world. He also knew what would happen if the world, especially his own government, ever figured out how to develop time travel. He understood why it was necessary to keep this project under wraps, just like it was right to keep the work at area 51 from becoming common public knowledge. Of course Dr. North and Dr. Lyle Green paid him handsomely to keep this knowledge secret. As long as the General had free run of this project he was willing to work with the two doctors and help where he could. General McPhee knew though, Professor Manning at Columbia, was getting close to learning the secrets.

If he did, then for sure the President and his boys would shut the operation down here at the Valley lab and he might be exposed. Oh well, he thought, I'll cross that bridge when I come to it. He had salted away quite a bank account from this project so far and if luck were with him he would have plenty more to go along with it. The General's thoughts were interrupted when Dr. North addressed him on his way out of the lab.

"General McPhee, myself and Dr. Green will be going to Chicago this evening. I want you to keep strict security on the lab. We have some urgent business to take care of in Chicago."

"How long will you be gone?" he asked.

"Probably a couple of days. There is a lot of work to be done and we need to be there to try to hurry things up a bit."

"You don't have to worry Dr. North. I'll put extra men on detail." The general said with authority.

Both Dr. North and Dr. Green gave the general a glance that if glances could talk would have conveyed their thoughts as to what kind of security he would provide, remembering the raid a few months ago.

Either the General did not catch the glance or he chose to ignore it, for he smiled and waved to them as he walked towards the room that held all his security apparatus.

The hours passed and soon it was time for the doctors to make the trip through the wormhole to the town of Chicago on the parallel world.

The lab techs were ready to assist when the doctors arrived.

"Lyle, there's one thing I have to get from my office. You go ahead and slide through." Doctor Alex North said.

"Ok, see you in Chicago." Lyle said as he stepped on the tripod and positioned himself between the three metal circles.

The lab techs were there to ensure everything went according to plan. The actual transmitting equipment was automatic and did not need any human assistance. The techs, who were all alien themselves, were there mostly to keep the humans away. The first few moments the Doctor was in the tripod, he would be unable to project his human form, thereby allowing his lizard-like appearance to be seen just before he popped out of sight. None of the humans working in the lab were allowed in the transmitting room. They were all kept busy running errands and assisting the aliens.

A smile, if it could be called that, appeared on the face of the doctor as he thought about the humans working there. If only they could see who they were working for, wouldn't they quake in their boots? At that moment the lizard genshee appearing in his alien form briefly, popped out of sight on his way to Chicago.

It wasn't long before Dr. North approached the tripod in his alien lizard like body, not bothering to utilize his ability to hide his alien form. For that matter, all but two of the lab techs were in their alien body. He stepped upon the tripod and was soon on his way to Chicago too.

Chapter Twenty - Six

Lank had called president Gordon on the private phone number assigned to him. When the president answered Lank switched hands with the phone.

"Mr. President, this is Special Agent Lank Miller. I need to see you at your earliest convenience." Lank said in a quiet voice.

"Well hello there Lank, Sounds like we are finally moving on this thing," the president said.

"Sure enough Mr. President. I have some urgent news to relay to you along with an update on the current situation." Lank told the president.

"Will you be able to use the encrypted secure telephone lines at seven pm tonight Lank?"

"Yes Mr. President I'll be at my office to receive your call at seven tonight."

"Ok I'll place the call and we'll talk then. How are your wife and daughter doing?" The president asked with genuine concern in his voice.

"They are ok sir, hanging in there like good soldiers."

"That's good, I'm glad for them. I know it has not been easy for Mary Ann to cope with you being gone so much."

"She understands sir, no problem." Lank advised the president.

"Ok then seven tonight." The president said.

"Right sir, I'll be ready."

Lank was glad he would be able to talk with the President tonight. This would give him more time to prepare for his trip through the wormhole. He could only trust Professor Manning and his team in getting him safely through and then bringing him back again. It would be a dangerous trip, not knowing what was at the other end.

He planned to take firepower with him in the form of his trusty nine-millimeter handgun along with an AK47 when he actually went through the space time machine. He hoped he would not have to use any force but it was always wise to be prepared.

He knew he should be more afraid than what he was of going through the wormhole, but he had been in so many tight and dangerous places he supposed it was his way of preparing himself.

Lank was at his office when the secure telephone rang precisely at seven pm. He picked up the telephone piece and heard the president's voice.

"Good evening Lank, glad to hear your voice again," the president greeted Lank.

"Good evening to you sir." Lank returned the greeting.

"Well you must have some important developments from the lab at Columbia for me Lank."

"I do sir. Professor Manning has duplicated the time machine and is ready to try it out in the morning."

"You mean he has perfected time travel?"

"Yes he and his team have been working 24/7 on the project sir.

"Interesting, I'm curious as how all this ties in with the rash of abductions we have been having over the past five years."

"We should have some of the answers, at least, in the next few days," Lank advised the President.

"Will it be you Lank that will be the guinea pig?" The President asked.

"Yes Mr. President, I am the logical choice." Lank responded.

"Lank, make sure you carry your trusty side kicks along with you. You never know what lies on the other side."

"I will certainly do that sir. That is my plan" Lank said.

"Good, I'm counting on you Lank, not only me, but the whole world, maybe the whole universe."

"I'll do my best sir."

"I'm sure you will. Well Special Agent Lankford, you have my best for a successful conclusion. I'll be waiting to hear from you in a few days," the President told him.

The connection was broken and Lank hung the receiver up and close the hidden door that hid the small black box that was used for the encryption of their voice.

Lank thought about his conversation with the President for a few minutes, then he dialed his home. He hoped Mary Ann would be home. He did not want to tell her he would be gone for a few days.

Lank dared not reveal his plans to Mary Ann. No use in worrying her any more than he had to. He had kept her in the dark in the past and things worked out ok. What a story he could tell her when he finally retired from government service.

Looking at his watch he noticed it was getting quite late, he decided not to go home tonight but to stay in a motel close to the lab. He wanted to be there early, to be briefed by Professor Manning before taking his trip.

Now that his plans were made, Lank decided to call his wife and let her know he would not be able to be home tonight.

When Mary Ann answered on the first ring it caught him off guard.

"Hi hon. How you doing?"

"Ok, I just got back from the school. You know I had to be there for the game, Jen is one of the cheerleaders and would have been very upset if I had not of come." Mary Ann informed him.

"Hey that's right. I forgot about the afternoon game. It wouldn't have made much difference though as I would not have been able to attend anyway."

"Don't worry about it Lank, I'm sure Jen understands."

"I know, but it still hurts knowing I'm missing out on so much of her activities while she is growing up." Lank lamented.

"Well I won't be able to come home tonight. I have something I am working on and it looks like it is going to take a few days," Lank told her.

"I was afraid you might have to go out again. Is it going to be dangerous?" She asked.

"Probably not, I won't be by myself."

"I hate it when you have to go off like this, but I knew that when I married a man that was in law enforcement."

"I'm thinking it will only be a few days at most and then I'll be back. Don't worry, I'll be ok." He assured her.

After the conversation with Mary Ann, Lank picked up a spare suit, shirt, tie and socks along with his travel bag containing his toiletry items from the locker in his office. He then checked into the motel he had used several times in the past. He left a request for a six am wakeup call and took a hot shower, climbed into bed and promptly fell asleep.

Precisely at six am the phone rang, awaking Lank from a deep sleep. He managed to grab the phone on the second ring, thanked the operator and replaced the receiver back on the hook.

Lank was never one that would linger long in bed once he was awakened. He swung his legs over the side of the bed and walked to the sink. He liked to shave first then take a hot shower. It always refreshed him to allow the hot water to pulsate from the top of his head and onto his neck, then down his back.

Finishing his shower he dried himself off, splashed his face with the aftershave lotion from his small travel bag. He dressed himself and walked from his room to the lobby to partake of the continental breakfast. That was one of the reason he liked staying at this motel chain. Their breakfast consisted of a variety of cold juices, milk, scrambled eggs, sausage and biscuits with plenty of white gravy.

Lank took his time finishing his breakfast, enjoying it immensely. When he had topped off the breakfast with his second cup of coffee he was ready to see Professor Manning.

It did not take Lank long to make the trip to the lab on the campus of Columbia and seeing the Professor as he entered the lab, raising his voice a trifle, Lank addressed the Professor.

"Professor Manning, How are you this fine morning. How long have you been waiting on me?" Lank asked in a jovial tone of voice.

"Well we put it to the ultimate test around four am this morning and everything checked out all right," The Professor told him.

"Good, then it is a go for me then."

"Yes, we put the last piece of the puzzle together last night. You know the medallion, well we found out we did need it after all. It is the device that will bring you back to this precise entry of the wormhole."

"I don't think I understand Professor. You mean I would not have materialized back here in the lab?" Lank asked incredulously.

"Maybe, then maybe not. You see it would all depend on you getting back to the tripod on the parallel world. With the medallion you can be miles away from the tripod when we activate the remote TSMD, because you have the medallion on your person, it will bring you back to this tripod here in the lab." The professor explained.

Lank, remembering a previous explanation of the Professor, asked.

"Professor, doesn't the medallion have to be programmed to be in tune with my nervous system?"

"That's right and if you will come over here and take a seat, I'll start the programming."

Lank moved to the other side of the professor and sat down in the indicated chair. The professor with the help of one of the lab technicians, turned the TSMD on and placed the medallion around Lank's neck.

"Now Lank, it will take a couple of hours for the programming, so you just try to relax, there is coffee on the table to your right. You can move around some, but stay within a ten foot range of the TSMD."

"You got it." Lank said as he settled down in the chair.

After the two-hour programming period was up, the professor returned, motioning to Lank to step up onto the tripod, he began to give him last minutes instructions.

"Lank I want you to know we have tested this time/space machine over and over again. Everything looks all right. I feel sure you will be ok. You will materialize at the end of the wormhole, which is located on the parallel world. What area we don't know. There are three tripods stations that we know about located on the parallel world you will visit. Which one you will arrive at first should not be too much of a concern to you."

"Do I understand you right, I should be able to transfer back and forth between the tripod here in the lab and two other tripods located on the parallel world?" Lank asked, feeling better about it all for now.

"Yes that is correct. This tripod is a duplicate of the one on the parallel world that is connected somewhere in the middle of the wormhole and the other tripod is located at the end of the wormhole. Now come over here and I'll give you instructions on how to work the tripod," Professor Manning told him as he gently guided him toward the electronic equipment that controlled the actions of the tripod.

After an hour or so had passed with Lank learning and practicing with the tripod controls, the professor thought he was knowledgeable enough now to actually go through with it all. Lank thought so too and was ready to make the jump through time and space to the parallel world. He was excited and pleased he would the one to maybe solve this five-year-old abduction issue.

His thoughts were interrupted when the professor motioned to one of the lab techs, who began to set the controls on the tripod.

"Mr. Lankford, do you think you are ready, any last minutes thoughts?" the professor asked, halfway laughing.

"None as far as I know. I'm ready as I will ever be," Lank said. "I have my trusty friends with me."

"Ok then, Ron, are you ready? The Professor asked the lab tech.

"I'm ready Professor, just say the word.

"Lank, here you go, happy trails," Professor Manning said.

Lank could see the lab tech, Ron, fiddling with the controls and then all of a sudden he felt himself falling. Falling faster and faster through what looked like a long tunnel. There were several moments in time Lank thought he had passed out. The end of his flight came fast. He abruptly came to a complete halt.

Slowly his surroundings came into view. The first thing he became aware of as his eyes slowly adjusted to the light in the room, were for sure he wasn't in the room with the Professor Manning. This room was laid out completely different from the room he was just in. More noticeably was the absent of the Professor from the room.

It must have been at least ten minutes before he was at himself enough to climb down off the tripod. The tripod was different too. It seemed bigger than the one he had stepped on at Columbia. Lank vision turned to a large door at the end of the building. He stashed the nine millimeter handgun and the AK47 behind some crates out of sight made sure he had his trusty friend hidden securely in the holster he wore on his belt in the middle of his back and walked toward the door, upon reaching it, he swung the door open, only to be confronted by two old men. They did not look threatening in any way.

Lank looked around for additional people but seeing none, he turned his attention back to the two old men. The two old did not seemed surprised to see him.

"Hello sir. Don't believe we have seen you before. You come from Dr. North?" they asked.

Lank was aware enough of his surroundings to play along with the old men.

"Yes. I come from Los Angels."

"You just missed the good doctor. He went back to Los Angels."

"That's strange, Dr. North promised to give me a tour of the facilities here." Lank told them hoping to find out just exactly where he was at.

"He did not tell us anything about a tour. One of the old men said. "I take it you haven't been here before."

"That's right. I needed to check out the facilities here, something has come up and we need to speed up operations." Lank said, carefully selecting his words.

"Yes, he did tell us that things were going to start moving fast pretty soon. If you like, we can give you a tour of the facilities here at Chicago." The second old man said.

Lank breathed a sigh of relief. He now knew where he was.

"Sure that would be just fine. Can we start the tour now, I am pressed for time?" Lank asked them.

"No problem, which facility do you want to look at first, children's area or the housing area for the women waiting to be impregnated again with fertilized eggs from the other Earth?"

"Lets start with the housing area and them we can tour the other area. Is that ok with you?"

The two old men looked somewhat surprised at the politeness in Lank's voice. They were used to being firmly directed by the other men that came from Earth. This was a pleasant change.

The two old men led him from the building across the lot to a high fenced area that enclosed a large building. It was a large enclosed area and Lank could see row after row of what looked like cars. The whole area, being encircled by a chain link fence did not look like it was for any security.

When they approached the gate another old man, upon recognizing the two with Lank, opened the gate and allowed them through into the courtyard. When they came to the first building, Lank waited until one of the old men motioned for Lank to get inside one of the cars. Lank opened the car door and entered and sat down in the bucket seat. One of the old men got in on the driver side and the other old seated himself in the back seat. The driver of the car spoke to the car.

"Children's area," the driver stated in a firm voice.

"The children's area is not far from here, but there is so much trash on the streets it will take about an hour to get there," he told Lank.

"Yes I'm aware of the condition of the roads," Lank said, with the implication he was familiar with the set up.

They drove in silence the rest of the way. Lank was surprised the car was driving itself and marveled at the height this society on this parallel world had climbed to. When they eventually turned into a street that led to a fenced in area with a large gate guarded by a lone old man. When the car had come to a halt, the guard approached the driver side and inquired their purpose. The driver stated the man beside him was from Los Angels and was sent by Dr. North. The guard pushed the gate open and they entered into a large parking area. As they continued on towards a conclave of buildings, Lank noticed there were no children about and mentioned this to the old man.

"Sir, the children are all kept inside. We have never seen any of the children, although we occasionally hear them at play.

Lank thought that was strange but did not inquire further. The car rolled up to the first building and a female voice, automated of course, came from the dashboard.

"Women's housing area, Do you wish me to wait?"

"Yes wait here till we return," the driver stated in a firm voice.

They begin to exit the car and Lank followed them to the door of the first building. When they reached the door of the building, Lank waited for them to open the door. Neither of the old men gave any indication of opening the door for Lank. Finally the old man who had been the driver informed Lank why they could not go any further.

"Sir, it is forbidden for us to enter any of these buildings. Dr. North only allows us to be the caretakers. Caretakers are not permitted inside the apartments."

"I know, I just forgot there for a moment," Lank said, hoping his choice of words would suffice.

It must have worked because they stepped back a step and motioned to Lank to open the door and go on in.

Lank opened the door and entered the building. The building was hospital clean in every respect. White walls, tiled floor. In front of him stretched a long hallway with doors on each side, just about as far as he could see. He passed a large room that must be the computer room.

He saw banks and banks of electronic gear lining the walls of the room, obviously in an operational mode. Walking on past this room he deliberately passed up several doors along the hallway until he came to the end of the hallway. The hallway ended with large double doors across the hallway.

Lank thought he heard children's voices in the distant. He listened carefully and decided it must be on the other side of these double doors. Upon pushing open one of the double doors he found himself looking at another long hallway with doors evenly spaced down the length.

He opened one of the doors and looked into a nice apartment like living space. Nice furniture, pretty curtains on the windows, a second closed door probably leading to the bedroom.

"Anybody home, Hello" Lank spoke in a raised voice. For a moment he thought the apartment was empty but just as he turned to leave, the bedroom door began to open.

"Yes, I'm here," a pretty soft voice came through the doorway, finally revealing itself to be a beautiful young woman.

"Hi I'm Lank from Earth. How do you do?"

"Earth, huh, the real Earth or the parallel Earth."

"I'm from the real Earth, what is your name?" Lank asked.

"My name is Ann Long. It has been so long since I talked with a man from the real Earth." Ann said.

"I'm here to try to get all of you girls back to Mother Earth and I'm going to need all your help. Can you tell me what is going on? Lank asked.

"You mean from the time I was snatched through time and brought to Los Angels, I mean the other Los Angels?" Ann began.

"Yes that will be a start, please continue on Ann."

"Well we were brought from the room we had arrived at to a large apartment complex in Los Angels, only it wasn't Los Angels as I knew it. I remember a bunch of orientation lectures we had to attend, telling us what had happened to this planet and the human race was dying off because the women could not produce any eggs to be fertilized. How the government had developed a time machine to go back into the past and snatch young women of childbearing age and bring them to this world. Only something went wrong. They found out they were not going into the past at all but to a parallel world in the same time as they were." Ann paused here to collect her thoughts. It was obvious she was distraught.

"Tell me Ann, when were you transferred here to Chicago?" Lank asked her.

"Well they implanted a fertilized egg into my body and after about nine months I began to show a little. That was when they took me into the clinic and ran a lot of test. Shortly after that they moved me here to Chicago," Ann told Lank.

"You mean you were just barely showing at nine months Ann?"

"That's right, you see for some reason it takes about a year and two months for a pregnancy to end in birth."

"You are not pregnant now are you Ann?" Lank asked.

"No. I was scheduled to be impregnated again last week but for some reason the old men never came for me." Ann replied.

"Ann, how did they transfer you from Los Angels to here?" Lank asked.

"The same way I was snatched to Los Angels."

"That's a good piece of the information I am looking for. Ann have you noticed any unusual activity going on lately?"

"There has been a lot of activity going on the past couple of weeks. I think they are trying to remove the children from here. We used to hear a lot of them playing but lately there have been fewer and fewer," Ann told him.

"You said you heard the children, Have you ever seen any of the children?" Lank queried her.

"No, none of us have ever seen any of the children, not even our own," Ann told him.

"I think I know the reason Ann. You see the real Earth's government found out what was going on and we were able to track the operation here to this parallel world. I am a government agent."

"Yes I remember before I was snatched I had heard of the abductions going on." Ann said.

"Ann have you heard of a Dr. Alex North?" Lank asked.

"Not personally, I do know the old men who takes care of us here in the apartment are afraid of him. They say he is not from this world. I mean they think he is an alien of some sort."

"That would certainly fit in with what has been going on."

"There is a story going around some of the old men accidentally witnessed the arrival of Dr. North a couple of years ago coming through the time thing. They said he looked like a big ugly lizard. In a few moments though he looked like the old Dr. North."

"Ann one more question. You said you had not seen any of the children, not even one you gave birth to. Is that right?"

"I'm sorry to say I have not. None of the girls here have ever seen any of the babies, not even the ones born to us."

"Doesn't that strike you as strange Ann? I mean surely you should have been able to see and care for you own baby."

"Well we didn't and I wish I knew why."

"I am beginning to get a picture of just what kind of operation Dr. North is running here but first I have to tour the area where the young children are kept. Ann are there any of the old men you can trust?" Lank asked, already formulating a plan in his mind.

"Maybe, there is Tom who cleans the floor, and Mac, the handy man, they are friends. Other than that we have not had much contact with any of the people. Not like it was when we were in Los Angels." Ann said.

"Ann I'm going to leave you here for a little while, I promise I will return. How many girls are there here that you know of?"

"There usually are about hundred in this apartment on each floor. Probably upwards of three hundred or so Mr. Lank." Ann answered.

"Ok. I want you to pick out two women that are good friends of yours that you can trust not to reveal what we know to any of the other girls. It will take a while to get you all back to the real Earth but it will happen. You and your two friends will be the first to return, and Ann you can call me Lank."

"Ok Lank. Do you want me to bring them here to my apartment?"

"Yes, I shall return as soon as I can. Do you think you can get Tom and Mac here with you by the time I return?"

"I think so, they usually come when one of the girls need their assistance." Ann replied.

"Ok then, I'm off and be ready when I return."

"You bet I will," Ann whispered as tears begin to well up in her eyes.

Lank gave her a reassuring pat on the shoulder and then departed back out the door he had entered.

The two men who had escorted him so far were patiently awaiting his presence. Both stood slightly back looking like two old dogs waiting on a biscuit to be thrown their way by their masters.

Lank addressed them in a voice that he thought they were expecting from a friend of Dr. North.

"I'm ready now to tour the other facility. All is in order at this one. After I tour the children's facility, I will need to explain some things that I want you to do for me." Lank told the two old men.

Without any hesitation on their part they readily agreed and told Lank they would be waiting when he got through touring the birthing facility. After they were all seated back in the car they guided him from the courtyard back through the gate and across the street to what looked like a large hospital.

When they arrived at the front door Lank knew what was expected of him. He opened the door and made his entrance. Nothing was amiss within his immediate viewing range. He heard some children playing further down the hallway and directed his steps that way. The closer he got to the children's voices, the more excited he became. Turning around the corner of the hallway he came upon a scene that was so bizarre he could not believe his eyes. Suddenly the whole plan of Dr. North's was becoming transparent.

It should have been obvious from the start, Dr. North would have had and ulterior motive. Lank could hardly wait until he got back to Earth to share what he had found out with Professor Manning.

Lank knew he was going to need help from Raymond, Lewis, and Jeff in this matter. Doug would have to take his team to Los Angels and take out Dr. North and his crew. Man this had turned into a galactic event.

Looking at the children in front of him playing, it was hard not to feel anger at a race of people that were willing to hoodwink another race into doing such a devious plot. It was not the children's fault, Lank knew, but still the innocent suffer, not only in the real Earth's world but in this world too.

The children, which were probably twenty-five or thirty in number paid no attention to him but went on playing their game.

Lank causally approached them hoping not to frighten them. He had not been close enough to hear whether or not they were speaking English. When he was finally noticed by one of the group Lank spoke to him, or her.

"Hi there. What kind of game is that you are playing?" Lank asked the one that had noticed him.

"We are playing genshee," He answered.

"Genshee eh, Having a lot of fun, are you?" Lank queried.

"Yes. We play genshee when we have to stay indoors."

"I see," Lank said. "How many are there of you here?" Lank asked hoping to get an idea of what he might be up against in the near future.

"I don't know, a whole bunch. When we are allowed out in the courtyard we hardly have enough room to play any games." He told Lank.

Mentally reviewing the size of the courtyard Lank figured there must be at least a thousand or so.

"Do any of you speak any language other than English?"

"We don't have to, What ever language you speak we will answer in it," He replied, surprising Lank.

Lank turned that little bit of information over in his mind and then asked one remaining question.

"Can you make yourself look like a human?"

"Sure we can, watch."

Lank watched as the lizard boy in front of him became a good-looking young Earth fellow about ten years old. Lank shook with excitement as he took all this information in. It sure would come in handy in the future.

Lank thanked the youngster and turned and walked back the way he had come. The two old men were still there when he came out the door. They gave him an expectant look, waiting on further instructions.

Lank told them he wanted them to escort him back to the women's housing area and then back to the laboratory. They nodded their heads in agreement and headed back toward the apartment building where Ann was.

Lank entered the building and went straight to Ann's room where he found her sitting talking with two other young women.

"Hi again. Lank this is Marie," nodding toward the darker complexioned girl, "and this is Wanda Williams. Girls this is Lank Miller. He is a special agent from the real Earth."

"Yes that is correct. I will be taking you back to the real Earth with me. Are you up to it?" Lank asked.

"Just try and keep us here," Marie said emphatically.

Lank reached into his pocket and withdrew the medallion. He showed it to the three girls.

"Have any of you every seen one of these?" He asked.

"Yes," all three girls answered in unison.

"Yes I bought mine in the mall, you know those little outside booths they put up in the middle of the walkways in the malls," Ann told him.

"Do any of you still have yours? Lank asked, looking at each of the girls.

"Yes, although we don't wear them anymore," Marie said looking at the other girls as she spoke.

"What would be the reason for not wearing them?" Lank asked, already knowing why.

"After three or four months the medallions began to leave a burned area on our necks," Ann told him, pulling her shirt back to reveal a discoloring of the skin in the shape of the medallion.

"I suspected as much," Lank told them. "You see they are radioactive."

"You know we kind of suspected as such but really had no way of knowing for sure." Marie said.

"Ok, you will have to wear them one more time. Only for a few moments though as you go through to the real Earth."

"Where will we be at when we arrive? I mean where on Earth will we be coming out at?" Ann asked for the other two girls as well.

"You will be at a laboratory located on the campus of Columbia, in New York City."

"Well that is too far from home. I was taken from a department store in Kent, England," Marie mentioned.

"I remember you now, Marie. I read about you in a clipping of a newspaper from Kent, England, a town called Borough Green, wasn't it when you disappeared?"

"Did anyone see me disappear?"

"Yes, there was a man by the name of Larry Culvert. I remember what he said. He said the second hand on his watch began to run backwards just before you disappeared." Lank said.

"I know him. Yes I was about to check him out and then the next thing I knew I was being help to a chair by some old people." Marie exclaimed.

"Ok Ann, where are Tom and Max? I need to talk with them."

"They are waiting in the community room just down the hall," Ann informed him.

Lank told the women to stay put while he was gone. He walked to the community room and upon seeing the two old men he introduced himself.

"Hi gentlemen. I am Special Agent Miller. I am from the real Earth," extending his hand. He was mildly surprised at the strength in the handshake of both men. The one called Tom evidently was the spokesman.

"Hello Special Agent Miller. I am Tom and this other gentleman is Max. What can we do for you?"

"Tell me what you know about Dr. North."

"Dr. North is the one in charge here. He directs everything that goes on here," Tom responded.

"The operation is? Lank pressed him.

"Well since our women lost their ability to produce any eggs, Dr. North began this operation of bringing young women from Earth to here and then using the sperm from the sperm bank. We are so thankful to the young women and sorry that Dr. North won't allow them to return home."

"Have you ever seen the babies born to these young women?"

"We did at first but after about a year this operation was started here in Chicago and we are not allowed to see the children," Tom declared.

"If you are not able to see the children, then how are they taken care of?" Lank asked.

"One of Dr. North's men come twice a week and we suppose he takes care of them. You see everything is automated here, even the dispensing of food and water."

When will this man be returning again?" Lank asked.

"He comes every Tuesday and Thursday."

Lank breathe a sigh of relief as this was Wednesday and he would have time to get the girls safely through the wormhole.

"How do you obtain supplies for the young women?" Lank asked, wanting to know if there were others of Dr North's helpers here.

"All supplies are stored in a building next to where the girls are staying," Max spoke, finally interjecting his voice into the conversation.

"How do they get there?"

"There is an airport close by and I suppose they all come from Los Angels.

"I see," Lank slowly said, forming in his mind the avenue he would use to try to obtain the help of these two men. Deciding the direct approach was the best way Lank begin to explain to them just what their Dr. North had done.

Lank watched the old men's countenance change as he progressed further and further into what had actually transpired. Finally, Lank stopped long enough to give them time to digest what he had told them and ask questions.

"Special Agent Miller, You mean Dr. North has stopped impregnating the young women that were snatched here against their will and started his own little operation." Tom said choosing his words carefully.

"Yes, Tom, You see what I think has happened is this. I think on Dr. North's world, which is not our Earth; their race has lost its ability to produce children also. When he found this world and the shape it was in, he turned it into a bonanza for his race. You see Tom, these aliens, and that is what they are, are bent upon producing a race of their own people here on your Earth. Eventually taking over when they had repopulated it with their own kind.

"Well I guess it wouldn't be too bad. They look just like we do. How would we ever tell them apart?" Max asked.

"No Max, they don't look like we do. They have the ability to either cloud our minds or somehow project a human image around their bodies, thereby causing us to see them as people that look like us." Lank explained to both of them.

"Well then, just what do they look like?" Max asked for both himself and Tom.

"They are a dark brown in complexion, the texture of their skin is leathery. The have a pointed head, large black eyes, more to the side of their head then in front like our eyes are set. Their arms are longer than ours, and a lot skinner too. Lank paused to let this sink in.

"You mean they look like lizards, don't you?" Tom asked.

"Tom, I knew those stories were true about seeing that lizard man when he appeared in that thing in the building," Max almost shouted to Tom.

"That's right Special Agent Miller. We were told that it wasn't true but a lot of folks believed it, especially the people that reside in the outlaying districts of Chicago," Tom said.

"Tom, Max, I need your help. All of these women were taken against their will and forced to carry the eggs of these Lizard aliens. They were not allowed to see their babies so they don't know what their babies looked like. I am going to try to send them back through the device that the aliens use to come and go, only they will return to the real Earth. It will be an ongoing operation and take six to eight months to complete, maybe more. I will need your help in bringing these women in twos to the building you see the aliens come from."

"Yes we will help. We know the women in our apartment complex but there other apartment complexes we are not allowed in."

"That will be alright. I'll handle that part of it. I will take you both into the building now and show you how the aliens bring the young women here. Will you come along with me?" Lank asked, anticipating a positive answer by turning and walking toward the building.

Both of the old men followed him down the hallway to Ann's apartment. Lank knocked on the door and upon hearing Ann's voice telling him to enter, he motioned to Tom and Max to enter before him. When they were all in the room, Lank began to explain that Tom and Max had agreed to work as a team in getting all the girls back to Earth.

"It's going to take months, maybe more than a year to get all the young women through the time device and back to Earth. I will need to have one of you stay here and work with Tom and Max. You see it is necessary to have one of you explain to the other girls what I am about to tell you. I have already explained to Tom and Max the situation that exists here on this Earth." Lank began the explanation, watching the faces of the three young women.

"Lank, what about our babies? I mean will we be able to take them with us when we go?" Ann asked.

"Ann, I was coming to that. I'm afraid you can't, and when I tell you why, I'm sure you will understand," Lank said, continuing with his explanation.

"You see Ann, Marie, Wanda, it is true the women on this Earth are barren and have been for a number of years, as evidence by the lack of any young people. Dr. North, who by the way is an alien, from some distant galaxy of which I don't know, somehow stumbled upon this planet when it was needing help to keep from perishing.

He made a deal with the men here and told them they would bring child bearing women to this Earth and by using sperm already stored in sperm banks here on this Earth they would be able to repopulate, thereby preventing the complete disappearing of their race."

"Well isn't that what happened," Wanda asked, interrupting Lank.

"Not exactly. You see there were babies born, but none of the women were able to see their sons and daughters. The old folks on this Earth were told it was necessary to keep all the children in special enclaves to prevent them from developing the same condition as women of this world had contracted. Even the old people were not allowed to see the children," Lank continued.

"Surely we can find the children, can't we Lank?" Ann asked.

"Ann, the children born to all you women are not your children. You have been acting as surrogate mothers. You see the aliens have been implanting fertilized eggs of their own race into the girls that have been abducted from our Earth. The aliens do not look like us. The babies that are born to you here on this parallel Earth, are of the race of the aliens. Their appearances are different from ours. I have seen them. They are in the conclave of buildings located across the street from here. I must tell you all, they have a thick leathery texture to their skins. I noticed the shape of their heads, they are elongated, with large black eyes set more to the side of their heads than ours.

Their arms are long and skinny, ending in fingers and an opposing thumb just like us," Lank paused to let this information sink in, keeping his attention on the faces of the three girls. Finally, after a long pause, Ann Long spoke up, obviously under an emotional strain.

"Lank, we gave birth to alien babies that has no connection with any of us, other than us carrying them for the year and five months it took until they were born. With that thought in mind, I think I can speak for Marie and Wanda also and probably for all the other women here. I don't want to even see them, let alone bring them back to Earth with me."

"I feel the same way. They would not be accepted on Earth anyway." Wanda said.

"You're probably right Wanda, Anyway there are thousands and thousands of them here on this parallel Earth. Even though each one has the ability to speak any language they are addressed in, and the ability to cloud our minds so that we don't see them as they are, but see them as good looking young Earth boys and girls. It would probably be a task beyond our abilities to relocate them to Earth."

"Lank what will happen to them, the children I mean?" Ann asked.

"I imagine the aliens will try their best to take them off this Earth. You see they are aware our Earth government finding out about them. They are going to be very busy the next few months trying to protect themselves and the children. I don't know, but I suspect this is the way they conquer other worlds.

Either finding a planet, or parallel world, of which there are an unlimited number I suspect, or stumbling upon a world dying like this parallel Earth. This allows them to manipulate and control the existing population."

"Sounds too weird to be true, Marie exclaimed, looking at the two other girls.

"Ok Now I need to know which of you are willing to stay behind for a month to help get the other women ready for transference."

"I will volunteer, since it will be for a month, I will be ok," Ann Long said, not looking at the other two girls.

"You sure Ann. I'll be willing to stay instead," Wanda said, looking at Ann.

"Yes I'm sure, you and Marie go ahead. Lank tell me what you want me to do?"

"I need you to talk with the women. I plan on taking Tom and Max with me when Wanda and Marie are transported back to Earth so they can be a witness as to what we are doing. I also intend to allow Tom and Max to visit the children and witness for themselves. You must be sure and tell the other girls they must keep their medallions close by. They will be need when they transport back to Earth. Any questions?" Lank asked Ann.

"No I think I got it," Ann responded to the question.

"One thing more. It will be at least two weeks before I return. Please don't panic. I promise you I will be back."

They were all silent for the space of a few minutes. Lank knew this was overwhelming them. He had no choice about telling them what was going on. They had to know as bad as it. A new thought crossed Lank's mind. He remembered the promise he had made to Mrs. Moulton concerning her daughter, Betty. He decided to ask these three girls if they knew her whereabouts.

"Ann, there was a young women that disappeared in New York a little over a year and a half ago. Her name was Betty Moulton. Have you ran across her or know where she might be?"

"Betty, of course. We were friends in Los Angeles before I was transferred here. There was another girl with her, I think her name was Lise. There were some complications with both of them, I don't really know what it was. I think it was something to do with compatibility with the egg implantation process."

"You have not seen either one of them since you have been here?" Lank asked.

"No I'm sorry." Ann said regretfully.

"That's all right Ann." Turning to the other two girls expectantly.

"No we haven't seen or heard of them either," Marie told him.

"Ok I'll find them no matter where they are, in Los Angels or here.

"Max, Tom, are you ready to accompany us to the transport room?" Lank asked the two men.

"Yes we are ready," Tom answered for both of them.

"Good, ok ladies come along. We are going home."

They had to take two cars to hold everyone, but that was not a problem as there were plenty of cars. Out of curiosity, Lank asked Tom what fuel these cars.

"They run on nuclear fuel cells, you know. We stopped using gasoline back in the early twenty century."

"Lank thought to himself how far ahead of the real Earth these people were, especially in fuel technology. His thoughts about the advanced fuel technology were interrupted as they rolled up to the door of the building Lank had first appeared in. When all had disembarked from the two cars Lank led the way inside the building holding the transporter.

He led them to the tripod and activated the controls on it. A whirring sound filled the air for a few minutes, until it finally faded away to be replaced with a low pitched hum. Lank glanced to where he had stowed his other two weapons behind the large crate, making sure nothing had been disturbed. He began to explain to Tom and Max what was going to happen. He showed them how to turn the tripod on, making sure the associated equipment, such as the TSMD was operating properly. When he was sure they understood all the procedures, he turned his attention to Marie and Wanda.

"Girls, you have to have the medallions around your neck. You see they are already programmed with your specific profiles," He told them, as he continued instructing them on how to stand on the tripod.

When he was sure they too understood, he told them to step upon the tripod. When both of the girls had taken their place on the tripod, Lank himself step upon the tripod and turning to Tom and Max.

"Tom, you or Max must pull that lever down that I showed you. When you do you will hear a popping sound and then we will be gone. Remember you will have to place the girls, three at a time, on the tripod, making sure they have their medallions around their neck, and then send them on their way.

Both Tom and Max nodded their head indicating they understood and would remember. Tom had his hand on the lever and was awaiting Lank's nod before he pulled the lever down. Lank making sure Wanda and Marie were ok he then gave the nod. This was the last thing Lank saw until he felt then became aware of someone helping him off the tripod. Becoming fully aware of his surroundings he noticed it was Professor Manning that was helping him off the tripod.

"Professor Manning, boy is it good to see you again," Lank said, filled with emotion. Then remembering Marie and Wanda he asked the professor about them.

"Came through just fine Lank. Look over to your left and you will spot them.

Lank looked in the direction Professor Manning was pointing and sure enough there sat Marie and Wanda waving at him.

He walked over and embraced both.

"Professor Manning, that guy with the long white hair and white beard, he will take care of you. The state department will fly you home so don't worry. I can't stay around I have so much to do before we can start rescuing the other girls. Good luck to both of you."

That was the last time he would ever see Marie and Wanda again.

Chapter Twenty - Seven

After Lank had briefed the Professor on what had transcribed on the parallel world and brought him up to date on what had to be done yet. Lank picked up his car where he had parked it before he had been transported to another Earth. He drove to his office, greeting Janet, his secretary. He gave her a quick synopsis of the situation on the other planet. When he mentioned the lizard boys and girls he had encountered, Janet gave out a little moan.

"Those poor women having to give birth to lizards."

"Janet, they did not know what their babies looked like, they were kept from their sight."

"You mean even until now," she asked.

"Yes. They never knew," Lank said in an offhand way. He was concentrating on what he would report to the president.

"Janet I need to set up an appointment with President Gordon as soon as possible. Will you set it up for me?"

"Of course Lank," Janet said on her way to the telephone encryption device hidden behind the false wall.

When the connection was completed and she heard the voice of the president's secretary, Janet handed the phone to Lank.

Lank greeted the president's secretary and stated desire to have an appointment with President Gordon.

"Special Agent Miller, the president told me when you called, for you to take the next available flight from New York and to report to the white house security shack. The president will see you in the oval office, no matter what time you arrive."

"That will be fine. I'll be there as soon as I can. Thank you," Lank told him. Turning to Janet, he asked her to make the earliest reservations on a flight to Washington DC.

The flight to Washington was uneventful. Lank stretched his legs out and rested his body for the short time it took before landing. He had just about dozed off when it was announced landing would be shortly. When he departed the plane and entered the terminal he heard his name called. Turning around he noticed a well-dressed man waving at him. He walked up to the man.

"That's me. Who are you?" Lank asked, not recognizing the man.

"I'm from the white house with a message for you Mr. Miller," the man declared.

"What is the message?" Lank asked, feeling himself becoming guarded. No one knew he was arriving on this flight, except maybe the President or some one from his office. Maybe it was just that he was so tired and tensed up after his dealings with the alien situation.

The young man gave him a coded sentence that was only privy between Lank and President Gordon. Lank was quick to acknowledge he had heard and understood the coded sentence.

"President Gordon cannot meet you at the white house. He has instructed me to ask you to go to the safe house. He said you would know which one it was," The young man said, a bit hesitant but managing to get all out.

"Yes I know which one he is talking about. You have a car" Lank asked.

"Yes I do. You show me the way and I'll drive.

"I don't think so, you show me the car and I will drive myself.

The young man smiled and said.

"The president said you would do that."

"Just being careful. What's your name?" Lank remarked.

"My name is Jim Tabor," the young man told him.

"Well Jim, lets go see what kind of car the government sent you off in,"

The car the young man drove to the airport was parked in the public parking area. It was a late model Buick. Lank approached the car cautiously, motioning to the young man to stay where he was. Lank begin to search the car's extremities for any evidence of a bomb of some type being attached to the car. Looking under the car and finding nothing, he began to breathe a little easier. He very carefully raised the hood, than asked for the keys. He began to check the trunk and the inside of the car. After a final check he was satisfied.

"Come on, Get in and we'll be off."

"That won't be necessary sir. The president is sending a car for me."

"Ok, thanks for bringing the car. Maybe I'll see you around sometime," Lank suggested.

"Yeah, maybe," Jim said in return.

Lank started the engine and backed out of the parking area and quickly exited the airport onto the main road leading to a small town of Suitland. The safe house was located on ten acres of prime real estate, hidden from view by a large stand of oak trees. Lank deftly drove the car down the long road with stately oak trees on each side. Reaching the house, a large brick two story home, he pulled the car up in front of the double car garage, cut the engine and opened the door.

He strode up to the front door, pushed the door buzzer and waited. It wasn't long before he was joined by two men dressed in dark clothing, one on each side of him. Lank waited until he was asked who he was and what was the nature of his visit. Lank told them who he was and the nature of his business.

"Boys, I'm here to meet with President Gordon."

"We know, we are just being careful. Mind giving us the password?" he was asked.

"Yes I do mind. If I give you the password, then it won't be secret any longer," Lank answered in the answer mode required by pre arrangements.

"Ok the president is waiting for you inside," one of the men told Lank.

Upon entering the rather large room, Lank took in the way the furniture was situated in the room. All the blinds were closed on the windows and heavy curtains were drawn not allowing any view whatsoever from the outside. Three additional secret service agents were stationed in conspicuous places around the room. Lank knew two of them, however he did not recognize the third agent. The agent nearest Lank raised his voice slightly and directed his attention toward the door as it slowly opened.

"Hello Lank, glad to see you are ok. Come on in and have a seat," the president said as he sat down himself on one end of the couch.

"Good evening Mr. President," Lank returned the greeting.

"I hear you have been rather busy. I thank you for rescuing the two young women."

"Yes sir, I have been busy but this is just the tip of the iceberg. We have so much more to do."

"Fill me in Lank, I'm listening," the president said.

"Ok. We have to get the FBI involved. You see we are dealing with aliens. Dr. North is an alien and most of his lab techs are aliens. I don't know at the present time what planet they are from, but I do know what they look like. Sir they appear as humans, just like an average Joe, but when they drop their cloak they show their true selves. I describe them as lizard like in appearance, maybe a little taller than us with a pointed head and wide set large black eyes.

They have the ability to cloud the minds of persons within eyesight of them so that they appear as ordinary humans. Sir what they are doing here, I suspect, is attempting to conquer the parallel world they are on now.

They have duped the old people into believing they are helping them to repopulate a dying race but in reality they are planting their own fertilized eggs into our women who have been abducted and using them as surrogate mothers. I have seen the offspring born from this procedure when I was in Chicago.

Our young women did not have a clue as to what was happening. They were under the impression, as the natives of the planet were, of the noble endeavor of using human eggs and then fertilizing them with sperm from the sperm banks already on this world. One other thing sir, our young women never saw their offspring. They were taken from them and put in a camp like enclosure at the moment of birth.

I visited this enclosure and actually talked with one of the youngsters. He was in his lizard form and volunteered to show me what he could be like if he chose to cloud my mind." Lank had stopped here again to allow the President to comment.

"This leaves me speechless. I would never have thought it. Thanks Lank, Tell me exactly what you will require and you will have it."

"I will need an FBI team to clean up the Los Angels Lab. Dr. North has to be taken out of the way. We will need complete access to the lab there in the valley to accommodate the rescue of the women still in Los Angels, I mean, sir, the Los Angels on the parallel world," Lank deliberately halted thereby giving the President the opportunity to interject any of his comments or questions.

"Lank I'm with you, go on."

"This is the scenario as I see it. If we do not secure the Lab facilities in Los Angeles then this allows Dr. North and his cohorts the ability to come through the wormhole and surprise my team, which will be in Chicago, transporting the abducted women back to this Earth. My team will consist of myself and three agents I have every confidence in. I will have them visit the lab here at Columbia and be trained on the techniques of time travel utilizing the medallion and the tripod. Also, the FBI team, will have to be trained by Professor Manning."

"How much manpower will be needed for the FBI to accomplish their task," President Gordon interjected.

"I will leave that up to the Professor to determine. Also Mr. President, I would like to have special Agent Doug Fields, who is the director of the local New York office, to be in charge of the FBI team."

"You got it. I will notify the director of FBI, and inform him of your request.

"Thank you Mr. President. That is about all I require right now. I will keep you informed. I would like to have both teams ready to go within three days. I believe Dr. North is aware of our interest, I just don't know how he much he knows about our plans for the future," Lank concluded.

"You're right Lank, Dr. Alex North needs to be eliminated. Lank for your information, there is an army General by the name of McPhee involved with Dr. North." President Gordon said.

"Yes I was aware of General McPhee and his security force he has employed to protect the Lab there at Valley."

"He is a retired General of questionable character. It will be a pleasure to have him removed," the President remarked.

"Sir, I will inform you just before we mount this rescue mission, which should be in three days time," Lank informed the President.

"Fine, fine, I'm counting on you Lank. The whole world is counting on you, along with the parallel world too."

With that, the President rose from his sitting position, effectively dismissing Lank without having to say anything. Lank stayed put while the President left the house and into a waiting nondescript car. Lank watched the car speed away and was thankful of his relationship with President Gordon.

Lank made his escape from the safe house shortly after the president had left. He called Janet, his secretary, from the car and being informed by his voice mail there were no messages for him of any importance. He decided to call Mary Ann, telling her he was in Washington and would be gone for a few more days.

After his chat with his wife, Lank quickly covered the few streets to his DC office to pick up a bag containing a spare suit, shirt, socks and underwear. From there he went to his favorite hotel in Washington. He was on good terms with most of the hotel clerks and was always able to obtain a room without reservations.

This time was no exception, the night clerk, whose name was Frank Bittle, greeted him with familiarity.

"Hi Mr. Miller, Good to have you back sir."

"Thanks Frank, yes it is good to be back in Washington. Do you have a room for me?"

"Of course sir, you will always have a room here. Would you like to have the same room you had last time?" Frank asked politely.

"Yes that will do fine. Wake up call for six am?" Lank asked.

"Six am it is sir. Here is your key card. Have a pleasant night and if there is anything you desire just ring the desk.

"Ok, thanks, its nighty nite for me," Lank said on his way to the elevator.

His room was on the second floor half way down a long hallway. There was not much of a view so he closed the curtains, then he turned the TV on and decided to take a much-needed shower.

Six am came sooner than he expected with a loud ring of the telephone, he was shaken awake. Answering the phone with a thank you, Lank rolled out of the bed with sleep still in his eyes. He headed to the sink and letting the hot water run for a while until he could see the steam coming from it before he levered the plug stopping water from going down the drain.

He washed his face with the hot water before he applied the shaving lotion. It didn't take him long to shave and splash his face with his aftershave lotion. Dressing quickly, stopping only long enough at the desk to check out of the hotel, he threw his small bag containing his old suit and shirt into the back seat of the car.

He knew a little all night-restaurant, a short distance from the hotel. He ordered his breakfast, which was not long in arriving, and enjoyed immensely the bacon and eggs with hash brown potatoes, toast and jelly, served with a hot steaming cup of coffee.

Lank spent most of the day making phone calls, running down his three friends. He had called Raymond first on his cell phone and had to leave a message. He then tried to contact Lewis but having little success there as well. He finally dialed Jeff in St. Louis. Jeff's voice came on the line.

"Hello, you've got Jeff, what can I do for you?"

"Jeff this is Lank. How you doing boy?"

"Hey Lank, I'm doing just fine. I've been wondering about you and what you have been up to." Jeff said.

"Busy, Jeff, very busy. I'll have to clue you in later on. Say, have you been in contact with Lewis and Raymond lately?" Lank asked.

"Not lately. I did talk with Lewis last week, I think it was probably last Tuesday. Why, you need to get in touch with him in a hurry?" Jeff asked with a hint of excitement in his voice.

"Yes it is very important I reach them today. Jeff can you make it to New York today, or tomorrow at the latest?"

"Hmm, let me see, Yeah, I can make it today. If I can't get a commercial flight, then I'll hitch a ride on a military transport plane or something from the base. Shouldn't be much of a problem. I'll be there." Jeff said excitedly.

"Good, in the meantime try to get in touch with Raymond and Lewis and relay to them the same thing I just told you. Ok?"

"Will do. Where do we rendezvous with you?" Jeff wanted to know.

"Jeff, when you get to the airport in New York, call me and I'll be there to pick you up. In the meantime I'll keep trying to locate Raymond and Lewis," Lank said.

"Gotcha. I gather we need to pack our traveling bag right?" Jeff said, figuring they would need some heavy firepower on this mission.

"Yes Jeff. It's going to be a long one, and a dangerous one at that. I can't tell you more than that right now. I'll be waiting on your call."

"Ok Lank, take care buddy. See you soon."

Lank decided to take an afternoon flight back to New York City. He called the desk at the terminal and was able to find a seat for that afternoon at four o'clock. He thought to himself he would go back to his DC office and lounge around there till time to go Regan airport to catch his plane.

He still had the car the president's guy had used. It was a nice car, not a family car though, but still it was transportation. He had forgotten to thank the President for the use of the car. Thinking to himself the next time he had the opportunity he would.

Arriving at his DC office he could see through the plate glass Pat was busy at the computer. Probably filing through the reports he had not seen or taken care of. Pat was very efficient. She was a hard worker too.

"Hi Pat, I'm back," Lank said as he entered the office door.

"Well good morning Lank, welcome back. You going to be able to stay for a little while this time?" she asked hopefully.

"No, I have a flight book this evening for 4 o'clock. You think you might give me a lift to the airport?"

"Of course, you said a 4 o'clock flight, right?" Pat asked.

"That's right, also Pat I have one of the President's cars down in my parking space. Do you think you might call the white house and have it picked up?"

"For a minute there I thought you wanted me to have a car towed from your parking space. You really did mean the car belongs to the president, didn't you?"

"Yes I was picked up by one of the President's men last night and he graciously let me use it." Lank told her.

"Sure, I'll call and get someone over here to get the car."

"Well, what has transpired since I was here last?" Lank asked as he strode toward his office.

"Larry Duiggs called and wanted to know if I had heard from you or knew where you were at." Pat said standing in the doorway to his office.

"What did you tell him?"

"What I always say when I cover for you."

"You're such a doll, thanks."

"Well exactly where were you this time, I know you were in New York for a while. Have you been anywhere else?"

"You wouldn't believe me if I told you." Lank said with a mischievous grin on his face.

"You just try me." Pat said laughing.

"Ok, well I was in Chicago for the better part of a day, then I returned back to New York that afternoon."

"Now wait a minute, what did you ride in, a rocket?"

"Not quite, but something similar. How about if I told you I went through time and arrived in Chicago the same moment I left New York." Lank said, watching the reaction on Pat's face.

"You mean you have a time machine."

"No, I don't, but Professor Manning does.

"I get it now. The Professor has built a time machine."

"Yes, he has taken what we got for him from the lab in Los Angels and duplicated an entry point into the same time warp that Dr. North had out in California."

"Lank, are you telling me you actually went through and came out in Chicago?"

"Well it is not the Chicago as we know it, but Chicago in a parallel world."

"Lank, tell me, does all this time travel and parallel worlds have anything to do with the abductees?"

"Yes it has everything to do with the abductees. I brought two of the women back with me. That is why we are going back and rescue the rest of them."

"I am so glad. This will put a stop to any further women being snatched through time against their will."

"Yes, Dr. North and his cronies will be routed out and dwelt with, you can be sure of that."

Lank spent the remainder of the afternoon bringing Pat up to speed on the aliens. He described them and their abilities to make themselves appear as humans. When he got to the part about the women not being aware of what the aliens were doing with them, Pat broke in with a loud sigh of remorse.

"Lank, you mean those women and the old men and women of that parallel Earth were being duped. Why that is disgraceful, them not being able to see their own offspring."

"It might be a good thing Pat, you see the offspring are not humans, they are Genshees, aliens from another world, Lizzard people, if you please. The two women I brought back were adamant about not wanting to see their babies." Lank told her with sadness in his voice.

"I probably wouldn't want to see mine either now that I think of it."

Pat noticing the time, alerted Lank they needed to be going if they were going to make the flight on time.

Pat drove Lank to the airport, dropping Lank off at the baggage area, she hurriedly sped away. She had several errands to run, one of them was picking up Lank's suits from the hotel and restocking his luggage he kept at the ready in the office. Also she had to get the car back to the President's car pool.

Lank picked up his boarding pass after paying the fare. He used his security clearance granted him by the Home Land Security Secretary, Larry Duiggs, to bypass the security post.

The flight was on time, for a change, Lank thought, as he heard the announcement. On boarding the plane he was directed to first class by the flight attendant. Lank had always preferred to fly first class, even when it sometimes took money he could not really afford to part with. He took his seat and settled back to read a magazine from the small table in front of him.

It seemed only a few minutes before he felt the plane descending in preparation to landing. Upon landing and taxing toward the terminal, Lank felt excitement course through his body. He was on the brink of the biggest mission he had ever been on. Later as he called for a cab, he had settled down somewhat in his thoughts. The cabbie was friendly and wanted to talk most of the way to the Lab. Lank acknowledged with a yes ever once in a while.

Finally the ride was over and he found himself entering the Lab. Looking around for the Professor, who was nowhere in sight, Lank walked to the room that had served as the Professor's office space but finding it empty he was on the verge of letting out a loud yell for the professor when he spotted the white hair and whiskers way back in the building. He walked the rest of the way and found the Professor busy setting up an additional tripod.

"Professor Manning, what you doing now?" Lank asked bending down to see just what part of the tripod he was working on.

"Hello yourself. I thought you would be gone for a few days."

"No way, you know me professor, I have to be in the thick of things."

"You got your team formed yet?"

"Not quite. But they should be here tomorrow afternoon."

"Well I should have this tripod hooked up by then, I'm hoping I can plug it in the same place the first one is." Professor Manning declared.

"I hope you can get it to work. That will double our rescue attempts."

"Professor Manning, I will have four in my team. We will transport from here to Chicago, and the FBI team will go to Los Angels and take control of it. We should have the worm hole to ourselves then." Lank said.

"The FBI team. How many are you going to have?" Professor Manning asked.

"I don't know right now. I think it will depend on our information we have as to how many will be needed. How many do you think we might need to take full control of the lab?" Lank asked.

"You better have at least twenty-five or thirty because that is what Dr. North has. That's just the aliens, not counting what General McPhee has as his security force.

"That sounds right to me. I had thought forty-five would be a good number. You know I'm going to have five or six FBI agents come here to the Lab and learn how to operate the tripod controls."

"Lank the faster we can get those young ladies home the better I will like it," The professor said, genuine concern showing in his voice.

"Same here Professor, but our second objective must be the eradication of the Gengsees. There is just something about a lizard that I find disgusting, especially when they parade as humans."

"Well if we work this operation right, I think we might become world-wide heroes. How does that strike you?" Professor Manning asked Lank.

"You can leave me and my team out of being heroes. I just want to get those girls home.

After talking with the Professor for a little while longer, Lank retired to the Professor's makeshift office and dialed Raymond's office number. The call was forwarded from his office to his cell phone. Raymond picked up on the fourth or fifth ring and grunted a hello.

"Hey Raymond, I glad I was able to run you down. Where are you out now?" Lank asked.

"I will on my way to New York inside an hour Lank. You going to meet me at the airport?" Raymond asked.

"Yes I will be there. What is your flight number and arrival time?"

"Lets see, yeah, flight NW597, arrival time ten Pm."

"Any word from Lewis. I was unable to reach him when I was in DC?"

"He is with me on same flight. You getting both of us, think you can handle us old man?" Raymond joked.

"I don't know, maybe, after you see what kind of mission we will be on and where we will be going you might not want any part of it," Lank told him.

"You know the answer to that Lank, the tougher the better. Has Jeff checked in with you yet?" Raymond asked, suddenly remembering Jeff was coming all the way from St. Louis."

"No, not yet, do you know if he is on the way?"

"No, he did not know his flight number when he called me. I'm sure he will be checking in as soon as he can."

"Ok Raymond, I'll be there at the airport to meet you and Lewis. Have a good flight."

"You betcha old man." Raymond responded in a familiar gesture of comradeship and broke the connection.

Lank happened to realize he was without transportation. He could call a taxi though and pick up Raymond and Lewis or he could ask the professor for a loan of his car. He decided it might be better to borrow a car from the professor. He might have to make an additional trip to pick up Jeff. It must have been mental telegraphy for at that very minute his phone rang. It was Jeff.

"Jeff, hey I was becoming worried about you, where you at now?" Lank asked.

"I'm sitting on the ground at Atlanta right now hoping my connection to DC won't be delayed." Jeff told him.

"Good, Jeff, give me your flight number and arrival time in New York and I'll meet you there."

"Ok. My flight number is Delta 877 arrival time in DC is supposed to be ten-thirty this evening."

"Hey that's great Jeff, Raymond and Lewis are arriving at ten tonight so we will all meet you there."

"Ok, it will be good to see them two owlhoots again." Jeff said.

"Right. Raymond told me a while ago he shares the same sentiment about you Jeff." Lank said laughing somewhat at the expression owlhoot. Only from a Midwestern would such a term spring.

"Ok I'll get off here and see you guys in a few hours." Jeff said.

"Yeah, see you Jeff." Lank replied as he broke the connection.

The Professor was overjoyed at the prospect of Lank using his car. He suggested the battery might be dead, for he had not started it for more than a week. Tossing the keys to Lank, Professor Manning went told him to keep it as long as he needed it because he would use one of the administration's car if he needed one, and with that he went back to work.

Chapter Twenty - Eight

Dr. Alex North was just getting off the phone with his second in command, Dr. Lyle Green, when he caught the hand signal of one of the techs who was assigned to monitor the use of the tripods located at various points around the globe.

"Yes, what is it?" he asked.

"The tripod at the Chicago terminal has just been activated again Dr. North, and our records do not show any Genshees that are authorized to use it."

"Ok, thanks for alerting me. I'll take care of it."

This was the second time the tripod in Chicago had been in use in a single day. He did not have any genshees that were authorized to use the tripod in Chicago at this time, so who had been using them. Only one answer came to his mind. It had to be a representative of the government of the USA.

Dr. North believed General McPhee would, or should at least, know who was using the tripod. He quickly dialed the General's office and when he answered he posed the question to him.

"General, the Tripod in Chicago has been in use. I have not authorized any usage of the tripod to anyone. Do you know of anyone from your government that would have reason to use it?"

"Yes Dr. North. There is only one man that is actively seeking to undermine this project," the general began.

"Well, who is it?"

"You know Professor Manning has been, for a long time now, interested in time travel. The man that has been seen going in and out of the laboratory there at Columbia is Special Agent Miller, who by the way, is Special Advisor to the President on Bio-terrorist affairs. I am almost certain he is the one that has been trained by Professor Manning and would be the most likely candidate to use the tripod," General McPhee said in responding to the question poised by Dr. North.

"This Special Agent Miller, Is he the one that was responsible for the raid on our facilities earlier this year?" Dr. North asked.

"The very same. He has three more men who are special agents that make up his team. They have been sent to many hot spots in the world in the past, and are still active today.

"Have you tried in the past to eliminate Miller and his team?"

"Yes, almost succeeded this last time. We engaged two Iranians to plant a bomb on his flight back to New York but somehow he got wind of it and the two Iranians were arrested and the bomb defused.

"Too bad, do you have any plans to eradicate this problem in the near future?" Dr. North asked out of concern for the project.

"Yes, I have something in the works, if successful, will eliminate any threat to your security."

"If your latest plan does not succeed?"

"I have enough men to protect you and the project here at the Valley Lab. It would not be wise on the part of Special Agent Miller to attack this place." The General responded with somewhat of a puffed up pride.

"I certainly hope so General McPhee. You know the success of this project rest entirely upon what we are doing here at the Valley."

"I understand and I will use all the tools available to me to protect you and this project," he said with resolve in his voice.

When Dr. North had hung up, General McPhee was already devising a plan of escape for his crew and himself if it came down to that. He was not about to risk his life protecting these doctors.

The General was crafty and cunning when it came to dealing with situations such as he found himself in now. He knew exactly who it was that had gone through the time machine, as he called it, and who came back through. He had a couple of men planted inside the laboratory that was constantly feeding him reports of how far along the professor was in duplicating the time machine.

The latest report notified him of plans to send Special Agent Miller and his team through to Chicago and set up a rescue program to bring back the women who had been abducted.

General McPhee was not too interested in the plight of the abductees. He had seen them many times and thought they were doing a fine thing in trying to repopulate the parallel world for the old folks there.

It did strike him at times though why he had not seen any children when he visited their world. He put it down to children's camps run by the aliens. As long as he could justify his budget in keeping the Quantum Physics lab open here in the Valley he would continue to do what he had been doing from the start. Any way, the payments he received from the aliens for keeping quiet their activities was more then adequate.

Dr. Alex North turned what he had heard from the General over in his mind. He did not have the greatest of confidences in the General, but he needed someone who was familiar with the government's way of conducting business in order to have the Lab federalized. This way, with the lab being under federal control, or so it would seem to the General, Doctor North could continue to operate the program he was sent to this world to do and bring it to a full completion.

He had his own version of security employed within the project. He had a plan to send a dozen genshees through to Chicago and have them placed around the tripod and to capture or kill those Earthlings that dared to come through. The only problem, their race was not a violent race. They conquered by way of infiltrating and overcoming passively.

He had been on this Earth long enough now and seen enough violence via the media and even first hand knowledge, that it had rubbed off on him and made him less resistive to the idea of taking a life, especially an Earthman.

The only other genshee he could count on was Dr. Lyle Green. They both were the first ones sent here and were of a like mind when it came to protecting the project. He had shared his concerns with Dr. Lyle Green on the phone prior to his talk with the General. Both agreed they must increase the security around the remote tripods and had talked about the best way to accomplish it. Finally it was determined Dr. Lyle would go to Chicago and arrange an ambush to surprise anyone that materialized on the tripod there.

Dr. Lyle Green thought about the conversation he had with Dr. North. He knew Dr. North was counting on him to secure the remote tripods before it was learned their true purpose. There was an idea in a remote part of his brain that was slowly blooming and for the rest of the day he nourished the idea until it blossomed into a full-fledged plan.

He approached the tripod with a small bag he had put together of things he would need in Chicago, knowing what he had to do. He set the controls to start automatically and stepped upon the tripod. The popping sound that always occurs just prior to the disappearing of the one on the tripod went unnoticed this time. Dr. Lyle was used to the trip and it did not bother him at all.

Arriving in Chicago, he stepped off the tripod, looking around and seeing no one, he carried his bag and walked toward the end of the room where one door was set in the wall. He opened the door and entered into a rather large room, obviously a storeroom of some sort. Dr. Lyle began to rummage through some of the larger crates that were stacked in one corner of the room.

Evidently finding what he was looking for, he removed a rather large piece of equipment from the crate and carried it to a table that had been, from the looks of it, a workbench. Dr. Lyle took some instruments from his bag and beginning to adjust some of the settings on the piece of equipment lying on the table.

About thirty minutes had transpired before he smiled and returned the instruments back into his bag. He carried the piece of equipment back to the tripod where he removed a similar piece then replaced it with the one he had adjusted to different specs. He then stashed the one he had removed back in the large crate the other piece had been. No one would ever know he had switched the parts until it was too late.

Dr. Lyle walked to the main door that opened out into the courtyard and walked toward the rows of parked cars. He selected one, not that one was any more desirable to him than any of the others, but just out of habit picking the one that was the nearest him. He got in the car and gave it a command.

The car backed itself out of the parking space and headed toward the gate. Stopping automatically while the old man that was operating the gate flipped some controls and the gate swung open.

"You seen any other men coming through here in the last day or two?" He asked the operator.

"No, haven't seen anyone since Dr. North came," the old man told him.

"Ok, I'm going to be gone for a while, I will be returning tomorrow morning," Dr. Lyle informed the gatekeeper.

"Right, Have a good day sir," watching as the car sped down the road.

Chapter Twenty - Nine

Lank was at the New York airport waiting on Raymond and Lewis to arrive. He had got there a little early and was making the most of the wait by reading a magazine someone had left in the seat next to him. He had read a couple of the stories and had thumbed halfway through the remaining pages when he heard the announcement of flight NW597 from DC had just landed and disembarking passengers could be met at gate 37.

He strolled down toward Gate 37. Mingling with other folks waiting on love ones. Lewis and Raymond were among the first to enter the terminal. They were engaged in a conversation, not heated it seemed, but lively and upon spotting Lank, they immediately broke off the conversation and approached Lank.

Lank shook hands with both of them and after rescuing his hand from Lewis's big paw led the way toward his car, or Professor Manning's car.

"Have a good flight?" he asked both of them.

"Yeah, didn't have much time to really get old Lewis here to going though," Raymond answered for both of them.

"You'd been up the creek without a paddle old man if this flight would have been much longer," Lewis said out of the corner of his mouth.

They had only a short wait for Jeff's flight to come in. They had to check the status board to see what his gate number was. By the time they had walked to gate seventy-one to where Jeff's flight would taxi too, the plane was already landing.

Picking up Jeff when he came through the gate and after the short reunion with each other, they walked down towards the baggage claims area and the three recaptured their bags. Lank led them out of the terminal and toward the parking lot.

Approaching Professor Manning's car. Lank opened the trunk first and the three piled their luggage in the rather large trunk space. After inserting his key in the driver side of the car, thereby unlocking the doors on the car. He slid behind the wheel and waiting for the three men to find their places in the car. Raymond walked around to the passenger's side and slid himself in. Lewis had already seated himself in the back seat. Jeff slid in beside Lewis.

Lank decided to wait until they were at the lab before briefing Raymond, Lewis and Jeff on what they had to do. Engaging in conversation mainly about what Raymond and Lewis had been doing, especially while working in the VIP lounges.

"Lank you know who we saw the other day come into the VIP lounge at the airport?" Lewis asked.

"No, I don't know, who was it?" Lank asked, obviously falling for the bait.

"None other than your boss," Lewis said.

"Which one?"

"Why John Farshaw, who else."

"Wonder what he was doing there, any idea?" Lank asked Lewis.

"Yep, heard him discussing his trip to the Bermudas."

"The Bermudas huh, I wonder if it was on official business."

"I don't think so, I heard him and his girl friend, yes girl friend, I've seen his wife, talking about their room at the hotel."

"Well every man to himself, I always say," Raymond said, getting his say in.

Their conversation abruptly came to a halt as Lank, braking a little hard, as he pulled into the parking spot by the side of the lab. They walked toward the door in the front of the lab and entered into a room that had electronic equipment sprawled all over the room. Looking for the Professor, Lank noticed there had been some additional equipment placed around the tripod.

Finally seeing the professor, Lank, with Lewis, Raymond and Jeff following behind him approached the Professor.

"Hi Professor Manning, how are you today?"

"Hi there yourself, hey who you got with you?" Professor Manning asked, then without waiting for an answer he grab Raymond and gave him a big hug.

"Haven't seen you in a while. You doing alright Raymond?"

"Yep how about yourself?"

"Working hard as usual," professor Manning came back.

"Yeah and I might add, without hardly any sleep too," Lank interjected.

Turning his attention to Lewis, Professor Manning grabbed his hand and pumped it up and down.

"Good to see you Lewis. You been keeping Raymond here in tow?"

"Impossible Professor, Raymond there is always one step ahead of me."

"I can imagine that scene Lewis."

"Jeff, how about you, hacked into any government computers lately?"

"Not lately, maybe a few months ago," Jeff said smiling.

"Yeah and a good job in doing it, I've heard," Professor Manning said with a hint of pride in Jeff's work.

"What you got here Professor?" Jeff asked, looking around the room at the banks and banks of electronic equipment.

"This is the time machine you've been hearing about. Quite a show, isn't it Jeff?" Professor Manning said looking around the room with a satisfied smile tucking at the corners of his mouth.

"I'll say, I'm interested in seeing how it works," Jeff said as his eyes lit up seeing the Tripod for the first time.

"All in good time. You will be sick of it by the time I get through with your training period, I bet."

"Yes, and each one of you will have to take a crash course in the operation of the tripod because we will be bringing back the young girls that have been abducted from all over the world," Lank advised them.

"Bringing them back from where?" Jeff asked, not being privy to Lank's prior trip to Chicago through the wormhole.

"Jeff I'll let the Professor get you up to par. Lewis, you and Raymond will have to learn how everything works also, so I am going to leave you here with the Professor until tomorrow sometime. I would like to get this mission on the road by tomorrow night," Lank told them.

Professor, have you been contacted by FBI Agent Doug Fields yet?" Lank asked.

"No not yet."

"I'll check with his office and see what the hold up is. I want Doug and his agents here by tomorrow morning if possible. They need to be trained also, because they will be taking over the Los Angeles Valley Quantum Physics Lab," informed all of them.

Lank left them to it, turned and left the lab on his way home. He would check with Doug at his office early in the morning. The drive home took longer then usual. Traffic was line up for at least a mile ahead of him and at a dead standstill. Seeing there was no exit close to him that would speed up the drive to his home, Lank sat there twiddling his fingers making a visible effort to stay calm. Finally, after thirty minutes of maybe going a hundred feet the cars ahead of him begin to move at a faster pace. By the time Lank had advanced to where the traffic jam had its beginning he was unable to tell what had caused it, no evidence of an accident. He thought to himself, isn't that just like it.

Most of the time it happened this way. Resuming the posted speed limit it did not take long to drive the distance to his home. He had decided not to call Mary Ann from the car. She would probably be asleep anyway and he did not want to disturb her. As he approached his house and coasted into his driveway he decided to leave the car in front of the garage and enter his home through the front door.

Entering the front door he immediately disarmed the security alarms by poking in the prearranged code into the box mounted beside the door and then resetting it before he walked to his bed-room door. He called out Mary Ann's name in as somewhat hushed voice, hoping he would not scare her. When she answered him he knew she was ok.

"It's just me hon, I'm back again for a short time." He said.

When Mary Ann started giggling from inside the room, Lank realized how it sounded when he had spoke to her.

"I mean I'll be here only a little while. I have to be back at the lab in the morning," Lank said, laughing a little himself.

Before Mary Ann could open the bedroom door, the door to Jennifer's room opened and she suddenly appeared.

"Daddy, you're home. I'm so glad, mom and I have really missed you."

"I'm so glad to be home too Jen, I missed you and mom," hugging her in a tender father-daughter embraced that encompassed all the love both had for each other, seemed to make up for the time he was away.

By this time Mary Ann had moved out of the bedroom and into the hallway. Embracing both Lank and Jen at the same time, they hugged this way for what seemed an eternity.

"I'm so sorry I have to be away from you so much," Lank whispered to both of them.

"We understand honey, Both Jen and I know it is your job. We are ok with it."

"That's right dad, but it still hurts when you are away," Jen said in a quiet voice filled with emotion.

"I know sweetheart. I keep telling myself it is for the good of everyone, but still I can't help but worry about you and mom."

"Hey, let's get off this merry-go-around and go into the kitchen and have a nice hot cup of hot chocolate," Mary Ann suggested.

"Sounds good to me, how about you Jen?" Lank asked.

"Why not, we're all wide awake I think," Jen replied.

Retiring to the kitchen and sitting at the bar, Lank and his daughter talked while Mary Ann made the hot chocolate.

"Ok. Let's enjoy this hot chocolate," Mary Ann said as she placed their cups in front of them on the bar. Pulling out the bar stool she sat down beside Lank and joined in the conversation.

They talked for the better part of an hour till Jen said she had to go back to bed. She had to be up early tomorrow. Her class was going on a field trip and had to be at school by eight o'clock.

Mary Ann agreed saying both her and Lank needed to get some sleep.

The morning arrived way too soon. Jen was already up as evidenced by the sound of a hair dryer whirring in the bathroom. Mary Ann was up also because of the aroma of bacon frying coming from the kitchen. Lank rolled over and debated whether to stay in bed for a few more minutes but decided against it.

He sat up and waited a few moments to clear the cobwebs from his eyes, then quickly began the usual morning ritual of shaving and taking a hot shower. After completing the shower he rummaged through the walk-in closet and removed one of his many suits, choosing a dark tie to go with it.

Emerging fully dressed into the kitchen, Lank decided he was ravished for food. Sitting himself down at the table, he waited until Mary Ann placed the plate of food in front of him. Not waiting until Mary Ann brought her plate to the table, Lank begin to eat heartily. The breakfast was scrumptious in his opinion.

Lank politely waited until Mary Ann finished her breakfast before he refilled his cup with coffee. They then engaged in conversation until Jen popped in finishing drinking the glass of orange juice she had poured earlier.

"Bye Dad, Mom. I have to run. I'll grab something to eat later this morning," Jen said on her way out the door.

"I worry about her, Lank. I know I shouldn't, but I do."

"I know you do. I do too. You know she is at that age," Lank said as he finished his last sip of coffee.

"You have to go in to the office today hon?" Mary Ann wanted to know.

"Yup, but only for a little while. I want to catch up on my reports and see Janet before I return to the Lab." He hesitated to inform her he needed to go by Doug Fields office. No reason to encourage more questions.

"Lank, Is everything going ok with your latest mission?"

"So far it is. I have Raymond, Lewis and Jeff here at the lab now helping me. I think the worst part is about over, we'll see.

"You mean you think the most dangerous part is over, don't you," Mary Ann quipped.

"In a way I guess. You have no cause to worry Mary Ann, I'm not alone on this one," he said softly, in an effort meant to calm her fears. About an hour had passed before Lank pushed his chair back from the table saying he had better get going.

"I wish you didn't have to go Lank."

"I know, but you know I'm a government man, and my time belongs to the government," He said straightening his tie while looking in the small mirror mounted in the door of the refrigerator.

Embracing each other and with a goodbye kiss, Lank headed out the door. He gave Professor Manning's car a good inspection as was his habit, especially since the car had remained out in the open during the night. Satisfying himself it was clean, he slid behind the steering wheel and with a wave of his hand, he was off.

Arriving at the UN building a good hour later, because of the early morning New York traffic, he was waved on through by the gate guard but had to park in one of the visitor's parking space. His car was still parked in his space. He remembered now, Janet had driven him to the airport in her car. After he had returned back through the wormhole he had borrowed the Professor's car from the lab. Well his car would just have to stay there for a while.

He entered the building through main door, going through the metal detector after being identified by the guard as to who he was.

Lank was glad when he walked into his office. Again he found Janet busy at the computer getting all his report ready for the briefing he would give the president. Janet knew she had to have two reports ready, one to go to John Farshaw, the director of Home Land Security, and one for the President. This was at the president's suggestion. There was no trust on the President's part about John Farshaw. The report the director would receive would not contain the detailed information prepared for the President. There would be just enough information in the report to keep the director off Lank's back.

Lank spoke to Janet and when he had her full attention he began to brief her and bring her up to date on all the events that had transpired since the last time he had seen her.

"Janet we don't need to include in the report to John Farshaw's anything concerning my team being deployed to the lab or the FBI team which will be going to Los Angels," Lank cautioned.

"I understand Lank. You going back to the lab today?"

"Yes when I'm finished here. By the way, I'm using Professor Manning's car. Mine is still parked in my parking space.

"I know. I saw it there yesterday and wondered why, then I remembered I was the one that took you to the airport in my car."

"The professor was good enough to loan me his car to go to the air port and pick up Raymond, Lewis and Jeff last night. I will continue to use it for the next few days. How about getting a visitor pass from security for the professor's car. I didn't have time this morning to get one. Allen Peters on the front gate waved me on through?"

"Sure Lank, no problem. Do you want me to send it to the lab?"

"Yeah, that would be fine. Well guess I will go by Doug Fields office and see if he has his team ready yet. I'll see you later Janet."

It did not take to long to drive to Doug's office. The traffic had all cleared out by now. Lank turned into the parking lot in front of Doug's office area. Upon entering the reception area Lank spotted Doug as he was just coming out of his office with some paper work he obviously had for his secretary. This was not Heather Banks for sure but the secretary Lank had known almost as long as he had known Doug.

"Hi Sharon, How are you today?"

"Why hello Lank, Where have you been keeping yourself these days?"

"Keeping busy that's for sure," Lank answered, turning towards Doug.

"Hi Doug, just in your neighborhood so I decided to drop by."

"Sure you did," Doug said smiling. "I know exactly why you are here."

"Of course you're right as usual. Can't hide anything from you, can I?" Lank said laughing, giving Sharon a quick wink.

"I don't know about that, however for your information, I have a team of twenty-five agents at the ready. What's the word Lank?"

"Five of the team and yourself, Doug, need to be at the lab on Columbia campus ASAP for special training," Lank told him.

"Special training eh, on that tripod thing you was telling me about?"

"Yep, your expertise will be needed at the Los Angles end to help in bringing the girls back."

"Good, I am so glad this thing is finally coming to a head," Doug said with fervor in his voice.

"I'm on my way to the lab right now Doug, You want to ride with me?" Lank asked.

"Might as well. Let me get my bag I have stashed in my office," Doug replied, then turning to Sharon. "You got the office until further notice. I'll check in when I can. Ok?"

"Gotcha Doug, Don't worry, I'll keep things under control.

"Thanks Sharon. I'll be getting back to you as soon as I can," Doug said as they were leaving.

In the car Lank clued Doug in as to what he could expect and what possible ramifications he might encounter.

"Doug I'm going to need your team, minus the five that will be at the lab here including you, to be in position around the Valley Lab in Los Angels and ready to go at my word," Lank told him on their way to the lab.

"I understand, Lank, they will be ready. They will be on their way to the valley lab tonight."

"Good, and as for you and the other four agents in your team. You will be learning how to operate the tripod and all its associated equipment from Professor Manning here at this lab."

"What will we be doing after that?"

"When you get word that the lab and premises are secured you will transport via the tripod to the Valley lab and assist in bringing back the abductees from the city of Los Angels on the parallel world. As you already know, there are approximately five thousand, give or take a few. You can see this is going to take a while," Lank said, giving Doug time to soak up what he had relayed to him.

"Lank, you mentioned a General McPhee that is in charged of security there at the Valley lab. You mean we will be going up against the army?"

"No, you see the general is retired but don't let that fool you, he has connections with the regular army, probably all the way up to the Secretary of the Army. You will have to play it by ear, don't let that hinder you. Our orders from the President are to take control of the Valley Lab at any cost."

"What are you going to be doing Lank, if I might ask?"

"I'm going though the wormhole to Chicago on the parallel world and start arranging the trip to bring back the girls. Raymond, Lewis and Jeff will be going with me to Chicago a little later on. You and the other four agents that will be trained on the Tripod will transport to Los Angels on the Parallel world and start sending the women back," Lank explained.

By this time they had pulled into the parking lot of the lab. Both men started walking up to the main door of the lab. Upon entering, they were stopped by a new security guard. Lank thought to himself that the Professor was being very careful. Now that the mission was about to commence, Lank was glad of the extra precautions the Professor was taking.

Lank identified himself and Doug, upon gaining admission to the lab, they walked the short distance to the tripod that was standing against the far wall. Doug eyed it for a moment before having anything to say about it.

"Why I never saw anything like it before Lank."

"Yes it is a remarkable piece of machinery. The professor has worked hard duplicating it from what we recovered from the raid on the Valley lab."

Professor Manning seeing them, walked over, noticing Doug, he looked at Lank for an introduction.

"Professor Manning, this is Doug Fields. He is in charge of the FBI team that will be taking control of the Valley lab."

"Glad to meet you Doug. Will you be staying here for a day or two?" Professor Manning asked.

"Yes and four of my team members will stay with me.

"Good. Lank, what hinders them from getting some training on the tripod right now? I have Raymond, Lewis and Jeff with their head in the books so they might as well join them.

"Professor my men should be arriving shortly. Maybe we can have the Security guard show them where to go."

Professor started to say something but was interrupted by four men entering the lab. The guard did his duty and stopped them only to let them go when the Professor yelled at him to let them through.

Lank finding himself alone after the Professor took everyone to the training room, thought about what was best for him to do. He thought about the sheer audacity of his plan. Never in this world had something like this ever been planned.

His plan was pretty well formulated in his mind. He would go through the wormhole this evening by himself and help Ann Long get the girls all set up for the trip back home. He could send three at once as long as they all had their medallions on. The rest of his team would follow the next day if the Professor had them trained enough to efficiently work the tripod. Lank had no doubt the Professor would have them raring to go by them.

He had advised Doug as soon as the Professor turned them loose, to give the word to his team, who by then, would have the Valley lab under surveillance, to take the lab by force. It should not take more than a few hours to accomplish this task.

The local police would be told it was a holdup for terrorist who was using the lab to exploit their agenda. This way, as far as the media were concerned, it would be a federal raid. Hopefully everything would be over by the time the media got wind of it.

Lank decided to go out and get something to eat while he waited till the time he had set for himself to transport to Chicago. Lank was really looking forward to the trip.

Later that evening Lank returned back to the lab and hunting up the professor, he told him it was time for him to go.

"Ok Lank. I'll get it all fired up, it will take only a few minutes to get it up and running. I'll call the students out and let them see it in operation," Professor Manning said hollering for his students to get a move on and come out and see something strange.

Raymond was the first to arrive followed by the rest of the crew.

"What's up Professor?" Raymond asked.

"I want to show you the tripod in operation. Lank here is going through to Chicago on the parallel world. Watch me now as I put this tripod into operation."

The men watched intently as Professor Manning adjusted and tweaked the controls until finally he was satisfied.

"Now watch. You notice Lank has a medallion around his neck. That is the piece that has been programmed to his nervous system. It is like a ticket you get on a city bus. The conductor punches a hole in the destination you want to go to.

Well this medallion directs the person wearing it in the wormhole to go to the destination that has been programmed into it. Lank's medallion has been programmed by the TSMD to send him to Chicago on the parallel world. Something we haven't told any of you yet is we only have the three medallions.

When we start getting the girls back we can use their medallions and reprogram them to send each of you to either Chicago or Los Angels on the parallel world.

Lank stepped upon the tripod and watched as Professor manually close the switch that would send him on his way. The last thing he remembered seeing was Lewis standing there with his eyes bulging out.

Chapter Thirty

Parking his car in the parking area he walked the remaining few steps to the entrance of the apartment complex that housed the female humans. Dr. Lyle Green had decided to have a look at his part of the project. He was the second in command here on this parallel Earth and the Chicago area had been assigned to him. He meant to protect it at any cost.

Dr. Lyle entered through the front door of the apartment and made his way down to the community room. He did not relish the idea of looking in on any of the Earth women. To him they were just cattle, and ugly at that. He longed for his mate back on Raael, his world in the galaxy of Pletia. This project should be completed within twenty-five Earth years at most.

By then all the old people will have dyed leaving only the Earth women who were being used as surrogate mothers. He would transport them back to Earth when their usefulness had come to an end.

He opened the door to the community room in this apartment building. As he surveyed around the room, taking into view three of the Earth women sitting at a table. One of the handy men was there waxing the floor. He thought it must be Tom, but then he wasn't sure, they all looked alike to Genshees.

"Good morning ladies, how are you doing today?" Dr. Lyle Green said in an attempt to open a line of conversation between them.

"We are doing fine, Dr. Green. How about yourself?" It was the red haired woman who responded, answering for the other two.

"Everything is going fine then, no problems with the clinical procedures being practiced here by my medical staff?"

"None whatsoever, we are just happy to help these people and keep their race from becoming extinct," Ann, the red headed woman told Doctor Green.

Ann Long thought to herself about what the purpose of this visit from Dr. Lyle Green to Chicago might mean. Ann had remembered how Special Agent Lank Miller had cautioned her about divulging any information at all to any of the aliens. Any person that looked young was suspect.

Lank had explained how these lizard like aliens could make themselves appear as humans. Dr Lyle had asked a question about any strange people visiting the apartment complex in the last few days.

The importance of this question caused Ann to return her attention back to Dr. Lyle.

"No, I haven't seen a soul till you came in," Ann Long stated, looking around at the two other girls for confirmation.

They both readily agreed that no one had been here. Ann had taught them well it seems. They would not divulge the fact that Agent Miller had been here and opened their eyes to what was going on. Ann was sure they were trying hard to conceal the anger they had for this alien creature. She just hoped Tom and Max would be just as subtle. Ann didn't have long to wait as Dr. Lyle turned to Tom.

Tom, How about you, Have you seen any strangers here in this Chicago complex?"

Looking up from a kneeling position of waxing the floor by hand, Tom paused a moment, giving Ann the fright of her life.

"No sir, Max and I have not seen any strangers at all. You and Dr. North have been the only ones we have seen."

"When was Dr. North here?" Doctor Lyle asked Tom.

"A few days ago sir. We didn't see him but Pete did, while manning the main gate.

"I see. Ok I'll let you get back to what you were doing. I have other business to take care of while I am here." He then, turned and left the community room, walking at a brisk pace on down the hallway to the front door. Getting into his car once again Dr. Lyle returned back to the terminal, which housed the entry point to the wormhole. When the tripod came into view, Dr,

Lyle could not help but break out in a big smile, although it looked like a big smile to any human looking at him, to the Genesee it was more in the attitude than in any movement of muscles in his face.

Anyone using this terminal to go back to where he came from would be in for a huge surprise. Dr. Lyle Green had seen to that. He planned to stay here in Chicago for a few days in the hope of catching someone unauthorized using the tripod.

Having made sure the trap was still set, Dr. Lyle turned and left the building and once again used the car to leave the compound. Stopping at the main gate to talk with the care keeper for a moment.

"Your name Pete?" Dr. Lyle asked point blank.

"Yes sir, my name is Pete."

"Well Pete were you on duty when Dr. Green was here last?"

"Yes I was, my shift was about to end when Dr. North appeared in the doorway of the building. I don't know where he went after that."

"I see, who was your relief and when will he back on duty?" Dr. Lyle asked.

"That would be Roger, he will relieve me in about two hours."

"Good I want to talk with him to. Let me know if you see anyone leave the building?"

"I certainly will," answered Pete.

With that, Dr. Lyle drove on through the gate and disappeared in the distance, leaving Pete to wonder where he was going.

Pete was proud of himself; he was able to convince Dr. Green no one had come through except Dr. North. Special Agent Lank would be proud of him. He had instructed Roger in what to say; in the event Dr. North or Dr. Green ever questioned him.

Doctor Lyle was traveling at a goodly speed, headed toward the stable, as the Genshees referred to the place that was home to the young Genshees that were born here on this parallel Earth. He was delegated the responsibilities of ensuring the health and welfare until they reached adulthood. It was a big responsibility but he was sure he could handle them. He had laid down the rules and regulations to the young genshees and so far they had shown respect. It was the same on his world, parents gave birth and then did not see their young again until they reach adulthood and was released back into the stream. Only one thing Dr. Green wished he could have witnessed. He was curious to see exactly how the people on this parallel Earth raised their young.

Of course he had seen videos of the children being taken on picnics and attending school, all in the company of adults. He really thought the Genshee way was far superior to the Earth way. He had seen how it was done on the real Earth and what a mess it was turning out to be. Crime was running rampant, committed almost entirely by the young people roaming the streets of the cities.

Pulling up to the building that housed the young Genshees, Dr. Lyle walked down the hallway and through the double doors across the hallway, the same doors Agent Lank Miller had gone through when he visited this area.

He was able to catch a small group of the young Genshees before they left to engage in their regulated exercises. Haling one of the youngsters Dr. Lyle Green spoke to him.

"Hi there, remember me?"

"Yes, of course I remember you Dr. Green. You are our guidance counselor," the young Genshee answered seeing Dr. Green in his natural body of an adult Genshee.

"How is everything going in here, any problems I need to know about?"

"Everything is fine. My group is looking forward to the time we can be declared an adult."

"Glad to hear that, it won't be long now until you will be able to go anywhere you want to. Just hold on a while longer." Dr. Green informed him.

"It will be an exciting day when we will be able to explore."

"Right, but right now I have to ask you some questions."

"What do you want to know Dr. Green,"?

"Have any of you seen anyone else besides Dr. North or myself, say, in the past week or so?"

"Yes, there was a man that came upon us playing a game inside."

"What did he want?"

"He asked us what were we playing and I told him Genshee. I don't thing he was a Genshee though.

"Did he ever tell you his name?" Dr. Green asked.

"No and it did not seem important at the time to ask him his name," the young genshee said.

"What did he do then?"

"He just turned and left. I don't know where he went."

"Ok, I'll find out who he was, don't worry about it." Dr. Green told the young genshee.

On his way back to the car, Dr Green, deep in thought, considered many possibilities as to who came through the wormhole. The most plausible explanation was that Special Agent Langford Miller. General McGhee had a large dossier on this Special Agent Miller.

He would have a look at what the General had. Maybe figure on a plan to eliminate this thorn in their flesh, so to speak.

Off in the distant was the old city of Chicago. He had taken a ride through the city when he first arrived on this world remembering how desolate it looked. A city desolate and empty, all the old people had long since left the city and moved out to the suburbs. Wild animals had taken over and roamed freely throughout the city. Dr. Green had visited the sears tower on this trip. He remembered seeing the destruction, the complete disrepair, of a city with all the life sucked out of it.

The plight of this world was so similar to the worldwide conditions on his home planet. The Genshees had a plan though, not like this backward world, which lay in the throws of a dying planet as far as human life was concerned.

At least his government had a plan, albeit a plan which out of desperation, and at all cost had to be kept secret from the humans on this world. Oh well, he mused, a few more years and all the humans would be gone and the plan could be executed in its entirety.

His attention returned to the present as he approached the car. He wanted to question the care keeper that relieved Pete. The information of whether or not the intruder had gained entry to the Earth women could be tantamount to the success of this mission.

Dr. Green drove the rest of the way to the building housing the tripod neither looking to the left or to the right. When he came to the gate, he stopped and called out to the guard.

"Gate keeper, come here I want a word with you."

"Yes sir, what is it you wish?" the gatekeeper said as he came and stood beside the car.

"Have you seen any one else beside me and Dr. North come out of that building?" He asked pointing toward the building where the tripod was located.

"No sir, not me. Pete told me though he had seen Dr. North for a few minutes the other day as he came out for just a moment."

"Your name is Roger, isn't it?"

"Yes sir, it is."

"Well Roger, if you happened to see anyone other than myself or Dr. North come through this gate, you write it in your log book and be sure to let me or Dr. North know when you see us again."

"Yes I will."

"That will be all," Dr. Green spoke to the car and it hurried away.

Roger was elated with himself. He had covered very well for the Special Agent Miller. He wanted nothing to do with these Lizzard people. Imagine using Earth girls to carry their lizard babies for them.

Dr. Green was sure he had all bases covered now. He only had to wait and the perpetrator would come to him. He parked the car and entered the building, walking up to the tripod he noticed it was just like he had left it. He set the controls for a three-minute delay and stepped upon the tripod. He adjusted himself and waited until the timer triggered which sent him through the wormhole.

Chapter Thirty - One

Lank realizing he had made the trip through the wormhole looked around. It was just as he had remembered. He stepped off the tripod and found the large crate he had stowed his trusty friends on. Yes there was the nine-millimeter handgun and the AK47 still stashed where he had planted them. That's good, hoping he would never have to use them but it was always best to be prepared.

Lank exited out the door into the street, looking toward the cars parked neatly in a row, he chose a pretty red one this time and gave it the commands. Immediately the car backed out and shifted into forward gear heading toward the gate. Approaching the gate the car came to a halt and Pete came out from the guardhouse.

"Hello Agent Miller. Welcome back," he said in a hearty but somewhat quaking voice.

"Hi Pete, good to see you again too. I'm on my way to see the women," Lank told him.

"Good, the sooner we can stop the plans of these lizards the better I'll like it."

"It won't be long now. We are working on the Earth end and getting things set up," Lank replied.

"Agent Miller, Dr. Green just left about an hour ago. He came and went toward the apartments of the women," I don't know what he wanted. He was gone for almost two hours before he came back and went into the building you just came out of."

"Thanks for telling me, has there been anyone else come through?"

"No he was the only one." Pete said. "I talked with Roger and he was the one that saw him leave here."

"Ok. I am going to the women's apartment now. I will be returning soon," Lank informed him.

"I'll probably still be here." Pete said.

Lank drove on to the apartment and entering at the same door he used before, he knocked on Ann's apartment door. It seemed to take her a while before the door opened to reveal her red hair.

"Hi Lank, You did come back," she said with a lot of enthusiasm in her voice.

"You weren't worried, were you?" Lank asked.

"Well you never know, you could have been stopped by either Dr. North or Dr. Green, you do know Dr. Green was here today?" She asked with concern in her voice.

"Yes Pete told me. What did Dr. Green want?"

"He wanted to know if any one other than him or Dr. North had been here recently."

"What did you tell him?" Lank asked smiling at Ann.

"We said we had not seen anyone of course. He even question Tom and Max but they told him the same thing. I think we convinced him that no one had been here."

"That is why I'm counting on all of you to help me. Now, Ann, how far along are you in getting the girls lined up?"

"Well you said we would be going three at a time and for us to make sure we have our medallions around our neck. So far I have this apartment and two of the other five apartments all ready to go. That puts the count at three hundred and sixty three or one hundred and twenty one groups."

"That's real good. We will be able to start and keep going until we get all of you out of here."

"Lank I have run into several women that don't want to leave. They don't believe me when I tell them about the lizard guys," Ann confessed.

"Ann I expected some of the girls would not believe us. That is alright, when we show them an alien without his human cloak on, then they will believe."

"Before we can get started I need to go back to Earth and check in with my team. They will be coming here to help send all of you back to Earth. I can't do it alone, I need their help. Professor Manning is training them on how to work all this equipment," he told her, watching for any sign of rebellion on Ann's face.

Ann took this bit of new information in stride. Without batting an eyelash she asked how long he would be gone.

"Only for a few hours I'm sure. You see, we only have three medallions, mine and the two the girls had when I took them through the last time I was here," Lank answered, than as an after thought he said. "It will be necessary for us to keep a few of the medallions in case some of the girls don't have theirs any longer."

It takes about two hours to program one before it can be used." I will need to take an extra medallion with me when I go back. I have three men coming back with me."

"No problem you can take mine. I trust you Lank to get me home again," she said handing him her medallion.

"Thanks Ann. You will be going home."

Lank hated to leave Ann but he had to get back. He wanted to start bringing his team here and get started on the rescue. Lank said his good byes and departed. He had his little car rolling back to the main gate in no time flat. Arriving at the gate. Pete met him again, waving him on. In a little while he found himself standing on the tripod waiting for the timer to throw the switch. If anyone were there to listen they would have heard a distinct popping sound and nothing else. The place would have been empty.

Shortly after he felt himself sliding through a dark tunnel the trip came to an abrupt end. He found himself standing on the tripod waiting until his mind was completely settled before he was able to step off the tripod.

Stepping off the tripod and looking around at his surroundings Lank felt a tingle of fright. Something was not right. Upon further checking and comparing with his memory cells, he came to the conclusion he was in a place he had never been before. Yes the building contained the tripod, yes there was the TSMD sitting there in its usual place, but other things in the room were not recognizable to Lank. A voice from the nearest corner of the room shattered the silence.

"Ahh so it is you Special Agent Miller. I thought as much," the voice addressed him.

Lank looked around in the direction of the voice. He had never met the owner of the voice but he certainly had seen pictures of him, along with Dr, North.

"Well if it isn't the infamous Dr. Lyle Green," Lank stated.

"Yes, I must confess, the same."

"How did you get me to materialize here at this point in time?" Lank asked him.

"Very easy Special Agent Miller. I simply removed the transponder and replaced it with one programmed to bring you here to the lab."

Well at least I now know where I'm at, Lank thought to himself.

If he was in Los Angels on the real Earth then the raid by Doug's FBI team had not occurred yet. He decided it was in his best interest to play ignorant of where he was at and what would be transpiring soon. Hopefully the raid would commence soon.

"Special Agent Miller, please accompany me to Dr. North's office. He will want to question you, I'm sure," Dr. Green said to Lank as he motioned him to follow him.

Dr. North's office was tucked away in the far end of the lab building. The office, itself, was not all that impressive, however some of the articles hanging on the wall reminded Lank of relics brought back from the interior of the African nation.

The man, or Genshee, sitting behind the desk looked up at last from a document he was looking at. Surveying the man accompanying Dr. Green with a quizzical smile on his face.

"Good evening Special Agent Lankford Miller. May I extend to you greetings? I am glad we have finally met face to face," Dr. Alex North said all the time watching Lank's face.

"Likewise, I am sure," Lank said in return.

"Dr, Lyle, how did this agent of this government happen to be here?" Dr. North said when he had tuned to look at Dr. Green.

"Dr. North. I have been suspicious of someone going through the wormhole to Chicago on the parallel world. I merely set a trap for him. I switched the transponders, replacing the one with a Los Angels programming only. He was able to transport to Chicago but he could only return here at the lab," Dr. Green informed him.

"This confirms our suspicions. We now know Professor Manning at Columbia Lab has duplicated our Tripod techniques. Well this puts a different light on the situation," Dr. North informed Lank.

"Dr. North, I think it would be wise on our part to keep Agent Miller here where we can keep an eye on him. I don't yet know what his plans were in visiting Chicago. It has not been reported he entered the building housing the Earth women. He did see the young genshees playing and talked with them. He knows about us, who we really are, How much more he knows I am not so sure."

"How about it Agent Miller, Just what are your plans now that you know who we are?" Dr. North said to Lank.

"I don't know why you are here doing what you are doing, but I do know what you are doing and why you needed Earth women to carry your young. Lank said looking at both of them as he spoke."

"When we have more time to talk I will be happy to sit down with you and explain why it is necessary to do what we have done," Dr. North told him.

"Yes, ok Agent Miller, please follow me and I will show you your temporary place of dwelling for a while," said Dr. Lyle Green, motioning to Lank to follow him.

Lank followed him to the far side of the lab where there was a door. Dr. Green opened the door and told Lank to go on in. He had no choice but to enter the room. He could have resisted, but had no idea how strong these aliens were or what manner of weapons they would use. The safest thing to do was follow their instructions until he could find out more about them.

Dr. Green shut the door and Lank could hear the key turning in the lock. Looking around the room, Lank could see it was being used as a storeroom more or less. There were boxes of small electronic parts, most of which were alien in nature stored in one corner. Various other pieces of gear could be seen lying where someone had dumped them just to get them out of the way.

Lank sat down on a crate to think of a way he might use this to his advantage. He needed a plan and right now his mind was blank.

Chapter Thirty - Two

Doug Fields, the FBI agent in charge of the raiding party had finished his training on the Tripod sufficiently enough Professor Manning turned him loose.

He had notified the Local FBI office there in Los Angels of the nature of the raid and had them enlist the help of the Local Police department. Doug had insisted the media be informed of the raid, giving the cover story of seven terrorists being tracked to the Valley. Tainting the cover story with reports of the terrorist intention to blow up the courthouse there in Los Angels.

That ought to be enough feed to keep the media satisfied and hungry for more details. This would not be the first time the media had been duped by the government, nor would it be the last.

Doug had instructed his team to surround the Valley lab but to lay low until he got there. He took a cab out to the airport where there was an agency jet waiting to take him to Los Angels.

Some hours later he was landing at LX airport where he had a company car waiting on him. The driver had been briefed and took off immediately for the Valley Quantum Physics Laboratory. It did not take too long to drive the distance, especially this time of night the traffic was not all that bad. The driver stopped two blocks from the Lab. There were several cars parked along the road but with the tinted windows all around it was impossible to tell if they were occupied. Doug slipped out of the car and walked to within fifty feet of the Lab. He slipped behind a large tree behind the Lab.

After waiting few minutes to make sure he was unnoticed, he emitted a low cat whistle, which was immediately answered in like manner from the corner of the lab. Almost at once a shadow appeared beside Doug revealing itself to be an FBI agent. The agent spoke only a few words but only a few words were needed to verify the plan.

Looking at his watch, Doug gave the order to proceed. The agent nodded in agreement and quietly disappeared into the darkness.

Doug waited for five minutes more and then slipped from behind the tree. He made his way towards the main door of the lab. He could not detect the presence of any of his agents yet, however he would have been upset if he had. Reaching the door and finding it locked proved no problem. With a quick few turns of his locksmith tools he unlocked the door.

Doug paused for a few moments hoping an agent had been successful in disconnecting the alarm system. When he did push the door open only dead silence greeted him. Pushing the door wide open he raised his hand in the signal to his team the raid was officially under way.

It seemed agents from every direction suddenly appeared. Even agents were already inside the lab came out from their hiding places. A mega-horn was handed to him of which he spoke the long awaited command.

"This is the FBI, Lay down your weapons," This command was repeated several times. He could see lab techs scurrying about, trying to evade the agents but not having any luck. Before any of the agents could reach the tripod area though, a loud popping sound was heard. Doug, being the only one of the FBI raiding party familiar with what the popping sound entailed wondered who it was escaping.

In a matter of minutes every one associated with the lab had been rounded up and handcuffed. By this time the local police sirens could be heard approaching the building. Doug knew the news media would not be far behind. He was so glad things went smoothly. His agents were now in the process of checking all rooms for anyone left that might be hiding.

Hearing a familiar voice, Doug immediately turned his attention in that direction. Upon seeing Lank displaying his badge and ID to an agent gave out a yell.

"Lank, what in the world are you doing here? You went to the Chicago area, I saw you with my own eyes."

"Hey Doug, yes it is me. Our Dr. Green sent me here. He swapped out the transponders in the Chicago terminal with a transponder programmed for the terminal located here at the Valley Lab. for the tripod," Lank informed his friend.

"Lank how are you going to get back to Chicago on the Parallel world."

"I'm hoping I will be able to transport back to Chicago ok. I think it only affects coming back through the worm hole."

"You say it was Dr. Green that switched the transponders?"

Lank, at the mention of Dr. Greens's name, remembered the two doctors were just here.

"Where is Dr. Green, and for that matter Dr. North?" Lank asked his good friend.

"I don't know I haven't seen them, hey wait a minute, I distinctly heard that loud popping sound always associated with someone using the tripod."

"That was probably them leaving here. Did you see General McPhee?" Lank asked.

"No he wasn't here. I feel pretty sure we can get quite a lot of information from his boys we arrested. What do you think Lank?"

"Both Dr. Green and Dr. North was here when I popped in, which was about two hours ago. That had to of been them that you heard popping out," Lank said, wondering himself how they knew about the raid.

"Well no matter now. What's your plan Lank?"

"I've got to get back to the Columbia Lab in New York. Professor Manning is going to have to go to Chicago and reprogram the transponder. We have to have that port and this port here in Los Angels in order to rescue those girls."

"Well I have a navy jet standing by at the LX airport, you can fly back with him if you want to," Doug said, hoping Lank would take him up on it.

"Sounds good to me Doug, can you call the pilot and inform him I will be his passenger instead of you, ok."

"You got it." Doug answered.

"One other thing Doug, do you have a car available to take me to the airport?"

"Sure, I'll have one of my agents take you, no problem."

Lank was thankful he was friends with Doug Fields. He was a find man and a good agent too.

The agent that took him to the airport was talkative; knowing who Lank was did not intimidate him in the least.

"Special Agent Miller, those two doctors that escaped, do you know how they managed it. We had every avenue blocked, even the roof was under surveillance. I just don't see how they could have gotten away." The agent said looking at Lank as he spoke.

"Well they did, but I have a plan and if it works out ok, then I think we will catch them very soon."

"That is good to hear," He said.

The bantered back and forth till the agent pulled into the fire lane of the airport where Lank disembarked from the car. Waving goodbye and thanks, Lank heading into the passenger terminal. Doug had told him who the navy pilot was and where he would be waiting for him. Lank spotted the pilot immediately standing by the entrance to the security area. Lank approached him and after identifying himself, the pilot's name was Leon Parker and he asked him about Doug. Lank filled him in on as much as the situation required.

"Well you ready to go sir. The plane has been serviced and raring to go."

"Yes I'm more than ready, Leon, I need to get back to New York City."

"I'll have you there in just under four hours. You know these jets go much faster now than they did a few years ago."

Leon did not lie, three hours and fifty-five minutes later he was landing at New York La Guardia airport. Thanking Leon for the ride, Lank walked through the gate and into the baggage claim area. Having no baggage to claim, he walked outside and tried using his cell phone. For some reason it would not work. He hunted up a payphone and after depositing the right amount of coins, Professor Manning's voice came on the line.

"Professor Manning, this is Lank."

The Professor was obviously flabbergasted.

"Lank, where are you and how are you calling me on the phone?"

"It's a long story Professor Manning, but I was sent back to the Los Angels port."

"You was sent, by whom and how?" Professor Manning wanted to know.

"Well I was able to transport to Chicago ok but when I used the tripod again, I wound up in Los Angels on the real Earth, I might add."

"How in the world did that happen?"

"Dr. Green had been to Chicago prior to my arrival and he switched the transponders with one programmed to terminate in Los Angels."

"Lank you still in Los Angels."

"No, I'm in New York City."

"New York City," Professor Manning repeated, sounding like one of those television ads.

"Yes I was there in the lab in Los Angels when Doug raided the place."

"That's great. I sure would like to talk with that Dr. North before they send him to the big house."

"Sorry Professor, but Dr. North and Dr. Green escaped through the wormhole."

"Escaped, I don't believe it,"

"You'll have to believe it Professor, its true. I am at a loss as to where they wound up at though," Lank mentioned, with concern in his voice.

"Should be easy enough to track them. An electronic image is left behind as to the port they would have arrived at," Professor Manning told him.

"That is all good and well Professor, but you will have to use one of the medallions and go to Chicago and somehow get that tripod back in operation again. I have those girls all lined up and waiting to come back to Earth."

"Ok I can do that, should be a simple thing putting back the original transponder in its place."

"Right, I knew you would be able to fix it. I'll wait until you come back before I transport again. Are you going right away?" Lank asked.

"Yeah I'm leaving right now. See you when I get back," The professor said as he broke the phone connection.

This would give Lank some time to catch his breath, so to speak, and collect his thoughts. He wanted so much to be in Chicago and start the rescue operation going. It should be under and hour and the Professor should be arriving back.

Lank killed time after he made the trip back in a cab to a little restaurant close to the Columbia campus. He ordered a sumptuous meal, feeling hungry after all the excitement he had been through. When there were left only a few scraps of food left on his plate, Lank finished his coffee and paid for his meal. He walked the rest of the way to the lab and finding Lewis at the tripod, obviously going through the procedures he had learned from the Professor.

"Hi Lewis," Lank called out to him.

"Hello Lank," Lewis returned the greeting, looking a little sheepish.

"What's the matter Lewis?"

"Nothing Lank, I just sent Professor Manning through a couple of hours ago and he ain't come back yet. He said he would only be gone a few minutes."

"Not to worry Lewis, the Professor knows what he is doing." Lank said, hoping to allay his fears.

The loud popping sound caused both Lank and Lewis to turn toward the tripod. Popping into view on the tripod was the professor.

Lewis let out a whooping yell at the sight of the Professor. He was so relieved the Professor was all right.

The professor, after climbing down off the tripod turned to Lank and Lewis.

"Lank I almost didn't find the transponder that Dr. Green had switched. I finally found it in a little room sitting on a workbench. If I had not found it I would have been in deep you know what."

You did fix it though, didn't you?" Lank asked, a little worried.

"Yes it will return you back here and the other girls too."

"Very good. I want to take Lewis, Raymond and Jeff with me. We will have a lot of work ahead of us," Lank told the Professor.

"Fine with me Lank, your boys are ready to go." He assured him.

"Ok Lewis, round up Raymond and Jeff and we will be off."

"Right. I'll get them. They just had to have a little nappy," Lewis said, hoping Lank would get the point.

Lank did but would not give Lewis the pleasure of his little poke at his cohorts.

The professor gathered the medallions he had programming for Lewis, Raymond and Jeff and handed them to Lank.

"Lank, your medallion should still be programmed."

When the three others of the team walked up to the tripod trying to wipe the sleep out of their eyes, Lewis handed them their medallions and watched as they placed it around their necks.

Lank told Lewis to wait till he went with Raymond and Jeff and he would come back for him. Lewis didn't relish the idea of him staying behind, but chose for once not to say anything that could be construed to be funny.

Lank, Raymond, and Jeff took their places on the tripod and Professor flipped the switch that sent them on their way, leaving Lewis standing with a look of consternation on his face.

Arriving in Chicago, the three stepped off the tripod. Lank motioned them to follow him as he walked to the front door. They walked all the way to the guardhouse. Lank was hoping Pete or Roger would be on duty but it was a new man.

"Where is Pete or Roger?" Lank asked the old man in the shack.

"You Special Agent Miller?"

"Yes that's right and this is three of my friends, they are agents as well. What's your name and what about Pete or Roger?"

"Pete will be relieving me in a couple of hours, Roger won't be on till tomorrow morning. My name is William Jorsen.

"Well William Jorsen are you aware of the mission we have come to do?"

"Sure am, I know all about those lizard men. Pete and Roger have told me all about it. Also Tom and Max are friends of mine too."

"Good, This is Raymond, and this is Jeff. They will stay here in the building until I get back. I have to go back to Earth and bring the last agent here to help us. When I return I will be escorting the girls here with Lewis, Jeff and Raymond will be sending them back to Earth through the wormhole," Lank told him, glad that he understood the situation.

It wasn't going to be easy repopulating this world but it was the responsibility of the people of Earth to do just that. Lank knew it would take a couple of generations to even get started on something as big as this was. He had talked this over with President Gordon and both agreed the best plan was to open this parallel world up to tourist and homesteaders.

Just let the media get hold of this and the sheer advertising by their coverage would be the shot in the arm to get this program off the ground.

After they had walked back to the tripod building, as it would become known as, Lank demonstrated how the cars ran. Raymond and Jeff were both impressed with all the automatic functions it had.

When the car demonstration was ended and they had gathered themselves back at the tripod, Lank bid them farewell and stepped onto the tripod. He watched as Jeff pulled the lever that sent him back to the lab in New York.

Professor Manning was not immediately in sight as Lank stepped off the tripod. Surely Lewis then, would not be too far away. Lank found them both sitting at the small desk in the Professor's office.

"I'm back," Lank said, approaching them.

"Hi Lank, Lewis and I are just going over something I found out about when I went to Chicago." The Professor said.

"What is that?" Lank asked.

"Well, remember when I told you I would have been in deep shit if I had not of found the original transponder."

"Yeah, I remember, you really seemed worried at the time," Lank replied.

"Yes I was worried. Lewis and I though have figured out how to reprogram the transponder to allow us to terminate at any of the ports in the wormhole."

"The professor did, Lank, I just watched," Lewis said out of modesty, or so he wanted it to appear to Lank.

"You helped Lewis, I needed your encouragement to spur me on," the professor said laughing.

"Lewis, I left Raymond and Jeff alone in the Chicago port. You think we might better go before they get into trouble."

"You mean again, don't you Lank," Lewis said evidently remembering the last time Raymond and Jeff had been left alone.

"Could be, but we need to go anyway. You know there will be plenty of work for all of us to do once we get started."

"Say the word. I'm ready."

"You guys go on, but promise me you will call on me if you need any help. Ok?" Professor Manning cautioned them.

"You bet Professor," Lewis chipped in.

When Lank and Lewis appeared on the tripod in Chicago, both Jeff and Raymond seemed glad to see them again.

"Hey Lewis, sure thought I had seen the last of you," Raymond said, not really meaning it.

"Grab your hats boys and straighten your ties. We're off to see the ladies."

"Lank you sure there is enough young ladies to go around, you know how Lewis is around women," Raymond had to get one last jibe in.

Lewis just grunted, letting this one go by.

They piled into two of the nearest little cars, Lank and Jeff in one and Lewis and Raymond in the other car. The cars were very comfortable to ride in. Lewis was so impressed with all the automatic features he just couldn't keep quiet any longer.

"Raymond, even you learned how to drive one of these in just one lesson, didn't you?" he said, an obvious dig at Raymond.

The car stopped on at the gate behind Lank and Jeff before Raymond could think up an appropriate answer to Lewis's dig.

William Jorsen was still on duty.

"Hello Special Agent Miller. I see you have a full crew now," he said in his quivering voice looking back at Lewis and Raymond in the second car.

"Yes, we are all here. We are going to get the ladies and start bringing them out three by three."

"Any thing you want me to do for you, just ask," William said.

"William, you, Pete and Roger are doing a good job. We still need you to watch out for us. Dr. North and Dr. Green escaped our net. As of right now, we don't have a clue as to where they might be," Lank informed him.

"Well I'll certainly let you know if I spot either one of them."

"Ok William, when we return with the ladies, I want you to come on over to the building we will be in. I want to familiarize you, Pete and Roger, how the aliens were getting around your planet. I've already shown Tom and Max."

William nodded his head and affirmed he would tell Pete and Roger.

Lank spoke the command to the car and it sped off in the direction of the apartment buildings with Raymond and Lewis coming close behind.

Ann was so glad to see Lank and the rest of his team. She introduced the three other girls with her.

Lank's attention was quickly turned to the last girl when he heard her name mentioned.

"Betty Francis Moulton from New York city, Queens, to be more specific.

The girl named Betty looked puzzled that Lank would know her full name and her address.

"How did you know that about me, we have never met, have we?"

"Yes in a way we have. You remember right before you were snatched through time to Los Angeles you passed a car and gave the driver a nice smile."

A smile broke out on Betty's face as the scene came back to her.

"Yes I remember now. I had not gone ten miles down the road when I started feeling funny and the next thing I knew I was somewhere else for a little while then I was off again, waking up in Los Angels, only it wasn't Los Angels as I knew it."

"I have been in contact with your mother in Queens and she is looking forward to being reunited with you again," Lank informed her, then turning to Ann he asked if they were ready to go.

Getting an affirmative answer, he led them all out to the two cars, since Raymond was the larger of the four men he indicated two of the women would ride with Lank and Jeff and the remaining women would ride with them.

Upon arriving back at the building and gathering around the tripod, Lank checked each girl to make sure she had her medallion.

He placed them on the tripod and described Professor Manning to them, giving the women something tangible to hold on to.

Looking at Lewis he nodded his head and Lewis flipped the switch. The all too familiar popping sound was heard and the girls were gone.

The rescue was now officially underway and going without a hitch so far. Lank hoped it would stay this way. He was still concerned about what Dr. North and Dr. Green might be up to. As weeks turned into months though his apprehension seemed to subside somewhat.

Every few days one of his team would go back to Earth and take a few days off, Lank looked forward to his time, spending it more with his wife and daughter than anywhere else.

The news media finally dug out the truth about the operation and every paper that was a paper herald the news about the abductions being solved and the women being returned back to Earth.

Word about the Genshees filled all available newspapers space. Most of them had a pretty accurate account of how and why the genshees were conducting their operation.

President Gordon had released a statement about the raid on the Valley lab and the escape of Dr. North and Dr. Green. The president went on in his statement giving credit to the FBI, keeping Lank and his team out of it for the president time. President

Gordon had cautioned Lank though not to expect to be unknown for long.

Lank's time was spent transporting the women and his time with his family on the few days he was able to get away. Doug was doing a great job at the Los Angels port, bringing the women from Los Angels on the parallel world to the Los Angels port on the real Earth.

There was still a lot of work to do. Already there were plans in the making of how to repopulate the Parallel world that was so desperate need of human souls.

Every once in a while, his thoughts would turned to Dr. North and Dr. Green, but finding them and learning what they were up to would have to wait.

THE END